When Time Flies

Acknowledgments

My heartfelt gratitude goes to:

Joe Hall, my invaluable and extraordinarily talented editor. Thank you for always believing in me. Your guidance has pushed me to grow as a writer, and for that, I am forever grateful.

To the incredible team at Infernal Moose—including Amy Odell, marketing extraordinaire, and Adrian Chen and Jake Keuhlen—thank you for your unwavering support and belief in this book.

And to Craig—the best husband in the Universe, who lets me be fully and unapologetically myself. *Te amo, always.*

Contents

CHAPTER ONE 1

CHAPTER TWO 9

CHAPTER THREE.. 14

CHAPTER FOUR.. 20

CHAPTER FIVE.. 23

CHAPTER SIX 36

CHAPTER SEVEN.. 48

CHAPTER EIGHT 57

CHAPTER NINE 61

CHAPTER TEN.. 69

CHAPTER ELEVEN 77

CHAPTER TWELVE 93

CHAPTER THIRTEEN 99

CHAPTER FOURTEEN.. 122

CHAPTER FIFTEEN 137

CHAPTER SIXTEEN 144

CHAPTER SEVENTEEN 152

CHAPTER EIGHTEEN... 158

CHAPTER NINETEEN 163

CHAPTER TWENTY.. 174

CHAPTER TWENTY-ONE 180

CHAPTER TWENTY-TWO 188

CHAPTER TWENTY-THREE 194

CHAPTER TWENTY-FOUR.. 200

CHAPTER TWENTY-FIVE 208

CHAPTER TWENTY-SIX.. 215

CHAPTER TWENTY-SEVEN 226

CHAPTER TWENTY-EIGHT 229

CHAPTER TWENTY-NINE... 233

CHAPTER ONE

The private jet engines hummed beneath me, low and unyielding, like a memory I couldn't shake.

Cabinets, fixtures, and countertops—every surface shone like it had something to prove. They had to. In this world, perfection was everything.

My eyes flicked to the cockpit, to the neat row of water bottles perched in their cupholders. All so pristine. All so orderly.

I tugged at my sleeve, hoping the storm inside me remained hidden.

If I had a mental weather app, it would say "100 percent chance of drama."

I glanced toward the captain. He sipped his black coffee as if nothing in the world could touch him. The co-pilot texted on his phone. Both of them, calm as rocks.

Me?

I needed calm wherever I could get it.

The biggest perk of the Gulfstream 650? It had a cabin door that separated me from the pax, or passengers, and their drama.

Ding! A text on my phone chimed. My screen shared it was 0900.

We're ready for breakfast. Thanks Indy.

I tapped the "thumbs-up" symbol.

As a corporate flight attendant, I had worked with these pilots many times before, so I knew their breakfast preferences. I opened the tiniest oven in the world and shoved in a tray of bacon. Later, I would prepare the eggs to serve everything hot.

I was flying one pax, Mr. Jacobs, who had preoccupied himself with coffee, the *Financial Times*, and a nap. That was why I liked flying businessmen: we didn't talk except for a "good morning" or "what would you like for lunch?"

With time to burn, I conducted the usual self-critical evaluation of my life and my attempts to fix it.

The old rage from my liver rose, and my intestines churned like an electric whisk on the lowest speed. I was a cliché of both Chinese medicine and Ayurveda. The fact that my shame, anger, and fear culminated into Inflammatory Bowel Disease (IBD) really made me textbook. As the spiritual experts would say: *You keep holding onto old crap.*

I'd tried everything to let go of the past. I talked about my feelings to numerous therapists—some good, some not. I even attempted the "woo-woo" including:

Inner child work.

A soul retrieval from a Native American shaman (Apparently my soul couldn't be retrieved).

Good ole fashioned journaling.

Cry therapy.

Ayahuasca in the Amazon jungle (The result? Shitting and vomiting at the same time).

Exploring my "shadow side."

Breath work while a didgeridoo played in the background (One word: painful).

Shrooms.

Trauma workshops.

Belief coding.

Vision boarding (I was desperate).

Transcendental Meditation.

Ketamine.

Visits to psychics, mediums, astrologers, and tarot readers, who all agreed…

I was pretty fucked.

Then I returned to the Western approach and did a one-week stint each with Lexapro and Zoloft, which only gave me migraines. I freakin' loved the *I-can't-even-get-anxious-if-I-wanted-to* feeling of Xanax…but alas, it wasn't enough.

Nothing worked.

I let out a sigh from my belly, as a multitude of yoga teachers had taught me. As I expelled the air, I felt strange…odd…not dizzy, not nauseous, but weird. I checked the monitor that displayed the airshow. Time To Destination, or TTD, was three hours to go until we landed in Teterboro, New Jersey.

The words and numbers on the monitor blurred into an astigmatism.

I rounded the corner into the crew rest and then plopped onto the club seat. Exhaustion crawled through my veins like slow lightning. My vision pulsed. The feeling was jetlag times infinity. I tried to stay centered and think through what was happening. I had been flying—almost nonstop—to save money to buy a house. Crossing all those time zones and the constant fatigue combined with the IBD did not make for a healthy lifestyle.

I'd let myself get *that* run down. Damn.

My body felt weightless. It was like the moment before a fall, that breathless pause—only it never ended. A newfound hum in my ears grew until it swallowed my every thought. My eyes darted over my lap to the khaki fabric wall and finally to the window. The sky brightened to an angelic white, nearly blinding me. I wasn't dizzy. I had the urge to stare straight ahead, yet I could not focus.

Am I vaporizing?

I stretched out my fingers. They were disappearing! I felt so airy, as if I could levitate off the seat. I grasped the armrests until…

I couldn't grasp them anymore.

The outline of my body began to blur. I lost the solidity of flesh. Tiny sparks of light flickered along my arms, breaking apart into floating specks, like dust in the sun. These particles—that were once me—scattered outward. Where I had sat, I was now only a swirl of luminous dust, leaving me somewhere between confused and terrified.

The world spun ahead of me, leaving no room for panic, no room to understand. In an instant, purple lightning hummed and sounded like the constant static of a bug zapper. The spinning intensified, yet I wasn't queasy.

What the fuck is going on?

I realized I was spinning through blackness, as if I was on an otherworldly plane. Then the particles of my body snapped back together and returned it to its human shape. I kept rotating and twirling until, out of nowhere, I smelled old wood and cleaning solution. And then…

There I was, sitting on a chair in a—was it a *courtroom*?

My mouth was so dry it felt like sand had settled on my tongue. A dull ache pulsed behind my temples, the kind that usually came from waking too early and too thirsty. My eyes darted across the courtroom, desperate to anchor on something steady, but every face seemed sharpened against me, a blur of judgment I couldn't decipher. My chest tightened, heavy as stone, and though I begged my body to move, shift, or raise even a finger, nothing obeyed. It was as if my body had betrayed me; every molecule refused to budge. Before I could get one thought together, I heard:

"Indy, doodoo, what's wrong?"

Mom.

Where am I?

I did the only thing I could think of in an emergency: the Ujjayi breath. Inhale up the throat and exhale down the throat, making a Darth Vader sound.

It wasn't working—my body wouldn't listen, my mind wouldn't quiet. The storm surged inside me.

"Indy! What are you doing? Brian, what is she doing? What's that noise she's making?"

I turned to see my father, and then—wait a minute…whoa. Mom, Dad, my lawyer, the prosecutor, and *the judge*? The old building was the courthouse in Brookline, Massachusetts, the uber wealthy part of Boston where I had attended private school.

My eyes widened like I just spotted free Wi-Fi on a transatlantic flight.

My parents appeared younger. I looked down at my outfit to discover I was wearing a skirt suit, and the only time I had worn a skirt suit was on the day of my plea bargain.

I investigated my surroundings until I stopped at a massive window with a mirrored surface on the opposite wall. It had the perfect amount of glare to catch my reflection. I recognized the Indy Kash from thirteen years ago with hair down to my bra strap and leftover baby fat rounding out my face.

I found myself trapped again in one of the darkest corners of my life, dragged to a place I had sworn never to revisit. That single moment had shattered everything—my trust in myself, my family's faith in me, and whatever fragile hope I had left for a future. Seventeen years old, branded guilty for a crime I did not commit, I felt the sentence jabbing into my bones like daggers. I wanted to scream, shout, holler…yet any feral sound was locked behind my ribs. And then, just as I braced to turn away from it all, I caught her—a young woman beside me. Her coal eyes pierced mine. White paint streaked her face.

Then, she vanished.

I was left staring at the ghost of myself in the reflection until Mom whispered from behind me, "Doodoo. Focus."

My mother with her West Indian tough love. It never ceased.

The judge said, "Miss Kash, are you all right? Do you need to be excused? The bailiff can take you to the restroom."

I shook my head, too stunned to do anything else.

"We will proceed then. Miss Kash, I understand this a lot for you to take in, but this is *very* serious." He turned his attention to the prosecutor and my defense attorney. "You have entered a plea bargain which I have accepted. Miss Kash is a first-time offender, and her character references, schoolwork, and activities are outstanding. Up until this point, she has shown good judgment, which makes her actions so surprising."

Was this really happening?

The judge continued, "Let the court recognize the submission of affidavits from the following: Trevor Stone, Brooks—"

I remembered this part clearly. The people who fucked me over. I was too numb to scream or cry or do anything.

"As the plea bargain states: India Jean Kash, you plead guilty to the crime of arson. Because there was only property damage, I am ordering: a twenty-five hundred dollar fine; three hundred hours of community service; and ten sessions with a court-approved therapist. I am also ordering probation, which will be lifted upon completion of paying the fine, the community service, and therapy requirements—all of which the defendant must complete by the time she turns eighteen— or within the next seven months. Usually with property damage, I would order restitution to be paid, but insurance is covering the damage. Several parents at Brookline Prep submitted a letter ensuring that they will pay for any damage that insurance does not cover. Miss Kash, if you do not complete the outlined requirements by your eighteenth birthday, the plea bargain is off the table. Do you understand?"

My mind flashed to the meme that went viral. "Pyro Girl" was me with horns and red eyes on a loop of setting fire to a building and two words that repeated over and over: *Pyro Girl!* "Burning Down the House" by Talking Heads played in the background. It resounded in my thoughts and nightmares. I could never escape the humiliation of "Pyro Girl" or the internet harassment that came with it. My mind then flashed to rejection letters from colleges that destroyed any chance of having an amazing career in STEM. After Brookline Prep expelled me, I returned to my old high school, where kids would ask me to set their ex's phone or locker on fire.

A tear trickled down my cheek, then another and another until I was bawling.

"India Jean, get yourself together right now!" Mom whisper-yelled from behind me.

I ignored her and spoke up. "Your Honor, I'm innocent! I was set up! I know exactly who did it—"

"Enough," the judge said as he raised his hand. "Counselor, I suggest you get your client under control. She is about to blow one of the best plea bargains I've ever agreed to."

My lawyer leaned over and whispered, "India, shut up!"

I didn't know what to do. Here I was again, about to accept a punishment I did not deserve. A punishment that ruined my entire life. But what was I supposed to do? This *was* the best deal, and the seventeen-year-old me had to stand by, again, and accept it while my parents, my lawyer, and everyone else believed that I was guilty.

The tears would not stop flowing. "I'm sorry, Your Honor. That will not happen again. I understand the terms of the plea bargain."

As if I was outside of my body, I heard myself plead guilty, the judge bang his gavel, and my lawyer and parents begin to talk. My intestines churned, and this time, the whisk was on its highest speed.

I grabbed my stomach and ran past my lawyer, pushed through the swinging door then the main door, and burst into the hallway. I sprinted as I desperately searched for a toilet. Then, I felt myself vaporizing again.

The angelic light beamed, the purple lightning hummed in my third eye, and I disappeared into the blackness. I twirled and floated, morphed into particles and back into my physical form, and landed right where I had started in the crew rest club seat.

The oven dinged.

What the—?!

I was gripping the armrests so hard that my forearm muscles bulged. My breathing quickened, but my stomach seemed fine. I touched it. No churning. I inhaled and exhaled deeply to slow my breath and released my grip on the armrests. The engines of the private jet droned as usual. I checked the monitor in front of me: two hours and fifty-seven minutes to destination. Several minutes had passed. I peeked my head out of the crew rest, and yes, those were the same pilots. Wait, did the oven ding?!

Shit!

All I wanted was to sink into myself, to unravel thought by thought until I could make sense of what had just detonated my world. My heart ached for the release of falling apart, for the luxury of losing my mind, even if only for a moment. But the air was too thick with urgency, and the weight of responsibility loomed. The job came first, whether I was ready or not.

I jumped out of the seat and scurried into the galley to smell overcooked bacon. If it did burn, the smell would engulf the entire plane, and the pilots and pax would be furious. If there was an actual fire, well, it would be Pyro Girl 2.0.

I threw on fluffy mitts, opened the oven, and pulled out the tray of sizzling bacon. It could pass as extra crispy. I didn't realize how long I'd been mulling over my life in the crew rest and then the—the *whatever-that-was* happened, but that only lasted a few minutes in present time—

STOP!

Indy, focus.

I shook my head and put on my game face. I cracked eggs, microwaved them in a glass cup, and scrambled them with a fork. For each pilot, I arranged eggs, bacon, and a cup of fresh berries on a separate plate. On trays, I dropped off the food in the cockpit.

On my walk back to the galley, I heard a ding. The service bell.

Mr. Jacobs needed a refill on coffee.

When Time Flies by Jennifer Moreno (Ciotta)

I carried the pot with trembling hands. For him, it was a quiet comfort in a cup. For me, it was a suffocating reminder that I could barely breathe.

#

The rest of the flight was unusually busy with Mr. Jacobs obsessing over the "floofing," or little tumbleweed balls sloughing off the insanely expensive carpet. I had to call Lily, the lead flight attendant who got me this job, to discuss the matter with her. Between calls to Lily, the head of maintenance, and involving the pilots, we sorted the matter. Mr. Jacobs was still annoyed but at least pacified enough to accept that the carpet company would rectify the situation this week.

The other kicker was Mr. Jacobs requested a late breakfast, which he had *never* done before since he was an intermittent faster. With only forty minutes left in the flight, I rushed to cook him a culinary feast using a microwave the size of a hotel safe and the equivalent of an Easy-Bake oven. By the time he had finished eating, I had to clean up the aircraft and prep for landing. This meant stowing away loose items and walking into the cockpit to give the pilots a thumbs-up that the cabin, pax, and me were ready for landing.

I was about to head back to the crew rest, when a thought occurred: that was where I had, well, "gone into my past." So maybe that wasn't the best choice of seats right now. Instead, I pulled out the jump seat, which resembled an awkward dentist chair, and sat behind the pilots.

My phone chimed with a text. It was from Ron, the owner of the management company.

"We're having computer issues. Can you screenshot the catering invoice and send it to me? The caterer cc'd you on the email. Thanks."

I gave the text a thumbs-up, searched my email and found the invoice, and screenshotted it. I opened the Photos App. But instead of the invoice popping up, I saw…

His face.

CHAPTER TWO

Impossible.

I blinked and looked again.

Jayden Mokashu.

How was *he* in my photos?!

The hair on my arms raised. My heart thumped like a rabbit with ADD, and the churning in my stomach that I knew all too well had returned. We would be landing soon, so I couldn't unstrap myself and dash to the lav. *Indy, it's okay. Relax*, I thought.

What did that annoying shaman tell me? The lady with the poofy blue hair…Oh yeah, the one from Trauma Workshop #3. Imagine myself as Dorothy as Toto pulls back the curtain to discover the Wizard, who is a small man manipulating a machine, and I'm Dorothy who has gone on the hero's journey and found courage, and that the Wizard represents the ulcerative colitis and—

What the fuck am I talking about?!

I returned to the reality in front of me and began the deep breathing techniques that I always fell back on. Hand over belly, inhale, exhale. At least all those restorative yoga classes were good for something. I glanced at the pilots. Thankfully, they didn't notice me freaking out behind them.

Once I was able to compose myself, I examined every detail of the picture: Jayden's coiffed dreadlocks tinted with honey blond that extended four inches from his scalp. The smooth black skin and twinkling eyes. A smile like Dwayne Johnson, confident and flashy. The merlot-colored suit only he could wear, with a midnight tie and crisp white shirt.

His face radiated goodness.

That was a lie.

But that wasn't the point. How did a person who hadn't been in my life for *thirteen years* suddenly appear in my photos?

Jayden was a narcissist of the highest degree, and he chose his victims carefully. At that time in my life, I was a fawn to his wolf…and like a wolf, he was agile, the leader of his clan, and trustworthy to his sycophants. But at first, he appeared compassionate.

When Time Flies by Jennifer Moreno (Ciotta)

For my junior year of high school, I had been accepted into the elite Brookline Prep. I was a transfer student on scholarship amongst kids from some of the wealthiest families in the country. To them, I was a sixteen-year-old girl who looked twelve, and wore shoes from DSW. I was the outsider, so they used their greatest weapon: they ignored me.

Until Jayden approached.

I remembered that first week of school:

Two and a half hours to go. And it's Friday. I slid my ham-and-cheese sandwich out of a Ziplock bag, bit into it, and then placed it on my lap. Air hissed as I opened a can of Coke. I rustled through a snack bag of potato chips. The upperclassmen at the nearest table dined on takeout sushi.

As I was about to pop a chip into my mouth, someone said, "You're cute. Who are you?"

The voice came from behind me. I glanced over my shoulder.

"Yes you. Eating the chips. And soda. And some equally unhealthy sandwich I bet. You're cute."

Jayden stepped into view. He was the guy everyone wanted to be. Tall, good-looking, a thin but athletic build, and colorful dreads. Those chocolate eyes.

"Thanks." I didn't know what else to say.

"You look young. I mean *young*. Are you a prodigy or the darker female Benjamin Button?"

"The darker female Benjamin Button."

He laughed. "You got jokes. What's your name?"

"India—well everyone calls me Indy. Indy Kash."

"Damn that's a movie star name for such a little girl."

I blushed. "I'm a junior—almost seventeen. I'm not a prodigy, unfortunately. I transferred in."

"Yeah, you did. You don't belong here, Indy. Not with that no-name backpack and shoes." He upped and downed me. "Yep, scholarship kid. We get a few of us a year. Helps fill Brookline's quota for 'diversification,'" he said while gesturing air quotes. "We black folk—or should I say half-black folk in your case—look good on paper."

"Yeah, my dad is white. My mom is from Trinidad. I'm a lot of things."

He nodded. "I'm the opposite. My mom is white and my dad's black, but no one ever sees the white part. Anyway, wait 'til Brookline Prep asks you to be a greeter for parents' night and takes your photo for the school brochure."

I gave a faint smile.

"That's better. By the way, I'm Jayden Mokashu. I'm on scholarship too. They call it 'academic' but I'm actually here for crew."

I raised my eyebrows.

"A black guy who rows? I know. I rowed in clubs around the city. The Brookline recruiter liked what he saw and here I am. It was tough at first, but you can't let these people run you down."

He sat next to me. "I'm from Roxbury, so I'm way out of place. A tip?"

What the hell. At least someone acknowledged me in five whole days. "Sure."

"Find your niche, your talent, whatever you're good it—and showcase it. These people remember that in the future. If they have a use for you, you'll benefit and get along. Look at me with the rowing. When I help them win, I get into a good college because of their parents' recommendations to the best schools. Then I help them win at college, then in the business world. That's how I look at it. We're outsiders. We'll never be inside their inner circle, so learn to use them as much as they use us."

Solid advice.

Before I could respond, he stood up. "Nice to meet you, Indy Kash. See you around."

On my walk home from school that day, I had thought about how unfriendly and quiet I was in our conversation. I could've been nicer to him, but I was suspicious about why this popular guy and beloved athlete would even talk to me.

As it turned out, my first instinct was *always* right.

A few weeks later, my science teacher saw my propensity for STEM, so I was moved into a couple of Jayden's classes. The day we had met he had made himself out to be "a jock," but he was actually brilliant—

Wait.

Why were we not landing?

As if he was reading my mind, the captain turned his head and pulled the microphone away from his mouth. "Indy, we're in a holding pattern for the next thirty minutes. Bad traffic. Can you go back and tell Mr. Jacobs?"

I nodded and walked into the cabin to deliver the news. Mr. Jacobs looked up from his newspaper and grunted.

Once I was back in the jump seat, I grabbed my phone, needing to checking his photo—proof he was real. But the image wasn't there. I scrolled, frantic, heart hammering with every swipe. Gone. Erased. As if he had never existed at all.

"WHY AREN'T WE LANDING?!"

I jumped. Mr. Jacobs had snuck up from behind me. The poor pilots.

The captain turned around. He seemed as collected as Sully Sullenberger about to land in the Hudson River. "Did Indy tell you about the hold, Mr. Jacobs?"

Another grunt. "How much longer?"

"Twenty-eight minutes, unless ATC holds us for longer, which they might."

"Did you tell them who I am?"

Oh, Jesus. We'd gotten to this level.

"Yes, Mr. Jacobs."

I had to physically stop myself from rolling my eyes. Somehow the captain's firm response told Mr. Jacobs to back off subconsciously, because he returned to the cabin.

I lifted myself up and turned around to make sure he was in his club seat. He was back to reading. The headline of his newspaper blared: "Boy Billionaire Woos It Girl." Was that the *National Enquirer*?! Really?

My phone beeped. A photo had been Airdropped to me. My pulse spiked—only the pilots could have done that. With shaking fingers, I unlocked the screen, every nerve braced for impact.

Another image filled the glass, dragging the breath out of me.

It was me. Not a memory, not a trick. Present-day—thirty-year-old Indy—wired into a metal box like a specimen. Cords sprouted from my body, anchoring me in place. I pressed the screen, half-hoping it wouldn't move, half-terrified it might.

It moved.

I watched myself suspended, arms splayed, a grotesque mirror of Da Vinci's Vitruvian Man—but skewed, twisted at a forty-five-degree angle, so my body was shown from every side. The wires pulsed against me, each one fastened to a point along my frame. My stomach dropped. They weren't random. They marked me like targets: the seven chakras.

I fought the urge to scream. My pupils scoured the details of the photo, while a lump formed in my throat. Even if I wanted to shout, my voice was stuck somewhere in disbelief.

Three wires connected to my spine along the first three chakras: the tailbone; below the navel; and the solar plexus. On the front of my body, the remaining wires connected to the last four chakras: the heart; the base of my throat, the third eye, and the crown of my head. I noticed a shadow along the side of the metal box.

I pressed again.

The photo disappeared, leaving me with my mouth hanging open.

"Indy, is everything okay?"

The co-pilot saw me. Shit.

I fake-laughed. "Oh, just some clickbait garbage. Sorry."

"That stuff sucks you in. We're five minutes from landing. ATC bumped us up."

"Thanks."

I checked my phone again. *Whoa, time flies.* Twenty minutes went by fast.

I couldn't risk the pilots observing more strange behavior or they'd start to talk. Pilots loved good gossip. Not as much as the mechanics, but still. I tucked away my phone under my thigh and then…the weightless feeling returned.

Everything happened in an instant: the vaporizing, the angelic white, the lightning, the bug-zapping sound in my third eye, rolling in black space…and then…

I landed in a place I thought I'd left behind forever.

CHAPTER THREE

The night of the fire.

Screams invaded. A rush of people in tuxedos and designer gowns ran for their lives. The heat intensified.

I coughed.

The disorientation of being teleported or whatever the hell just happened finally dizzied me. I had the urge to run for *my* life, but instead, I put one hand on a wall and the other over my mouth and nose. My eyes watered and I blinked incessantly. Down below, the orange flames and gray smoke engulfed the stage. The blaze swallowed the gilded chairs, off-white tablecloths, and circular wooden tables. Fire crackled and whooshed, while in the distance, firetruck and police sirens blared.

I could barely open my eyes. I was choking on the smoke that rushed onto the balcony.

I had no choice but to run.

I grasped the train of my satin evening gown and dashed down the stairs in three-inch heels. When I reached the bottom, I swung my head left then right.

Where is that exit?

Smoke streamed into the enclosed area. Everything felt tight: my lungs, the hacking cough, how I squeezed my eyelids shut. There was no time to take a beat. My frenzied mind attempted to rationalize: *Is this a side entrance or the service hallway?* I remembered an exit.

It was here the last time…wasn't it?

The inside of my elbow shielded my mouth and nose, and with my right hand I touched the warmth of a wall. My heart quickened. I reminded myself, *Indy Kash, you survive this fire. You find a way out.*

Down the short, narrow hallway was glass. I sprinted toward it.

Wait.

It's not a door.

I remembered one with a silver handlebar that pushed easily onto the city street. With both hands, I felt around the perimeter of the warm glass. *It's a window!* I looked left and knew that was where the door should be.

Instead, I faced a wall. Blank. Silent. To my right, another stretch of off-white, as if the room itself had swallowed every exit. Behind me, smoke coiled higher, blotting out the world, while glass shattered in the distance like a countdown I couldn't stop.

My fingers fumbled over the window frame, frantic, searching for a knob, a latch, any proof that escape was possible. Nothing. The smooth surface mocked me.

Panic slid icy fingers down my spine. My breath came too fast, too shallow, my own body betraying me. The harder I tried to breathe, the more it felt like I was inhaling fear itself. My heartbeat pounded in my ears, louder than the coughing fit that wracked my chest. The thought struck sharp and merciless:

There is no way out.

As the smoke rushed in, my legs wobbled. I wasn't going to make it. The truth would die along with me.

This thought drifted outward, cold and eternal. My whole existence had turned against me and wrapped me in silence. I was dissolving into the weight of it, as if the world had already begun to forget I was ever here.

"STAND BACK!" I heard a person with a bullhorn.

I scurried from the window, now able to see blurry figures outside. The next thing I heard was glass breaking as an axe chopped through the window pane. It shattered into large pieces that crashed to the floor. I covered my eyes and huddled in a corner. When the breaking stopped, I looked up. A glove reached inside.

"COME TOWARD THE WINDOW!"

I jumped up and moved toward the gray-soot, black-gloved hand. As I grabbed it, a strong person pulled me through. On the way out, a shard of glass pierced my right ankle. I winced.

I stepped onto the sidewalk, facing my classmates, their parents, and my teachers. I had attended this school fundraising event alone. My parents certainly couldn't afford any of the auction items, but I was certain that someone called them once people realized I was missing.

The female firefighter who rescued me said, "We gotta fix that cut on your ankle and make sure your breathing is stable."

I nodded.

"What's your name?"

"Indy Kash."

She murmured to the police officer next to her. They examined a clipboard with sheets of paper.

She flipped through the papers and looked up at me. "Your name isn't on this attendee list. How did you get in?"

"How did I *get in*? I go to this school!"

She made a stop signal with her hand. "Calm down. You've been through a lot."

"Why would I be here in a fancy dress if I wasn't invited?"

I didn't care if this brave woman came to my rescue. I was completely offended that not one classmate or teacher thought to check if I was safe. Was I *that much* of an afterthought?

"India Kash. Yes, she was at the event. I'm sorry, India, but you weren't on the list for the auction. Neither were your parents," the headmaster explained. "The list at the door only includes those who are participating in the auction."

The officer said, "How did she get through the front door then?"

They stared at me.

The first time I had attended this fundraising event—when I was actually sixteen years old—I was on the list. I had checked in at the front door with my history teacher Mrs. Hen—yes, her real name. This time I wasn't sure, but how was this *possible*?

How was *any* of this possible?

When I had returned to the plea bargain hearing—at surface level—things appeared the same. Now that I was thinking about it, there was the young woman. Her eyes seemed to spear the air itself, and her face was painted into a haunting perfection. Who was she?

Everything was off.

Then I heard the unmistakable laughter of Jayden Mokashu. Friends and parents surrounded him as they huddled in blankets and sipped hot coffee. I glared.

Why had I attended the fundraiser that night? I had asked myself this many times throughout the years. I'd concluded that it was a last attempt to fit into this elite, prep school world. I thought if I could dress up and look like everyone else, people would finally see me.

When I had arrived at the event, I saw that everyone had their groups and knew each other. I had no one to talk to. I realized the mistake I had made. To pull myself together, I slipped backstage and plopped down on the scratched wooden floor. Between sniffling away my tears, I heard the sound of…was it rustling?

I peeked around the red velvet material. Jayden and his friends talked quietly and laughed. He puffed on a cigarette. I smelled weed and saw them pass around a bottle of brown liquor—fine, whatever.

Jayden looked away from the group and straight at me.

I froze as if I was interrupting a Skull and Bones meeting—which I probably was. At least the prep-school version.

He turned back to the group as his best friend, Trevor Stone, handed him a joint. He puffed and told a story with his hands, while Trevor slapped him affectionately on the shoulder.

"Would you like a blanket?" a sympathetic firefighter asked, interrupting the memory.

Upon recalling Jayden and Trevor, a surge had pulsed through my bones. I shuddered, which the firefighter mistook for the cold Boston night.

I shook my head.

The police officer said, "We have contacted your parents"—great—"but first, we have some questions as to why you were backstage and then in the balcony."

In my original past, after I ran into Jayden and his friends backstage, I'd retreated to the balcony for some alone time. Besides not wanting to appear a frazzled mess, I didn't need my mom asking why I was home so early. I stayed on the balcony until the fire broke out, and then I had to escape.

The Brookline police and fire departments had concluded that I was backstage with cigarettes. A lit cigarette had set the curtain on fire, and it spread. Somehow the video surveillance showed me heading backstage, but conveniently, Jayden, Trevor, and their friends were nowhere to be found. My guess was Jayden had tampered with the video.

I had told the detective, the fire chief, my defense attorney, and my parents the truth, but no one believed me. It was them—meaning the rich families who owned Brookline—versus me, a scholarship kid with nothing to offer.

My parents then grounded me, took away my phone, and removed all flammables from the house. My life had consisted of meetings with my lawyer, disappointed glances from my parents, internet humiliation, and an ongoing deep depression.

The police officer repeated, "Why were you backstage and on the balcony?"

"What are you getting at, officer? I'm tired. Cut to the chase."

"Miss Kash, watch your tone. Several invitees witnessed you go backstage."

"I'm sure they did."

"This is very serious, Miss Kash. It's evident that the fire started backstage. But no one was back there for the short duration of the event. No one except for you."

"Why are you believing these 'invitees?' They're trying to set me up. Isn't that pretty obvious?"

"Whoa. I'm just asking questions."

"You know what? I'm not dealing with this bullshit thirteen years later. I know how it ends."

The officer winced in confusion or fear that a teenage girl was about to unleash on him and that my parents were influential like the others.

"I'm a minor. Stop asking me questions. The next person you talk to is my lawyer."

About to hobble off with blood dripping from the deep cut on my ankle, I transported through time and space, back into the jump seat of the private jet.

Thud!

The pilots had landed the plane, not smoothly, but we were safe and on the ground.

I grabbed my right ankle. There was no sign of blood and I couldn't feel a scar through my compression stocking.

My head spun as we taxied the runway. I had to keep my shit together, if only for five more minutes until Mr. Jacobs deplaned.

So, I kept my shit together, wished Mr. Jacobs a "good afternoon," gathered all my things, and handed the cleaning crew the leftover food.

I thanked the pilots and then drove my ancient convertible out of the parking lot.

It was then that I allowed my mind to settle for the seven-minute drive to my apartment in Hackensack. A little voice in the back of my head said something I did not want to hear:

I needed to call my mom.

In our relationship, I was always teetering—one misstep from tumbling. However, her West Indian upbringing gave her metaphysical knowledge.

I wasn't sure if any of these events or occurrences were meta, but no other explanation fit. I mulled over the logical or not-so-logical options:

Did I suddenly develop a split personality?

Not that I was aware of.

Low blood sugar?

I would feel faint.

A seizure, dementia, an alien jumping into my body?

None of these options seemed likely.

I sighed. I had to talk to Mom.

Fuck.

CHAPTER FOUR

"It's the kokma."

Here we go.

My mother said in her sing-song Trini lilt, "You know the *kock*-ma. You grew up with her. Sometimes she'd step on your chest while you were sleeping. I had to shake you to wake you up. It's just an evil spirit trying to steal your soul. That's all."

Oh yeah, that was all.

It was only the legend of a West Indian ghost baby, the kokma, who jumped on a person's chest while they slept and attacked their throat. Very subtle.

"Mom, I don't think so. I was wide awake."

"Maybe you *think* you were wide awake. Did it feel like the kokma?"

"Not really. I've had sleep paralysis before, and this felt different. And again, I wasn't asleep."

Did she ever listen to me?

"You've been working a lot. Where are you now?"

"I'm home."

A pause then the usual. "Your father and I worry about you. This job, it's a lot of travel, especially with the UC"—ulcerative colitis, my unfortunate specific brand of IBD—"You know what happened last time with the flare. You were so sick, baby girl. You have to be careful. We're hoping you will find a *real* job soon."

There it was. The compassion-insult sandwich. How could I get a real job if no college would accept me? She knew my circumstances, and yet she buried the knife in my heart a little bit deeper with each conversation.

"Your father tells me he hasn't heard from you in a long time."

Oops. I kept forgetting to call my dad. We got along fine but didn't have much in common as adults. I gave him his space to do his thing, while I did mine.

"How's Dad?"

"He's good. It sounds like the job is good, and he keeps himself occupied with his books and listening to old records. He's taken up birding."

"Huh?"

"Bird watching."

Holy shit did that sound boring.

"Awesome."

The fascinating part was how my parents formed a united front. They cheated on each other, divorced after I graduated from high school, and sold the house. My dad took a job in the Berkshires, and my mom retired from her exhausting nursing career and moved back to Port of Spain where she had grown up.

"Anyway, Mom, can we get back to the reason I called?"

"Are you dating anyone?"

"Mom!"

"I'd like to hear about my daughter's life *first*."

There was no swaying this woman. I sighed. "Everything is good: work, Snowball, my apartment. I'm not dating."

Snowball, my white Persian cat, was prancing across the counter. I grabbed her fluffy tail and wiggled it. She meowed.

Mom made that West Indian tongue-sucking sound. "India Jean, when is the last time you've had a boyfriend? You gonna dry up down there."

"Really?! Are we *really* talking about this?"

"It's fine if you're gay. Or asexual. Your father and I don't care, as long as you're happy."

Oh My G—*don't let her throw you off track*, I thought. "I'm straight. I'm in a dry spell."

"You gotta take care of that soon, or you're gonna be humping Snowball."

Nice.

"Mom, let's move on to why I called—"

"Okay, okay. One more thing…back in my day, those rich white men you fly, they wouldn't have wanted an ethnic girl, but today's different. These men have fetishes for ethnically ambiguous women. And you're beautiful! All those years when you were a teenager of looking so young and developing so late"—thanks Mom—"they've paid off. You look like you're eighteen, India. This is the time to strategize and snatch one of those men. I was reading the other day that many of these rich men don't want to date in their caste anymore. They want a woman who knows how to work. That's you! You have to be open to the possibility. I was gonna forward you the article, but I know you hate that."

I was praying this lecture had an end.

"Any other ideas for what happened to me today?"

She paused. "You're exhausted, doodoo. Get some rest and the answers will come to you."

I decided to save my sanity and give up on this conversation, and said goodbye.

That was a serious waste of time.

Why couldn't she ever see my side of things? She had been so preoccupied with her career, her shitty marriage, the public humiliation of having an arsonist daughter, and the divorce that she wasn't there for me when I needed her.

She was right about one thing though: my couch was luring me. Its soft white fabric enticed me to lay down. If I were to close my eyes for a five-minute power nap, I could then continue my search for answers.

I pushed the kitchen stool away from the counter, walked over to the couch, and laid down. Snowball jumped next to me, curled into a ball, and settled in for a nap too. My eyelids tugged themselves closed as I finally drifted off for some much-needed brain rest.

My head sprang off the decorative pillow. Even Snowball was startled; she leapt off the couch with a defiant meow.

I tasted the dryness in my mouth, blinked a few times, and reached out to pet Snowball. "I'm sorry that I startled you, Snowy," I said in a baby voice.

I rubbed her furry head, which she usually loved, but she was distracted. She had turned toward a corner in my living room and fixated on something with saucer-like eyes. I tapped a finger on her fluffy skull. "Miss Snowy, you in there?"

I followed Snowball's gaze and jumped when I saw a glowing figure. My skin prickled, while my mind scrambled for yet another explanation that didn't exist. She stood there, impossibly radiant, the air bending around her. It was not a shadow or stray reflection. She was a painted being that should not exist—at least not in my living room.

CHAPTER FIVE

It was the young woman from the mirror-window.

My chest swelled and a sob rose before I could swallow it down. I didn't understand why. Relief, terror, wonder—all of it tangled inside me. I felt like a child again, exposed and unguarded before something greater than myself.

Her painted face resembled that of a warrior. Underneath were radiant black eyes and flawless caramel skin. Silky midnight hair flowed down her back and her chest, covering her naked breasts. A pleated, school-girl skirt encompassed her hips down to her upper thighs, and a red sash wrapped around the skirt to form a tied belt. Two beaded necklaces rested on her clavicle. Her scent was the freshest coconut and breadfruit.

It wasn't just that she was beautiful—it was that her beauty claimed me. I knew, even as I stood trembling, that I would never escape it. Every flaw in me screamed louder, every scar felt raw again. Her perfection didn't dazzle me—it exposed me.

I just told my mom I was straight…but this creature standing in front of me was pretty spectacular for any human to take in.

Even through the war paint, I could see she was a mixture of different ethnicities: East Indian, another type of Asian, and black. Actually, we looked alike, except for my curly hair and the violet and white glow emanating from her physical form, which wasn't quite human. There was a hazy quality to her, yet I could easily distinguish her features. Snowball couldn't look away either. I'd never seen her that entranced.

I was barely able to utter the words, "Who are you?"

"I'm Kai, your spirit guide."

"My what?"

"You heard me. Kai. Your. Spirit. Guide."

Her voice…it reminded me of Mom's. It had that Trini quality, like she was singing as she spoke. Light and smooth with a quiet power.

I closed my eyes. "I must be dreaming."

"You're not dreaming. You weren't dreaming in the courtroom either."

My eyelids popped open. I couldn't think of a breathing technique for this situation. My human urge was to panic, yet steadiness prevailed. This spirit guide had an energy that invoked, well, not pure joy. No, I wasn't getting that vibe. Instead, I felt an otherworldly stillness.

Okay Indy, get your shit together. This a dream, only a dream. A weird dream that feels 1000% real.

I needed to ground myself back to reality.

What was that technique?

The thing Cher and Christina Ricci used for acting to feel emotions?

Yes, *that* Cher.

Touching surfaces.

Touch different surfaces to bring myself to the present moment.

My left hand wandered over a couch cushion, while my right hand stroked along Snowball's spine. All the while, I stared at Kai, mouth agape.

"Close your mouth, Indy."

I obeyed.

"What are you doing?"

I looked like a nutter stroking both my couch and Snowball at the same time. I halted.

"Your grandma and mom reacted the same. It must be a family trait."

I froze. Did she just say my grandmother *and MOTHER*?

My head swam in the chaos.

Brain fog made me slump into the couch.

All I wanted was to take a nap in peace and then piece together the puzzle. Instead, a glowing spirit stood before me.

Annoyed, frustrated, and simply exhausted from this entire day, I relinquished any logic of the situation and decided to do something uncharacteristic of me.

To go with the flow.

"So, you're the spirit guide for my mom and grandma?"

"I'm happy to talk, but first, could you make me a PSL?"

I sat up.

"A *what*?"

"A Pumpkin Spice Latte. Humans love them this time of year and I love the smell."

Did she not know about the UC or that I wasn't a barista or that I didn't have *any* of the ingredients?

In an instant, they appeared on my counter, including an espresso maker, a royal blue mug that read "Kiss Your Spirit Guide," and a container of milk…from an actual cow. Who drinks real milk anymore?

I blinked hard, thinking, *I must be imagining all this*. I wasn't.

She turned to me. "I'll show you how to do this once and then you can do it the next time."

"If you can instantly materialize all of this"—I swept my hand across the ingredients—"why can't you materialize the latte?"

"Because I enjoy watching baristas. It's like being at a real human coffee shop, without being at a real human coffee shop, like on *Friends*. You know?"

Wait, she watched…? I decided to let that one go.

As she ground the beans and frothed milk, I said to myself, meeting a celestial being, you'd think this experience would be all healing and shit. But instead, I had a spirit guide in war paint humming as she made herself a PSL.

I had spent a small fortune on all those metaphysical workshops, online courses, and experiences in other countries, so of course, I knew the concept of spirit guides. Had I believed in them?

Not really.

"Now you know how to make my favorite drink. Please sit," she said as she pointed to a kitchen stool. She took a long whiff of her latte, giggled, and put it down.

The giggle. Whoa. Kai morphed from a hard-ass into a giddy teenager.

"Unfortunately, I can't drink it because I have no physical body to absorb it. I'm jealous of humans sometimes. I would love to taste."

I eyed her with curiosity, because she now seemed young, very young. Eighteen? But if she were immortal, she wouldn't have an approximate age. For all I knew, she was 6,000 years old.

I pulled out a stool and sat. Snowball perched on the one next to me, still entranced.

Kai stirred the drink. "You, your mom, and grandma can time-travel, as I'm sure you've figured out."

I held my breath. The words *time travel* resounded in my head.

"Exhale Indy"—I did—"I assumed you had figured it out after today?"

I'd loved taking science classes in high school. While I was grounded, I even went through a *Star Trek* phase. In the science and technology magazines which I still read, time travel was discussed as more of a theory, a distant concept— not a concrete thing. It was popularized in books, movies, and TV, so I naturally assumed it leaned toward fiction.

How could *I* be a time traveler?

She picked up her drink and breathed it in. "Your time-travel gift is inherited. It 'turns on' when you turn thirty. Happy belated birthday."

I shook my head, barely taking in the words.

"The same thing happened with your mom, grandma, and all the women in your maternal lineage before them. You time-traveled at work today. That's because air travel activates the gift for the women in your bloodline. Before humans invented air travel, your Native Carib ancestors would astral travel."

In a few of the meta workshops I had taken, the leaders had discussed astral travel. My ancestors could intentionally send their astral or spiritual body to another place.

"Because humans have devolved metaphysically, time travelers now use other means, like air travel."

Logic prevailed once again. "Why wouldn't Mom tell me that I could time-travel?"

My voice broke on the word "travel." How could she not tell her only daughter about this?

"You have to ask her."

I sighed. More games, more waiting for answers, more my mother not telling me a damn thing.

I studied Kai. "Why are you wearing war paint?"

"This is the traditional ceremonial paint and dress of the Native Caribbean people. My natural state as a spirit guide is an amorphous light. But to appear to humans, I must take form, so this is the form I choose. I think it is unique, powerful, and beautiful."

It was.

"Why were you in the courtroom?"

"I contacted you too early. My bad. Sometimes I'm an eager beaver." She laughed. "The other spirit guides are like, 'Kai, slow down!' But I get too excited. I have to work on patience."

Did she just say *eager beaver*?

I shook my head and refocused. "When do I travel next? Will I travel every time I'm at work? Because that'll be a huge issue. And what about the mysterious photos popping up on my phone?"

"We'll work on controlling it. You will learn how to go back and forth, but for now, you have to simply get used to it. I bet you feel exhausted."

I nodded. I really did.

"Tell me about the mysterious photos."

I explained the pictures of Jayden and the metal box with wires that appeared and then disappeared from my phone. A shudder rippled through my body.

Kai pressed her lips together. "I need to gather more information. I will have the full story once I'm back on the plane."

"You travel by *airplane*?"

She giggled. "No, silly. I meant the *astral* plane."

Of course.

"I expect a piping hot PSL next time." Her eyes bored into mine. "You *can* do this, Indy. I'll return with more intel."

She vanished into thin air. Snowball darted her head left and right and hissed loudly. When Kai left, I also noticed a shift in energy, where now it had a denser, more grounded quality. Snowy had noticed it too, because she rarely hissed. The natural, heavier energy of myself had returned, which meant my negative emotions had returned along with it, and I was *pissed* at my mom.

I swiped my phone off the counter and clicked on her contact. She picked up.

"Wow, twice in one day."

I could practically feel the rage kick up in my liver.

"Hey Mom, guess who stopped by today?"

"Who's that, doodoo?"

"Kai."

Silence.

When she finally spoke, she said, "Oh."

"*Oh*?! That's seriously all you have to say?! Seriously?!"

Silence again.

"Why wouldn't you prepare me for this—this LIFE-ALTERING situation? Maybe the fact that we can *time-travel*? Why would you waste THIRTY YEARS nagging me about dumb shit or hardly talking to me or whatever?" I cleared my throat as I felt the tears forming. "You really and truly don't care about me."

"That's not true, Indy. I dreaded the day you turned thirty—" She sighed. "I knew this was coming."

"Then why? How could you not prepare me for this?! My job is a corporate flight attendant for Chrissake. I'm always on a plane!"

"I know you can't understand this, but I was trying to protect you."

"You did the complete opposite."

"You don't know what you don't know, India."

"What the hell does that mean?"

She paused for too long.

"Mom, you better explain everything, or so help me God, I will never, and I mean *never* speak to you again."

She spoke slowly, as if choosing her words as carefully as possible. "Do you remember that random trip I took to Michigan in 2010?"

I frowned. Where was she going with this? "Okay. Yeah."

"I visited this town called Ypsilanti. A former coworker of mine offered me a head nursing position there with better pay. After touring the hospital and meeting the staff, I knew I would like it, but was it enough to uproot my family? As I pondered the decision, I drove the rental car to a grocery store to grab a snack.

"That's when the time-travel experience started. The parking lot turned into something…odd. The cars were new but from 1980s; there was even a DeLorean."

"Okay."

"When I opened my car door and got out, time stood still. There was no breeze, no sound. No birds chirping, people talking, or the smell of hot asphalt on that summer day. The air was so dense, as if I could slice through it. Something was off."

Welcome to my life.

"There was a long, almost tunnel-like passageway with a burgundy carpet between the outside entry door and the door to enter the store. As I passed through this tunnel, a creepy feeling surrounded me, yet I kept going. Then I entered the grocery store and froze. Everyone and everything looked as if they were straight out of the 1980s. The teased eighties hair, the punk makeup, the men wearing knee-high socks."

"You time-traveled then?"

"It was more than that. The air flow ceased. I could hear the ringing of the cash register and people walking—all the normal sounds. I smelled cleaning solution and harsh perfume. But the air around me refused to budge. I couldn't shake the eerie feeling."

Mom's voice dropped an octave. "I turned around, ran, and threw open the door. But I couldn't pass through the tunnel. The air held me there and began to suffocate me. Imagine air squeezing you to where you can't breathe, doodoo."

I couldn't.

"I yelled and couldn't hear my own voice. I struggled and tried to wrestle myself out of the air. Finally, I gave up. I fell onto that burgundy carpet crying. I was stuck like someone trapped in an elevator without an emergency button. My breathing slowed, and I was gasping. My mind raced through my entire life, until the next thing I knew, I was back on the plane flying home."

"What! How?"

"I don't know."

These words kept repeating themselves today.

Mom sobbed into the phone.

Finally, she said, "India, that experience was so terrifying that I stopped traveling on planes. When I moved back to Trinidad, I drove to Florida, took a cruise to Port of Spain, and shipped my things here."

She'd always said she was afraid to fly.

"Mom, I'm sorry that happened and that does sound horrible, but that's still no excuse for why you didn't tell me."

"I didn't want to revisit that experience. I knew Kai would come to you when you traveled, and she did. She can explain things much better than I can."

"I disagree."

"Just be careful. Time-traveling is serious business. It's not for me, and it may not be for you." She raised her voice. "India Jean, I am *not* discussing this with you anymore. This conversation is over."

The line went dead. The door known as Mom slammed in my face.

It had happened many times before. When Tina Kash was done talking, that was it. There was no talking to her now. She wouldn't answer calls or texts for days, possibly weeks.

I wished my grandmother was still alive so I could ask her.

Thank God for the internet.

I searched for my phone until I realized Snowball was lying on it. She meowed as I reached under her.

Just then, it chimed with a text from Ron. "Just emailed you the trip sheet for tomorrow. Thanks."

My heart skipped a beat. I would be flying again, possibly time-traveling to who-knows-where…and after listening to my mom's story…geez. *Ping!* The email had arrived. To assuage the panic now coursing through my body, I forced myself to study the trip sheet.

Fourteen pax from TEB, Teterboro, to LAS, Las Vegas. Show time: 0900.

It was a drop-off, which meant the return leg was a deadhead, or no pax. Thank you, Jesus. A Vegas trip was never good with the usual rowdy pax, and I was the constant bartender…and even worse, now I could be the constant time traveler, too.

Ugh.

I clicked Reply, wrote "received," and hit Send.

I texted Mrs. Albright, my upstairs neighbor and Snowball's pet sitter, to see if she could feed Snowy in case I got delayed in Vegas. Mrs. Albright texted, "Of course, honey."

At least I could rely on something stable in my life. Everything else had been turned upside down. The sun had barely set, and in the course of today's events, I had time-traveled to my past twice, met my spirit guide, and outed my mom. I couldn't imagine what tomorrow would bring.

Back to my mission: research time travel.

Internet, movies, TV.

I mean I couldn't just straight call someone and be like, "Hey, do you time-travel, or do you, by chance, know anyone who time-travels?"

Yeah. No. It wasn't like finding a good gynecologist.

I snatched my iPad off the counter, walked over to the couch, and sat cross-legged. I had to stay in an upright position to keep myself awake. My back ached, my head pulsed, and my mouth had been dry and pasty ever since my first trip through time and space. But I had to suck it up. If I time-traveled tomorrow, I wanted to be prepared…or as prepared as I could get in one night.

Snowball snuggled next to me as I searched on my iPad to find *Back to the Future*, which I hadn't ever seen—good movie. I now understood Mom's DeLorean reference. Then I watched a couple episodes of the 1989 version of *Quantum Leap*. I felt kinda silly using movies and TV for my research, but what else could I do?

I thought about the messages in the writings of HG Wells, Octavia Butler, and Audrey Niffenegger. I had watched the current season of *Outlander* a few months ago. What I realized was this: the time traveler has to change something in the past in order to help others in the present and future.

It was all…so much for one human to absorb in one day. So much so that I decided to crawl into bed and sleep until my alarm went off at 7:00 a.m.

#

My alarm chimed melodious tones, yet an alarm was still an alarm. I wiped the sleep from my eyes and realized that I'd been actively dreaming all night. My lucid subconscious had swirled with dreams of being born into a lineage of time travelers…and that I had my very own *spirit guide*.

Then I pinched myself. Yep, this was real life.

I reached for my phone on the nightstand, knocked over a cave-looking purple amethyst, and stood it back up. I removed Do Not Disturb and opened my home screen to reveal a bunch of missed calls, and several texts from Ron saying, "call me!"

He was on the west coast, so I couldn't imagine the drama he had to deal with at 4:00 a.m. That was corporate aviation, where unfortunately, pax with their last-minute trip changes and demands could easily take away a good night's sleep.

I called.

"Hey Indy, change in plans today. I wanted to reach you before you left for the hangar. I assigned another FA to the Vegas trip."

I frowned. "Okay."

"I have a special request. It will take a couple hours of your time; it's located at Aire Aviation—you know, the giant new company that just moved into Teterboro?"

Yeah, but I hadn't worked for Aire yet.

"I'm paying you a full daily rate for a couple hours of work."

Nice.

A thought popped into my head: *No air travel, so that meant no time-traveling for now*. Thank God.

"What's the job?"

"You know how I occasionally get these on-the-ground requests when potential buyers wanna buy an aircraft? Well, this time they're looking at a Citation X for their executive team. Small, I know, only eight seats. I tried to convince them to look at something bigger *and* newer—anyway, they'd like an FA to do a lunch setup on the aircraft. All the food has been ordered and will be in the fridge at the hangar. All you have to do is unwrap it, present it, and serve them lunch."

"They don't want to take the aircraft for a spin?"

"I guess not. Can you do it?"

"Sure. I'll be there at eleven?"

"Perfect. They'll be there just after twelve o'clock. And Indy, this is an *important* account for Aire. If they get this business, there's a lot more to follow for us. So please, impress them like you always do, but a step up."

"Got it."

"Thanks. Bye."

I eyed the stack of technology magazines on my bedroom floor. Sometimes I would find a profile on a female engineer, rip it out, and save it in a folder. I attempted a vision board with photos of women in science and tech whom I admired, but looking at it was too painful.

I wasn't getting admitted to any college with my juvenile criminal record. Though it had been sealed, anyone who searched me online would discover my past. I had ripped up the vision board and dropped the fantasy.

I had learned to be grateful for this job. The court had assigned me to volunteer at different organizations to fulfill my community service requirement. I'd seen meth addicts who couldn't afford food for themselves or their children eventually succumb to the disease. I'd seen others be given a second chance and turn their lives around. I had been given a second chance too.

Volunteering at a food pantry when I was seventeen was my one lucky break. I had met Lily, the lead FA on the Mr. Jacobs account and cabin service manager at Ron's company. She had taken a liking to me because I worked hard, never gave her shit, and was hospitable to the food-pantry clients. She was having trouble finding good flight attendants; most of them were super flaky and unprofessional. She knew my situation but said Ron could work around a sealed record, and that pax or their companies rarely background-checked a flight attendant once the management company approved her. When I was eighteen, Ron hired me as a contractor and I'd been working for his company ever since.

Even so, when I turned the pages of those glossy magazines and watched videos online about women in STEM, my heart ached. I'd come to terms with the fact that I wasn't living my Plan A, B, or even C. I wished I could finally accept my life path and move on, but I couldn't. Most days I felt like I was drowning in stillness, desperate to move but unable to break free.

#

I unwrapped a silver tray of chocolate-covered strawberries, which I added to the display of finger sandwiches with mini condiment jars, individual charcuterie boards, crudités with plain hummus dip…and, yep, glazed donuts. I *zhuzhed* the snack basket and then did a once-over of the fruit basket to ensure I had removed all the price stickers. Water bottles rested in the cupholders.

The aircraft sat on the tarmac with engines running. The mechanic and I were inside the plane, while the director of aviation had disappeared into the FBO —Fixed Based Operator or private jet terminal—to greet the pax.

The mechanic shouted into the cabin, "Pax are here."

To provide the full effect, I waited atop the stairs, like on TV and in the movies, which usually wasn't realistic. We would wait inside the aircraft, next to the door. But hey, for today, I'd go the extra mile for Ron, because he was the reason I wasn't living in a cardboard box.

A group of men in dark business suits ambled toward the aircraft. Right on time, a little past noon. They laughed and gestured. They were in a good mood, which would make my job easier. An hour of them eating, drinking, bombarding the director and mechanic with questions about finances, maintenance, warranties, budget, etc.—and then I'd clean up and would be back home. The best part was: no surprises today. The plane was grounded.

From a distance, the businessmen appeared youthful, which was usually the case as they were looking to purchase a *used* aircraft. I already felt bad for their future pilots. If the businessmen's company were to allow them the plane for personal use, forget it. The pilots would say goodbye to their families and home lives.

The director chatted with a young man in a power blue tie and newsboy hat. He wore designer sunglasses and carried a leather-bound notepad. I assumed that he was the CEO, because the other men surrounded him.

Oh, crap! I forgot the hot towels!

I rushed into the aircraft. The towels were already in the microwave, so I pushed "ten seconds" and Start.

The microwave beeped. I opened its door to a fresh lemon scent and quickly ripped open the package. I grabbed miniature tongs, scurried back to the aircraft stairs, and flashed the mandatory smile with a tray of hot towels perched on one hand. I peered down as the director extended his hand so the lead pax could ascend the stairs first.

I smiled.

The lead pax then removed his hat and sunglasses.

My smile collapsed, replaced by a detonation in my chest.

It was Jayden.

CHAPTER SIX

"Indy? Indy Kash?"

Jayden Mokashu. In the flesh.

Not in a visit to my past.

Not in a random photo that mysteriously popped up on my phone.

My heart nearly failed to beat and my lips fell open. I almost dropped the tray of hot towels.

He still had penetrating chocolate eyes, flawless skin, and bright teeth. He wore designer everything, donned a buzz cut, and walked with even more swagger. He appeared taller, too. Maybe he wore lifts in his shoes? I wouldn't put it past him. A silver wedding band encircled his ring finger.

Did I somehow unknowingly manifest him onto this plane?

I closed my mouth. My heart continued to thump.

Here I was, a servant to a person I absolutely despised, who had destroyed any chance of hope or normality in my life. My skin crawled seeing him. My gut quietly howled, and stress began to build.

"You two know each other?" the director asked.

Shit.

Jayden replied, "We went to the same school."

"Oh wow."

Jayden continued into the entryway. Though I wasn't violent, I wanted to sucker-punch him right in the solar plexus. Unfortunately, this job had me by the short and curlies. I couldn't screw up today, no matter how I felt and no matter how much he deserved it. Tears pricked my eyes. Dammit.

To begrudgingly give credit where credit was due, Jayden had stuck to his plan. Prep school, college, his apparent flourishing career—he had used the people around him to advance his position in life.

The rest of the businessmen boarded the aircraft, including Trevor Stone. Of course, I should have guessed that.

I could vomit upon having to see these two lowlifes again.

Trevor was on his phone and acknowledged me with a wave but no glance. Remembering his youthful preferences, if I was a tall blond, I would've definitely received an acknowledgement. He still resembled Edward Cullen with more melanin, but his dark blond hair grayed at the edges and he was even thinner than in high school. He looked tired and tweaked—an ancient thirty-year-old. I didn't see a wedding ring; I couldn't believe he hadn't groomed some gullible Instagram model.

Once the six pax had boarded the aircraft, I followed. Usually, I would offer to hang up suit jackets, but honestly, the seething anger had subsided to a low burn combined with no fucks to give.

A Citation X, pronounced "Ten," was confined. It had an unusual setup with the eight club seats on a raised platform and an extremely narrow aisle. There was a seat on each side of the aisle with two sections of four seats. Everyone squished onto the plane and sat down, including the director and mechanic, who faced aft, directly in front of Jayden and Trevor in the forward-facing power seats.

In the galley, I closed my eyes and took a breath. I reminded myself, *this is only a job*.

I wished I could spit in their food.

Instead, I placed the tray of hot towels back in the microwave to be used for later, since they remained untouched. I opened the coat closet and removed an ice bucket with a bottle of champagne. I had the urge to shake it and pour it all over Jayden and Trevor or maybe pop the cork straight into their eye.

Alas, I let go of that fantasy, opened the bottle, and poured the bubbly into flutes.

Jayden and Trevor engaged in an intense conversation with the director and mechanic, who both refused the alcohol, since they were on the clock. I set a flute of champagne in front of Jayden. In turn, I mustered all my mental strength not to stab him with the dull knife in the silverware roll-up.

I moved on to deliver all the drinks and pass out hot towels. I then placed the trays of food and offered the fruit and snack baskets. I returned to the galley and glared at Jayden in my head, while really, I was cutting an apple for…well, no one.

"Hey Indy," the mechanic said.

I stopped chopping and turned. "Yes?"

"Please get Mr. Stone another champagne. Thank you."

Trevor focused on his cell. I wondered if he had recognized me? You know, the person whose life he had ruined.

Normally I would fold a cloth napkin around the bottle as a fancy touch to serve pax, but part of me didn't give a shit, especially when serving it to a known scumbag.

I walked over to Trevor. I cradled the bottom of the champagne bottle in my right hand and then glanced at the mechanic who was checking his phone. I leaned in as close as I could get to Trevor's ear and whispered. "Remember me? Take a good look."

His face rotated slowly. He examined me as I gave him my coldest, hardest stare.

"Indy, is everything okay?" the mechanic asked.

My face switched to a polite smile. "Oh yes! I used to know Mr. Stone from a previous flight company. I really enjoyed working for them, and I was reintroducing myself."

Without missing a beat, Trevor said, "Yeah, yes, she's great."

The mechanic's shoulders dropped with relief. He and Trevor resumed their conversation.

I felt Jayden's eyes boring into the back of my head. By the time I turned around, he and the director were immersed in discussion.

I poured more champagne, removed half-eaten trays of food, and served the dessert trays. The entire time, I caught Trevor peeking at me. Not in a creepy or sexual way, but in a way that showed he was curious.

As lunch winded down, I cleared the food, passed out more hot towels, and stowed the tray tables. The pax stood up and roamed the cabin, lavatory, and cockpit to see more of the aircraft. To give them space, I moved beside the entry door and checked my phone. *They should be out of here in five minutes. Ten max.* I'd do a quick wipe down and vacuum of the aircraft, throw out the trash, hand the dish bins to line service, and then I could move on with my life.

I observed Jayden's signature charm. He touched the director's shoulder like he was talking with a friend. His broad smile radiated trust and familiarity, though I knew better. I was sure he was telling the director and mechanic everything they wanted to hear.

Disgusted, I looked out to the tarmac.

How had Jayden—what would the meta gurus say—entered my "energy field" three times in the past twenty-four hours? Before yesterday, I hadn't seen him in thirteen years. The gurus would call this "synchronicity." I call it complete and total fuckery.

My blood started to simmer again. I had to compose myself. Now.

Okay.

Ground.

The 3-3-3 rule for anxiety. I scanned my environment, the tarmac, to name three things I see, to identify three things I hear—

Someone squeezed my shoulder. "Good to see you, Indy. I'm glad life worked out for you."

My skin crawled at Jayden's touch. I wanted to vomit yet again, but instead I stepped aside. As I watched his cocky stride across the tarmac, I thought, *I'm glad life worked out for you?! What an asshole.* I scowled as he disappeared into the FBO.

"Thanks, Indy," Trevor said.

The way he examined me…again, as if he had something more to say. Back in high school, he didn't so much as glance in my direction. The only time he acknowledged me was in that affidavit. I obviously hated him with every fiber of my being…it was just…I didn't know. I couldn't put my finger on it.

The director was behind him. I forced myself to smile and say "Have a nice day."

My eyes followed Trevor. He glanced over his shoulder, turned back around, and disappeared behind the automatic doors of the FBO.

Ever since their arrival, the air had been strangled from my lungs. Now that they were gone, oxygen seeped back in— measured and reluctant. All that remained was to step into the cabin and start scrubbing away the wreckage of this awful day.

#

"Indy, you did a great job today. Thank you for doing this last minute," the director said as he shook my hand.

"My pleasure. Thank you."

"Oh, and there was a pilot out there in the lobby asking about you." He winked. "Just a heads-up."

I laughed it off. "Thanks."

The director and mechanic headed into the maintenance office, while I exited through another door. I passed through a hallway and pushed open the heavy metal door into the lobby. I waved to the front desk staff. A pilot filling out paperwork gave me a huge grin. In turn, I gave him a polite smile.

Oh, if this guy only knew.

The last time I had sex—man, it had been *that* long—was a year ago?! Yeah, it had been almost twelve long months since I had a boyfriend. Before him, I dated men in my twenties, never attracting anyone serious. I had trust issues, and my parents "modeled a loveless marriage," which were a therapist's words, not mine.

To sum it up, I was broken.

The doors parted and I exited into the sunny, late fall day with a slight breeze. I loved this weather for November. My face tilted toward the warm rays. I felt like Snowball, a creature who lapped up every last bit of unseasonably favorable weather.

I pressed the key fob and my car beeped. I heard the beep but couldn't see it, since a huge truck was parked to the left of it. As I walked around the truck, I froze.

Trevor Stone leaned against my driver's side door.

He uncrossed his arms and stood up straight.

I bet he charmed the ditzy front desk girl to find out which car was mine.

"I think we can help each other."

My jaw dropped. A guy that never acknowledged me in high school, and now here we were. As if we were old friends getting reacquainted.

I don't think so.

"You think that *I*"—I said as I pointed to myself—"Can help YOU?"—I pointed to him—"When you, Jayden, and all your friends and their parents had me convicted, expelled, and then ex-communicated from all of society? Do you *not* remember the affidavit?! Stay away from me, Trevor, no joke.

I don't care how much money you have; I *will* get a restraining order. Get out of my way."

"I know it must be hard seeing me…and Jayden. But I really do think we can help each other."

I narrowed my eyes. "Leave me alone, asshole."

I associated Trevor with stupid antics and a JFK Jr. wish fulfillment—minus the authentic charisma of an actual icon. He had glided through life on his family name, and though creepy to me, good looks. But instead of his memorable goofy grin, his features were hardened. Was Trevor Stone serious?

He did not budge.

"I'm having some issues with Jayden."

I searched his face. He *seemed* truthful. "Interesting."

"Listen, can we talk somewhere else?"

"No. Move."

He stepped away from the car. I pulled the door handle and slipped in the driver's seat.

"I can help you if you help me." He paused. "With my family connections, I can get you into any college you want."

I stopped with the door halfway closed.

"What did you say?"

"I remembered you were in the dork classes"—I rolled my eyes—"the honor ones with Jayden. I realized that after what happened"—His voice quieted—"you couldn't get into college. I can get you in."

I remained quiet, mulling over the prospect and watching another FA roll his suitcase across the parking lot into the FBO. I'd never had an offer like this. I could not only get into college but get accepted somewhere *good…*

I looked up at Trevor.

I'd be making a deal with the devil.

"Hard pass!"

I got in my car, slammed the door, and drove off. I stole a glance in the rearview mirror—a flicker of regret for the offer I had left behind. But then I remembered how these animals devoured anyone they deemed unworthy. My foot pounded the accelerator with every fiber of my being, certain that I had made the right choice.

#

I chopped carrots with such fury that even Snowball distanced herself from me. I was preparing a beef stew to throw in the slow cooker. Once I moved to browning the meat, she would become interested again.

I mean, the *audacity*, the fucking entitlement to approach me like that. Who did he think he was? The angrier I became, the more scratches I carved into the wooden cutting board. The poor celery resembled hamster food.

My phone rang. I halted mid-chop and glanced at the screen.

Mom was FaceTiming me.

She only FaceTimed me on a holiday, such as Christmas or Carnival, or to tell me an older relative I barely remembered had passed.

I slid my finger across the screen to answer.

She looked beautiful. She'd lost weight. Her cheekbones protruded, yet she still had those luscious ruby lips that I, unfortunately, didn't inherit. Caramel braids cascaded past her shoulders. Was that a nose piercing?

The aqua hue of the Caribbean Sea lapped behind her.

"India. I realized after talking to you, I'd made a mistake."

Was Tina Kash going to apologize?

"I told you that I avoided time travel and flying because of my fear. That's true." She paused. "I don't want you to be like me. I want you to be like your grandmother. Fearless."

Her stern face told me everything. Her right brow furrowed and created multiple wrinkles. I hadn't seen Mom this serious in a long time—probably since telling me she was divorcing Dad.

"Learn everything you can about time travel. Whatever advice Kai gives, soak it in. Knowledge is power and could save you from my experience."

Someone banged on my front door.

"Mom, I have to go."

What I presumed was a mixture of love and concern spilled from her eyes. "Think about what I said. Bye, doodoo."

I hung up, walked to the front door, and yelled, "Who is it?"

"Trevor Stone."

Are you KIDDING me?!

He banged again. Damn it! Mrs. Albright would call the cops if he continued.

I turned the deadbolt, unlocked the door, and threw it open. "You have TWO seconds to get out of here, Trevor. I can't stand the sight of you at my job, and *definitely* not at my home."

"Kai visited me."

I took a step back. He did not say what I thought he said. "What?!"

"Kai. Visited. Me."

I heard the words, but all I saw was a disheveled mess of a human. Hair in disarray, purple bags from lack of sleep, five o'clock shadow, and a crumpled white business shirt half-tucked into faded designer jeans. Though I'd kill for those distressed Johnny Depp-style boots.

"Can I come in?"

"How do you know Kai?" I asked. "Wait—had Kai visited you before lunch today?"

"Yes."

"Why did you play it cool? Why not talk to me as soon as you could?"

Mrs. Albright squeaked open her window. She stuck out her head and peered down. "Hey honey, is everything all right?"

"Yep, totally fine. Just some guy who's spending the night"—The words tumbled out of my mouth—"Sorry for the noise, Mrs. Albright."

"Good for you, honey. He's cute."

"Thanks, Mrs. Albright."

The head retreated and the window creaked shut.

I grabbed Trevor's wrist and pulled him inside. "You're lucky I used the 'guy sleeping over' excuse or she'd call the cops."

As I closed the door and locked it, he said, "Must happen a lot for her to not even be fazed. Indy Kash, female Casanova. You *have* aged well, I'll admit that."

I rolled my eyes. "I live alone with my cat in a studio apartment in Hackensack. You honestly think a lot of guys come around here?"

"Why not? A good piece of ass is a good piece—"

"Jesus." Same ole Trevor. "You didn't answer my questions. How do you know Kai? Why did you play it cool this afternoon?"

"Do you have coffee? I'm exhausted."

Really? Who did he think he was, Kai?

"I don't drink coffee. Actually, come to think of it, I have an inflammatory bowel disease that *you* and your friends gave me."

"Sounds rough. Tea?"

"I'm not serving you in my home."

He scanned the apartment. "I like how you decorated. It's very free spirit. Very you."

He was referring to all the crystals, the drum that served as the coffee table, and the hanging stars amongst the other spiritual décor. *I guess all those meta workshops and experiences influenced me.*

I turned to Trevor and said, "You don't know me. Answer my questions."

He strolled over to the kitchen stool, pulled it out, and sat— without an invitation. My gastro juices churned. *This better be good.*

"Kai visited me yesterday. She said that I would see you today and that you could help me."

"How do you know her?"

"You and I are time travelers. My spirit guide, Erik, knows Kai."

I sank to the couch.

"It's a lot. I know"—Did Trevor give me a sympathetic look?—"But I couldn't let on in front of Jayden. The guy is always ten steps ahead and has eyes in the back of his head, I swear."

That made sense, though I hated to admit it.

"What I did to you in high school—" He paused. "I'm sorry. It was a fucked-up thing to do. Really bad. I swear I'm not that person. My dad pressured me into it, and I felt like I had no choice. I was a kid, but so were you."

Damn it. I was getting choked up. I couldn't let him see me cry. I looked away.

"I'm truly sorry, Indy," he whispered.

I couldn't look at him.

We were quiet until I cleared my throat and asked, "Are you actually sorry because you mean it, or because you want my help?"

"Both."

Well, that was honest.

"I researched you and saw all the news stories…and Pyro Girl"—it was as if the past was stabbing me over and over—"I found out you didn't go to college. That's fucked."

"Yeah."

"I—" He stopped and grabbed a tissue box off the counter. He gently threw it in my direction. I caught it and yanked out a lone tissue to wipe under my eyes.

"I inherited time-traveling from my father's side of the family. Once I turned thirty."

"Did your dad tell you ahead of time?"

He shook his head. "Not really. My grandfather doesn't talk about anything. And my dad sat me down as a little kid and told me in a drunken stupor. That was it. I thought it was a story until I started time-traveling a year and a half ago. My family can be pretty cold. I'm grateful for Erik."

Was Trevor Stone my only prospect for a human time-traveling coach?

For the time being, it looked that way.

I closed my eyes to think. Though he seemed a *somewhat* changed person, I had to remember that he was responsible for the trauma of my past. It was *him*, his friends, and the parents who had destroyed my life.

I heard rustling and opened my eyes.

Trevor was rummaging through a kitchen cabinet. Snowball meowed at his feet.

"What are you doing?"

"Looking for coffee. You really don't have any. I'll make myself some—" He examined the box in his hand. "Mycotoxin-free, mold-free, caffeine-free—and apparently taste-free—hibiscus tea."

He lifted the stainless-steel tea kettle under the faucet and ran the water. After filling it, he placed it on the stove and turned the knob. The orange-blue flame flickered and glowed. He then pulled two mugs out of another cabinet—how did he know which cabinet?—and set them on the counter. One was mud brown and the other was cotton-candy pink that said: "The Cat's Meow." He dropped a tea bag in each.

We remained in awkward silence until the kettle whistled. He then removed it from the burner and poured the steaming water into the brown mug.

"How did you know the tea and mugs were in those particular cabinets?"

He stopped pouring and shrugged. "Girls always have the coffee, tea, mugs, whatever near the stove."

Did they?

He sipped. "Wow, it's good. It doesn't taste like tree bark."

Snowball stared at him with wide eyes and meowed. I said, "Come here, Snowball."

She brushed against his leg and purred.

Traitor.

He walked over to the meditation chair and was about to put the mug on the coffee-table drum but instead reached for a rainbow-colored coaster. He placed his mug on it. At least he had *some* manners.

"There's so much girly shit in this place."

Scratch that.

"Because I'm a girl."

He reached down and grabbed Snowball, who looked shocked. He put her on his lap and stroked her head. She purred.

Trevor Stone liked cats? "You like cats?"

He shrugged. "They're cool. My sister's had one forever."

Huh.

He said, "I have to take you into my past to show you what I found."

"How's that possible? We're not on a plane."

"Huh?"

"I can only time-travel when I'm in air."

"I do it through a doorway."

"That's it?"

He laughed. "It's not *that* easy. Do you know how many doorways I avoided when I first started traveling? I've learned to set my intention and walk through the doorway."

"Geez. I have no control over when I travel."

"You will. It takes a lot of practice and patience."

Great.

"Anyway, Kai said I have to show you what I saw, so you can fully understand." He released Snowball to the floor and said, "Let's go."

CHAPTER SEVEN

We stood at the doorway of my bathroom, looking straight ahead at the tub-shower insert that I hadn't cleaned in a while. Snowball perched between us, glancing at Trevor and then at me. At least the bathroom smelled of rose potpourri.

Trevor closed his eyes; he reached for my hand.

"Let's see if this works. I've never taken anyone into my past before…*but* Kai implied that it is possible."

My stomach knotted. This was too…much. A person whom I absolutely loathed was about to hold my hand and guide me to wherever? Was this a trap?

"Stop!"

His eyes flew open and his hand dropped.

"What?"

"All you've done is ruin my life. Why should I trust you?"

"You're right, but you can trust Kai."

He closed his eyes and reached for my hand again.

I glared. I didn't have to like it…but like Mom said, *knowledge is power and could save you from my experience.* I sure as hell didn't want air strangling me and not know what to do.

Kai sent me Trevor for a reason. I could learn from him, keep my cards close to the vest, and cut him out of my life after I got what I needed.

I could use him the way he, his friends, and their parents had used me.

I smirked.

I heard Mom's voice again. *I don't want you to be like me. I want you to be like your grandmother. Fearless.*

Reluctantly, I put my hand in his with the loosest grip possible.

In an instant, Kai stood on the other side of me, holding my right hand in her indistinct grip. It felt unlike a sweaty human palm and fingers. Instead, hers were airy and comforting.

"You're doing the right thing, Indy. You must crawl before you walk."

She winked.

"I'm working behind the scenes on the astral plane; I can't be here most of the time. Trevor will help you. Though he's still learning himself."

She continued, "I will hold your hand as we pass through time and space. It will be a strange sensation at first—faster than when you travel by yourself. Breathe in and out, like in therapy."

Ocean breath. In through the nose, hold for four, out through the mouth as if I'm blowing out a candle.

"Good. Keep going."

As I breathed, I repeated a mantra: *be fearless*.

We stepped through the doorway.

Everything moved at warp speed, like a movie time-lapse, except we were immersed in it. My senses could not keep up. The neon colors of transcending time and space and the discordance of all sounds mashed together made me squeeze my eyes shut. I felt warm and cold breezes, wind, heat, icy temperatures. My mouth dried, frothed, and dried again.

My body jolted and then we were there.

On a random street, Trevor stood next to me. Upon entering wherever we were, I must've lost my balance. I lay on the ground and my tailbone stung. It was exactly like that time I went snowboarding and fell on the icy slope. This would hurt for a while.

"Sorry," he said as he lent a hand to pull me up. "I should've prepared you for the jolt at the end."

"You should have," I grumbled.

The night was chilly. I shivered. I looked down at myself to discover that I was present-day, thirty-year-old Indy.

Did I smell burning?

"Like I said, I've never brought a person into my past. I can see you, but I don't know if you're invisible to other people. Follow me and stay quiet."

Nothing looked familiar. We stood across the street from an abandoned building painted with graffiti. A dim light flickered inside, the only sign of life. We crossed the road and entered. The acrid tang of hot metal nauseated me; I retched silently. I used the streetlight to guide me, but that barely helped. We tiptoed across the crumbling cement floor until we reached a column to hide behind.

Trevor whispered, "Watch."

I peeked my head around the column. Someone was working in an exposed room.

Jayden.

Clearly an electric bill hadn't been paid in decades. A floor spotlight tilted upward. A propane heater ran.

Jayden leaned over a wooden table and maneuvered a large piece of metal. The burning continued to overwhelm my nostrils. Had Jayden been welding? It affected him too; he coughed as he worked.

Suddenly, crunching footsteps and the beam of a flashlight appeared. I held my breath. Trevor kept watching. I crouched farther into the shadows as best I could. The person walked into the room and Jayden looked up.

He set down and…what was he holding?

The photo that was sent to my phone. Was this it?

I squinted.

It resembled…a group of wires.

Yes, this had to be what I saw in the photo.

"What's going on here, Jay?"

The voice was female and light. A tall, lithe figure stepped out of the shadows and more into the room. I leaned forward for a better glimpse. Permed African-American hair, a knee-length shearling coat, and a straight-leg jean with flat loafers—she didn't need the height.

"Who is that?" I whispered to Trevor.

"Jayden's wife, Tameka."

I still couldn't believe someone would marry that monster.

Jayden dropped the metal. "What are you doing here?"

"I got sick of waking up without you there. I guess you ain't cheating on me." She sniffed then coughed. "What's that smell?"

"None of your business. Go back to bed."

"What are you working on?" She stood on her tiptoes and peered over at the metal.

"Goddamn it, woman! Leave me alone!"

"One your experiments?"

"Tameka," he said in a metered voice. "Leave!"

He hurled a screwdriver at the wall. Tameka did not back up. He didn't throw it at her, but it wasn't that far from her either. My heart pounded.

Destroying his own marriage and others' lives. This was Jayden's M.O.

"Tameka, Jayden!" a voice yelled.

They both peered into the dark at the footsteps coming near them.

"What's going on? I've been looking for you everywhere."

It was Trevor from the past. Present Trevor whispered, "Keep watching."

"Oh, hey Trev. What's up, man?"

"What is this, Jay? Why are you working in an abandoned warehouse?"

"You know I like to build prototypes on my own. I don't need the office sycophants looking over my shoulder."

"That's fine, but why wouldn't you tell me, your business partner and closest friend of *fifteen years,* about this workshop?"

He wheezed and cleared his throat. "Some things I gotta do on my own. That's how I create, and that's how our agreement works. No questions, just results. How did you find me?"

"Honestly, I followed you. I knew you were up to something."

"If I'm up to something, come over here. What do you see? Some wires and metal."

I glanced at present-day Trevor and started to open my mouth, but he put a finger over his lips.

Past Trevor stepped farther into the room. "Sorry for doubting you, man. When I arrived in this neighborhood, I thought you were in deep shit. Meth or heroin or something."

Jayden burst into a fit of laughter. Tameka gave a meek smile.

"Wow Trev, you really got my back. Thank you, man. I'm fine. Just working on a surprise for our company. You'll like it—I promise. It's not ready, though. Give me some time."

Trevor grinned. "Fair enough. Sorry to disturb. I won't follow you again. Night guys."

Tameka waved. Jayden beamed until Trevor turned around and disappeared into the darkness of the warehouse. Then his face morphed into the ugliest, most sinister look.

What he didn't see was that past Trevor had vanished into the shadows but was walking in place, to sound like he was walking away.

"Fuck that guy," Jayden said.

"Yeah, I'll see you at home," Tameka replied.

She spun on her heel and marched out of sight. Past Trevor's footsteps quickened and left the building.

Jayden loomed over his work table and then paced in a circle. Present-day Trevor kept watching him as I thought, *damn, that's a fifteen-year friendship flushed right down the tubes*. I couldn't imagine the hurt that Trevor must've felt when he originally witnessed this. He looked intense but not upset.

"Let's go," he whispered.

We carefully tiptoed to the nearest doorway. Then it was time-lapse in reverse. In an instant, we were in my apartment, with me on the couch and Trevor on the meditation chair. Snowball cuddled in his lap.

"I nailed it this time."

I spread out my arms on the couch to catch my balance. Yet I wasn't imbalanced. I smelled the red onion I had cut for the beef stew. Snowball licked her paw. I was okay. Actually, more than okay. I felt clear and alive.

"Huh?"

"The soft landing."

The couch was much better than falling onto the cold, hard street. My tailbone didn't throb anymore. Instead, a dull energy buzzed through it and started to move up my spine. This was a new sensation among all the other strange ones I had encountered in the last thirty-six hours.

I eyed Trevor as he tickled Snowball's ear.

"You heard Jayden's parting words to you?"

"Yep, and I saw the worst look you can give another human. I knew he was hiding something. You were going to say something back there. What was it?"

I described the photo in detail with me hooked up with wires to a large metal box. Then I told him about the photo of Jayden that had come through first.

He spoke up, "You said the wires were hooked up to the chakras?"

My eyebrows raised.

"Yeah, I know what the chakras are. I did some research after I started traveling. Did you see an extra wire extending to the eighth chakra?"

That was an interesting question, because the eighth chakra, the soul star, was not attached to the body. It floated above the head. It represented the gateway of spiritual connection to higher realms of consciousness. I thought of it as the seventh chakra on steroids.

"No, nothing connected to the eighth chakra. Why?"

"You'll see."

He nodded toward the bathroom doorway. We got up, held hands, and went through it.

In a flash, we time-traveled to the abandoned building, except this time I saw Jayden in the exposed room with the metal box fully intact. It looked exactly as it did in the photo.

Jayden removed his shirt and began to hook himself up to the machine. I squinted. I couldn't see anything that resembled a patch that would suction to the exposed skin of the throat chakra and the crown chakra atop his buzz cut. I assumed tiny magnets at the end of each wire somehow connected energetically to each chakra, because they stayed put once they contacted his skin.

I shuddered at both the anticipation of whatever he was doing and the night chill. Trevor put his pointer finger over his lips to ensure we didn't speak. He removed his coat and draped it over my shoulders.

It took Jayden a while to complete the task of hooking up all the wires to his body, both front and back. He could only move a touch, or he'd knock the other wires loose, curse, and start over again. When he had connected what I thought was the last wire to the crown chakra, he picked up one more. It came to life, danced like a snake above his head, and plugged into an invisible outlet.

An angelic light flashed, split into bright white particles, and warped into what looked like the Star of David rotating in the center of a flower. The image of the soul star chakra.

My heart slammed against my ribs. I couldn't move or breathe. The sight of that power unraveling in front of me was too much, too vast—and too devastating to comprehend.

Careful of the long wires, Jayden maneuvered his arms and legs into the position of the Vitruvian Man. Violet lightning sparked from the box and boomed overhead. And then…Jayden was gone.

He had vanished into thin air.

I was paralyzed with awe, as if I had watched the world break open into something both magnificent and monstrous. Trevor tugged at my sleeve and then pulled me to the doorway.

We were back in my apartment.

"That's what I saw," Trevor whispered. His breath seemed to be snagged in his throat. "I-I returned a third time, but everything was gone. He moved his operation to another location. I haven't found it yet."

We didn't speak for quite some time, both of us rooted in dread.

I didn't know whether to gasp in wonder or cry in fear. To perform magic like that and science at the same time, it was inconceivable.

Finally, when I able to think and feel again, I realized Trevor's jacket was still draped around my shoulders. I moved to take it off.

"Nah. Don't worry about it. I'll get it back later."

"Do you know anything else about the box?"

"I got lucky. After I saw him disappear, I ran into his work room and looked through his plans. He had all these drawings and math formulas. It was like reading Greek. I spent less than a minute taking photos and ran out of there. I didn't know how long he'd be gone.

"I showed them to a quantum physicist and a scientist friend. I didn't know how to explain the genius-level work; they sure as hell knew it wasn't mine. I paid them *very* well and made them sign NDAs. The friend was at a loss, but the physicist told me it had something to do with timelines, but that's all he could make out. My guess? It's a Time Machine."

I couldn't believe what I was hearing. Even Snowball's eyes widened.

I squeaked, "If that's true, that's *really* bad in Jayden's hands."

"I don't know for sure, and the physicist was only guessing, but that makes the most sense."

"Was that photo on my phone from the future?"

"Did you see Jayden in the photo?"

I shook my head.

"That could be right—about the future. I'm not sure."

"And Trevor," I whispered. "The eighth chakra wire moving *by itself.* I mean, how?"

"I know."

"Did you save the photos of Jayden's plans?"

"No. I was afraid he could tap into my phone. I showed them to the scientists and deleted them."

"Did you print them out?"

"No. I was too nervous about Jayden finding them. I figured if a quantum physicist was guessing, what help would they be?"

"Why didn't you go into your past again and retrieve them?"

"I tried, but they were gone."

"Oh."

We remained silent for a while. I didn't know what to think, and obviously, neither did he.

Snowball was nuzzling his face. She trusted him. I didn't. The gesture of the sports coat was chivalrous, and I could see he had grown out of the stupidity of our high school days…but he was still Trevor Stone. I had to know the truth before we moved forward.

"Tell me how Jayden, you, your friends, the parents—how all of you framed me for arson."

Snowball stopped nuzzling, jumped off his lap, and hid behind the meditation chair. My tone was *that* serious.

"When the fire happened and we knew we caused it, Jay suggested a scapegoat. He'd thought we'd blame him."

"Was he right?"

"Partially. The other kids and parents would have, but not me. Jay was like a brother to me. I trusted him like the idiot I was—like I've been for a while." He paused. "Out of nowhere, video surveillance of you going backstage appeared."

Exactly as I had suspected.

"Conveniently, only a cigarette was found at the scene—no alcohol or weed. My dad paid off the building owner to keep him quiet and that money came out of my trust."

Snowball peeked her head around the chair.

I stared at the rug. "And no one gave a second thought to the powerless, innocent girl whose life was destroyed."

"Only me."

I looked up. "What?"

"My dad knew the judge and the prosecutor. I convinced him to negotiate the best deal possible."

I was at a loss for words. Trevor helped me, despite it being his fault. That showed an ounce of character. What I couldn't get over was how the people who destroyed my life went on with theirs as if nothing happened?

Because it didn't. Not for them.

"Not good enough."

"Yeah." He cleared his throat. "I know how wrong that was, but I was a different person. Lately, the Universe has been teaching me a lot of lessons."

"The Universe?"

He laughed. "Yeah, well, you travel through time and space, meet Erik and Kai, and you start believing in all that shit. You know?"

I did.

Trevor's cell rang in his pocket. He answered it. "Hi, Serenity."

I heard a womanly voice chatter away. I couldn't make out anything she was saying. Snowball jumped next to me and purred. I stroked along her spine.

He ended the call. "I've gotta go. The company is in big trouble and my sister wants me in the city now. What's your number?"

I told him, and he texted his number to me.

"I'll be in touch. Soon."

CHAPTER EIGHT

After Trevor rushed out, I hopped on my iPad and researched his family. Damn, they had a lot of drama. I even listened to an episode of *Boston Celebs Podcast*—Trevor and his family lived in Boston and had second homes all over the world, including the city. The podcast host said:

I think we all know, nothing is set in Stone. Haha. Today, I'm discussing the potential downfall of the Bostonian dynasty. First, let's start with some good ole fashioned history, but don't worry, no dates and facts to memorize…however, there will be blood and mud-slinging.

God this guy was perky.

In the 1800s, "Sir" Reginald Stone built his empire from nothing. He started with railroads, and through the decades, he expanded into media, air travel, shipping, and textiles. By the 1980s when Sir Reginald's great grandson, Steven, took the reins, Stone Corp's power and influence extended globally, as they opened textile factories in Southeast Asia. Due to ghastly workplace conditions, clothing manufacturers stopped doing business with Stone Corp. Steven was forced to sell off parts of the company to keep the family afloat.

As I very well knew, this was the Stone motto: not give a shit about the little guy and take care of your own.

By 2010, he had rebranded by investing in virtual reality, AI, and electric cars. He focused on renewable energy and other lucrative, environmentally conscious businesses. The media had dubbed him the 'Green Goblin.' He earns billions from his sustainable empire, but alas, his luck is wearing thin.

Good. Fuck 'em.

Steven Stone is old. He must hand over the empire that he rebuilt one solar panel at a time to either his son Steven Jr., SJ, or his grandson, Trevor.

The problem?

They both lack any kind of business sense.

The shiny gem of the family is young Serenity, who refuses to be a part of her mother's Housewives of Boston shenanigans and is earning her executive MBA at Tuck. If

Serenity took over, that would disrupt the Stone patriarchal system of succession.

Even worse, there have been rumblings of racism and sexism in the Stone Corp workplace. It's no wonder considering old, white men have dominated this company for centuries. Let me state the facts: there is one woman on the board and no people of color.

As I close out, I wonder what will happen to the Stone Corp empire? Who has the balls big enough to succeed Steven Stone? Will it be:

His son, the seemingly altruistic and dim-witted SJ?
His grandson, the handsome but brainless Trevor?
Or the talented but inexperienced Serenity?
We're on the edge of our premium leather seats.

Trevor's family sounded like a clusterfuck. I had seen clips of Kiki, Trevor's mom, pop up on my YouTube feed every so often but chose to ignore them. Anything to do with my past, I pushed it aside.

Despite my reasoning, I researched more. According to *Forbes*, Jayden had started a tech company for green computing that Stone Corp had acquired. Business insiders said the real reason Steven greenlit the purchase was to give Trevor a job. He was the Chief Business Development Officer of the company, which meant he did marketing, sales, and business growth. Plus, it added to the Green Goblin's sustainable fortune.

At least I had acquired more knowledge of my enemies. To me, right now, Trevor was the enemy of my enemy, which made him a *very* temporary friend.

I had been in the public eye before, and it took *years* of therapy to not wake up every morning thinking about Pyro Girl. I couldn't return to that dark place, because if it happened again, I didn't know if I could come back from it.

Yeah, this time-travel thing I could figure out on my own. The Time Machine? I could leave that to Trevor and Kai. It was too much for me to handle.

"You're not leaving it to me."

Kai appeared in her glowing Native Carib form, yet this time, the war paint was missing. Instead, I saw her beautiful face with a small chin, high cheekbones, and the eyes of an Asian woman. She frowned.

"Where's my PSL?"

The ingredients appeared on the counter. I went to grab the bag of coffee beans. *God, this is ridiculous.* My life was now making a drink that I couldn't drink for a spirit guide that I never knew I had.

In my haste, I knocked it over. The beans spilled onto the tile floor. Kai rolled her eyes.

"I'll pick them up."

I glimpsed the floor again; it was clean.

"Please make the drink."

I was barely watching when Kai had made the PSL during her first visit, yet my hands magically worked. I even intuited the extra dash of vanilla extract.

She grasped the cup with both hands and inhaled the sweet aroma.

The last time I saw her, she exuded confidence, poise, and omniscience. But now, I watched her glow fade and her aura freckle with black specks. I remembered from a metaphysical workshop that when the aura had black spots, they were blockages or disruptions in the person's energy flow.

Storm clouds formed in her eyes. Did she look—scared?

"What's wrong, Kai?"

"You saw the Time Machine that Jayden built. Or what we think is a Time Machine."

"Who is 'we'?"

"Trevor, Erik, me, and the Spirit Council."

"The Spirit Council?"

"The highest group of spirit guides who only interfere in human matters when it's absolutely necessary."

Why should I be surprised that there was a Spirit Council? Everywhere had a hierarchy.

"Jayden is planning something dark and I don't know what. I don't have the ability to see anything around him. His energy field is blocking me. I don't know how, and neither does the Spirit Council."

"You really think it's a Time Machine?"

"Yes. We had a meeting on the plane where we all discussed this sudden darkness coming over Earth. This energy that we cannot harness. We think it stems from Jayden." She looked away. "The elders haven't seen a darkness like this in eons; it has the potential to destroy many lives. That's why we need your and Trevor's help."

The sound of my swallow was loud, grotesque, as though fear itself has lodged in my throat.

She continued, "You and Trevor have the metaphysical abilities to help. And there's someone else who has different abilities and human smarts to help you."

I furrowed my brow. "Who?"

"You'll find out soon. First, the Spirit Council has requested your presence."

CHAPTER NINE

Traveling with Kai was similar to the time-lapse feeling with Trevor, except gentler. She didn't need a doorway; we just…went.

A peaceful breeze entered the room. Snowball curled up and fell asleep. I smelled lavender, rose, and honey, but it wasn't overpowering. The scents blended perfectly, fresh and light. The air morphed into a luminous cloudy haze, and the angelic white enveloped me. My surroundings resembled a version of heaven, or soaring at warp speed through cotton candy.

Then I saw, as if we were coming upon a mountain, the most beautiful convergence of vibrant, otherworldly colors. Every hue of the rainbow sparkled, danced, and illuminated with such magnificence that it was difficult for my human eyes to absorb. The ambient sound was the familiar roar of the ocean, as if I was holding a seashell up to my ear.

Light beings appeared so tiny within the vast astral plane. They drifted closer to us and sat there, floating in space amongst the colors. Some were balls of yellow-white light, while others had human forms, such as a person with dangling limbs wearing a ball gown. More glided to the forefront.

Kai whispered, "A few of the elders like to take human forms."

A Native American chief sat cross-legged alongside an older woman with a dog licking her face suspended in midair.

"There's Erik, Trevor's guide." She pointed to a blinking yellow-white light. "He's saying hi."

"Should I wave—"

"The Council has convened. Shh!"

The light beings immediately rearranged themselves in a hovering circle. I could hear a dull buzzing from the light beings and the colors. It reminded me of when I visited above the Arctic Circle in Finland; I stood alone by a remote lake as the Northern Lights swirled overhead. They buzzed like a faulty electrical switch. I couldn't believe that I'd had a similar experience on Earth.

The beings lit up as they "spoke" but they weren't speaking aloud. I could somehow understand their telepathic conversation.

Kai whispered, "We think the arson event may have sparked Jayden's interest in time travel, but we can't figure out why. He started drawing prototypes shortly after."

The turquoise being said, "We thought the idea was youthful and that he would never build anything of significance. To us, it was merely a child playing with a toy. Even if he had started to go too far, we agreed that we could easily stop him. However, we grossly underestimated Jayden's understanding of time travel and his metaphysical gifts. Together, they're a dangerous combination."

My body tightened at the confirmation. He was *One of us*.

A hologram appeared. Jayden worked on the Time Machine in the abandoned warehouse. As he twisted a screwdriver into the box, he was muttering to himself, "Leave me alone." He motioned like he was swatting a fly. "I'll have rules. Stop bothering me."

The hologram disappeared. I heard sniffling. A glowing white tear fell onto Kai's glowing caramel skin. I could only stare, dumbstruck. It was like seeing an angel weep, a grief too pure for my human self.

My instinct was to turn away from Kai, because I didn't have the emotional bandwidth to comfort a fellow human, let alone a spirit guide. Listening about Jayden, I was surprised, and then I wasn't. If anyone could turn both the spirit and human worlds upside down, it was him.

The turquoise guide said, "Kai tried her best to reach him, but he would not listen to her."

"Were you Jayden's spirit guide?" I whispered to Kai.

"No, but I knew his guide well. His name was Fabio. Now, no one can find him." She whimpered. "We don't know what Jayden did to him."

Jayden could take out a spirit guide? I gulped. He was capable of doing anything to anyone. He was an actual monster.

The turquoise guide continued, "Kai only saw Jayden build the Time Machine and nothing more. He didn't discuss his plans with anyone that we know of. The main questions are: why did he invent it? What is his intention?"

A being spoke up, "If he blocked us from his energy field, what can we do?"

In the distance, Erik blinked and said, "We have enlisted two humans to help us. India Jean Kash and Trevor Reginald Stone. India is here."

Reginald? I knew it was a family name, but geez.

The turquoise guide whirled around like a mini tornado. "They're here? They're not supposed to be here. Who invited them?"

I shot at Kai, "I thought the 'Spirit Council requested *my* presence'?"

She hesitated. "Well, kind of, not really. I'll sort it out."

Erik said, "Don't be angry at Kai or India. It was my idea to bring India here. Trevor is attending to serious matters in the human world.

"Both Indy and Trevor are connected to Jayden and his past. We are their guides and know we can trust them. However, time is not on their side. We feel that Jayden is about to make a move, and if he does, both the human and spirit worlds could be destroyed. We imagine it would look something like this."

Another hologram appeared. The place was black and smoky and reeked of dead animal. I made an about-to-vomit face and then swallowed hard. The smell dissipated. I witnessed the chaos of people writhing and howling in pain. Everything looked jumbled, mixed-up, a post-apocalyptic version of Earth. Worse than *Mad Max*. The sky was absent of stars, and beyond that, the astral plane was void of beings. It was an ominous, infinite black space, and it sent a chill through my spine.

The hologram disappeared.

It felt as if the beings were staring *hard* in our direction.

"How can you help us, India?" asked the turquoise guide.

"Uh. I-I have no idea."

"Well, that's comforting," the Native American chief said.

"I'm sorry. I really don't know. I just found out about everything—even me being a time traveler."

Murmurs ensued.

"Wait!" interrupted Kai. "We don't have a plan yet, but we're working on it."

We were?

Even spirit guides gave lip service to their bosses.

"We are piecing everything together in the human world"—more murmurs—"Quickly. We will be ready soon. I will report back."

The turquoise being nodded. "We are doing everything in our power here. Indy, are you ready for the challenge of your human life? To save both spirit and human kind?"

"No."

Kai tried to jab me with her formless elbow.

"You better get ready. Go!"

In a millisecond, Kai whisked us back to my apartment. Snowball yawned and pawed at the air.

Kai whispered through tears, "I tried using every wormhole, portal, or anything I could think of to reach Jayden. I enlisted the other guides, but he had become too powerful."

I didn't know what to do, so I walked over to the tissue box and offered it to her.

"My tears don't wipe away."

"You did everything you could."

"I failed."

It was awkward seeing her like this. I hadn't connected with a human, or non-human, in a long time. I did the most compassionate thing I could think of and touched her glimmering shoulder.

"Sorry I lied about being invited to the meeting," she said through sniffles. "But I wanted you to hear everything unfiltered."

"It's okay." I tried another emotion: empathy. "Kai, it's not your fault. Jayden fooled all of us."

"I'm a newer spirit guide, Indy. I was so confident in thinking that I could fix the Jayden situation, because I felt I could relate to younger humans. That's what I had told the elders. They believed in me, and now all I see is disappointment in their blinks."

"How old *are* you?"

"Younger than the creation of the Universe."

That narrowed it down.

She remained quiet for a while. As she thought, she fell into a trance where her body resembled a mannequin. If I touched her, I swore she would tip over.

All of a sudden, she clasped her glowing hands together. "I know! You need protection!"

"What?"

"You need protection if you're going into the depths of evil to fight Jayden!"

"I'm doing *what*?"

"I have to make sure you're protected if you get into a, uh, precarious situation."

"Kai, what do you mean 'depths of evil' and 'fight Jayden'?"

She waved me off. "Oh, those are just expressions. Humans use them all the time."

"No we don't. Not those."

She threw me a stern glance. "The Spirit Council needs *your* help, and like I told you before, you can do this. It's time to stop doubting yourself, Indy. The past is over, well, kind of. You must start believing in yourself. The Spirit Council does and so do I." She paused and said quietly, "You're our only hope."

Fucking fantastic. No pressure there.

This idea of self-confidence was a foreign concept. I'd been beaten down so many times, I wasn't sure any belief was still there. Somehow, I'd have to find a way to muster it. If both the Spirit Council and Kai believed in me, that had to say something.

I gave her a meek half-smile.

"That's it! You're getting there! I'll return with protection, and I don't mean condoms."

In a poof, she was gone. Snowball slumped to the floor and moped.

Depths of evil.

Fight Jayden.

Kai was a young spirit guide with a flair for the dramatic…but what the Spirit Council showed me was harrowing. Jayden would destroy everything from here to the astral plane. Was it an exaggeration? I noticed my right hand wouldn't stop shaking. That last hologram…was too real. The stench of dead animal sank its claws into my temporal lobe, refusing to let go.

A text chimed on my phone. It was from Ron. "Here is the trip sheet for tomorrow. Safe travels."

In the midst of everything, I'd forgotten that I was flying with the dreaded Amanda Karrington. She was a nightmare to flight attendants, but at least I was headed to London for a few days. I texted Mrs. Albright to remind her to take care of Snowball.

That meant that I could be time-traveling.

Shit.

I guess I'm in this.

Whether the Spirit Council's premonition was true or not…I knew for sure that Jayden was about to destroy people's lives like he did mine. I couldn't let this sociopath become the tyrant of both spirit and human kind. His sick, twisted plan—whatever it was—had to be stopped, and unfortunately, I had been chosen as the one to stop him.

I understood the Spirit Council chose Trevor because of his proximity to Jayden, but I wasn't close to him. Why me?

I intuited that the answer was in my past, the last place I wanted to go. How could I get over my past if I kept returning to it?

I sighed and checked my phone. It was eight o'clock at night but still a decent hour to make a phone call.

My fingers clicked as I texted Trevor: "Call me when you can."

A few seconds later, Trevor was FaceTiming me.

I picked up. His tired face popped on the screen.

"Hold on, Serenity," he yelled to the background.

A female voice said, "I'm taking the jet back to school—oh, who's that? I see a girl."

"None of your business. Get out of here."

A door shut.

He turned back to me. "Sorry about that. What's up?"

I told him about the Spirit Council.

"Erik mentioned the Council before, but I never visited. Wow."

"They said Jayden is a time traveler."

He was silent for a moment. "Yeah, I suspected he was like us. I should've brought it up to Erik, but I was so overwhelmed with navigating Jay and the situation at my family's company that I never asked. At least now it's confirmed."

That's right, the Stone Corp drama. I attempted compassion. "I heard about the company. How's everything going?"

He looked away from the phone screen. "Not good. I don't know what's going to happen. My dad is MIA. He must be upset because he won't be named successor. My mom's in her own world as usual. I have to stay quiet about the details, so there's no one to talk to." He snickered. "Not even my therapist."

Did Trevor Stone deserve my compassion and sympathy? Not really. "That sucks."

"Yeah…What else did the Council say?"

I told him about the world-ending prophecy, and then the depths of evil-fight Jayden comment. "Have you ever seen anything like the prophecy in your travels?"

"No. This is way bigger than I could've imagined."

I thought for a second. "I feel like I'm missing something about my past with Jayden that has to do with the Time Machine. Can you think of anything?"

"When did you and Jay have contact in your past?"

"That time I met him at lunch, and we did take a couple classes together. I was only at Brookline Prep for a couple months, though."

"Anything significant happen at lunch?"

"Not really, except for showing me he's an asshole."

"What classes did you take with him?"

"Trig and AP Physics C."

"I straight D'ed trig, so I know what that is. What's the other class?"

"AP Physics C? We learned about electricity and magnetism."

As the words fell out of my mouth, I thought, *how could I have overlooked that*? I was so preoccupied with discovering that I was a time traveler. All those sessions with a hypnotherapist, they'd actually worked to suppress past memories.

I had begun to take AP physics. Then I got expelled, and my public high school barely offered honors classes. The physics teacher at Brookline Prep was excellent, and I remembered being extremely sad about having to leave early into the semester.

"What's wrong? You look upset."

I shook my head. "Nothing. Good spot, Trevor. Electricity and magnetism…that sounds pretty time-travel-esque."

"See if you can visit that class again."

I laughed. "You know it's not that easy for me. I can't walk through doorways like you, and I don't have control of where I travel yet." I paused. "Can you take me into my past?"

"It doesn't work like that. We can only visit our own pasts."

"But you took me into your past? How did that happen?"

"I tried to take my sister into my past once—she knows about my, uh, unique talent. It didn't work because she isn't a traveler. We can only take other travelers into our past."

My schedule would be packed for the next few days. If I time-traveled on my work trip, I didn't know where I would end up or if I would return to the present. I assumed I would, because Trevor and Jayden returned to the present.

How could I get on an airplane now, so I could travel back to that class—

"Do you have a family jet available at Teterboro? One that would be available to fly right now?"

"Uh, we have a helicopter."

"I live less than ten minutes from there. I'll try and summon Kai to help me. It's worth a shot to return to my past and see what I can find from that AP class."

"I'll contact the pilots and meet you there at 10:00."

Before hanging up, I hesitated and then said, "Thanks Trevor."

CHAPTER TEN

The helicopter blades twirled. Standing off to the side were a pilot and Trevor, who was waving. I grasped my handbag as the wind from the blades guided my body.

The pilot escorted us to the helicopter and opened the door. We cut through the wind and stepped inside. The creamy leather seats, plush carpet, snack basket, and bottles of water, well, this *was* a nice way to time-travel. The door closed, and I saw another pilot in the right seat. We fastened and adjusted our headsets.

Trevor spoke through the headset and pointed at the pilots. "This is your big surprise. I thought it would be romantic to do a night helicopter ride of the city for your belated birthday gift."

The pilots could hear our conversation through the headsets. Trevor's fabricated story made sense. He pointed to the pilots again.

Oh. That was my cue. "Really?! Thank you so much! I'm so excited!"

"Anything for you, babe."

I giggled. Trevor Stone would do something *exactly* like this to get laid.

Wait, did I actually *giggle*?

We lifted off and ascended over the uninspired buildings of Teterboro. Then we flew off into the night sky. The city began to appear with its golden and pale blue lights. It reminded me of the astral plane with twinkling luminosity amongst the darkness of the space, or in this case, skyscrapers.

Though the scene in front of me was breathtaking, I had to focus.

"I wish Kai was here. She's been such a guide to me lately."

"It wouldn't be a romantic date if it were the three of us, would it? What do you think of the skyline?" His finger darted to the pilots.

I mustered girlish enthusiasm. "Amazing, babe! I can't thank you enough."

I pulled the microphone away from my mouth, covered it with my hand, and leaned across the seats. I shouted into Trevor's ear as best I could. "Can't the pilots turn off their ability to hear our conversation?"

He said, "They can, but I don't trust it. You never know. I always keep conversations in this bird light and fluffy."

I sat back and gave him a thumbs-up.

Kai suddenly appeared in the seat between Trevor and me.

"Whoa! You can't be here, Kai!" I said.

"Why not?"

"Can't the pilots see and hear you?"

"No, they can't. Just you and Trevor."

I glanced at the cockpit. The pilots were engrossed in flying.

"You called?" she said.

I heard her clearly despite the helicopter noise.

I said "yes" and explained the situation.

The black speckles enveloped her more, and they were unnerving. I didn't want her to feel worse by drawing attention to them. Her glow had lessened too. She donned the war paint. I guessed it was permanent now that we were in battle.

"I don't have your protection yet, so you must be careful."

"How can I be careful if I don't know what I'm doing?"

"Be aware of your surroundings. If anything feels off, follow your gut."

I nodded.

She turned to Trevor. "Hi there."

"Hey, beautiful." He winked at Kai and nodded toward the pilots.

She faced me again. "It's early for this skill, but I have a feeling you may be advanced for a beginner. Your grandmother was the same way. You remind me of her."

My mother used to say that all the time.

"You have to completely silence your mind and focus on where you'd like to return. Try to visualize every detail you can."

Trevor pulled his headset away from his mouth, reached across Kai, and squeezed my arm for a second. "We're here for you."

I hated to admit it, but Trevor's touch of support felt nice.

I shifted in the club seat and closed my eyes.

The physics class crept into my mind. I breathed in and out, detailing the sensory aspects of the classroom. I heard the squeak of the whiteboard marker and the shuffling of feet underneath the desks. I inhaled the musky scent of a popular cologne that male classmates spritzed on themselves. I even tasted the root beer that I often drank at lunch.

It was happening again.

The angelic white consumed me, along with the non-dizzy spinning and the purple flashes in my third eye. I tumbled around the outer depths of space until I fell gracefully onto a wooden floor.

The grace ended there.

There were semi-glossed wooden floor planks, a desk facing the window, and a slanted ceiling.

It was my old bedroom.

This house had once held commonplace memories. My father had gathered me on his lap and read to me as a small child. My mother baked chocolate chip cookies, and Grandma and Grandpa would stop by to share those cookies and milk with me. Then the arson event occurred, and I could barely recall the happy memories. They were replaced with my parents frantically removing matches and lighters from our home. I wasn't even allowed to ignite the flame on our kitchen stove. For a reprieve, I'd hide in my room, away from the humiliation, falsehoods, and accusations.

That reprieve never came.

As I had done countless times, I was staring at a screen that blared Pyro Girl. I would weep and scream into a pillow. One of the few helpful things that came out of therapy was I now recognized this action as self-torture and self-abuse.

This time, I closed out of the app.

My old Nokia phone sat next to me. After days of being a teenager without a cell, I'd searched my parents' room and found it hidden in a shoebox. I'd take the contraband to my room and put it back before they came home.

The phone blared the date. It was right after the Ruin-Indy's-Life arson event. Late 2011 and not much was on Netflix, compared to today. Later on, I'd concluded that was why Pyro Girl was a major source of entertainment for Boston teens. I was a victim of shitty timing. If it happened today, my infamy would be celebrated. Hell, I'd probably be offered my own reality show.

Fuck. I wasn't in the AP physics class with Jayden.

How could being a hermit in my old bedroom help me in the present?

And why couldn't I ever revisit the *happy* parts of my childhood?

Then *swoosh!* I was whisked again, floating through space much faster this time—not at Kai's or Trevor's time-lapse speed, but faster.

I leapt into my body, into a classroom.

I was there.

I think.

"Indy, you had your hand up? What's the answer?"

I did a quick scan of the room. That was the physics teacher, Mr. Glen. Kids in uniforms now turned around to stare at my awkward silence. Uniforms, good.

Where did Jayden sit?

Only two rows in front of me, he was scribbling in a notebook.

"India? Your answer?"

I blinked and checked the dry-erase board. It was an extremely complex math equation, that I was sure I once could solve, but right now…ugh!

Why was I such a nerd and always had to raise my hand?!

"I'm sorry, Mr. Glen. I thought I knew the answer, but I don't."

He gave me a puzzled look. "Okay, India. You get a pass this time. Anyone else?"

Jayden's hand shot up.

"Jayden?"

He rattled off the answer, and of course, he was correct.

It was all coming back to me.

Mr. Glen's marker squeaked as he wrote on the board.

He drew an upside-down triangle. In a separate equation, there was a symbol that resembled a musical note.

Maxwell's equations.

One of the foundations of electromagnetism and magnetic circuits.

Perfect for the Time Machine.

Besides me, Jayden was the star of the class. If I had stayed at Brookline Prep, we would've been locked in academic battle.

I craned my neck to peek at Jayden's notebook.

What was that gibberish?

I could make out a few strange doodles or drawings. I squinted, trying to glimpse a clearer shot. Alas, my vision wasn't that of a hawk's.

My eyes returned to my own notebook. God, this brought me back to all the science and geeky stuff I loved. I actually enjoyed solving equations. Being such an outsider at this school, this, right here, was where I had received validation.

I picked up the No. 2 pencil and began to scrawl these equations in my notebook. I noticed that my stomach was motionless. No gurgling or small pangs from eating something junky at lunch. My lips formed a smile. I felt actual contentment. It had been forever. Being a flight attendant was fine and had its perks, but expressing my true self was so much better.

Then I whooshed again. This time, I was back in the present, in the helicopter with Trevor. Kai had left.

We both pulled our headsets away from our mouths and covered them.

"You have this huge grin on your face," Trevor yelled.

"I finally revisited a good place."

"What did you find out?"

"I found the start of something."

"That's better than nothing."

I nodded.

"Kai mumbled something about 'working on the protection' and left right after you. You were only gone for a couple minutes."

"My body was still here?"

"Yeah. You looked like your normal self and were fidgeting, except you had this distant expression. I asked you a question and you answered robotically. To others, they'd think you were spaced out but normal."

I gazed at the lit-up city. "We'll lose our voices if we keep yelling. I'll tell you everything when we land. Let's enjoy the last of the ride."

#

Trevor Stone sat on my carpet and leaned against my couch. He bit into an ooey-gooey slice of pizza. It smelled heavenly. I was dying inside.

"You sure you can't have any?"

"Yep. You couldn't have picked something else to bring over?"

"Sorry, I forgot about your issue."

"Normally I wouldn't care, but pizza is the one thing—"

"I get it. It's cool."

He got up, closed the pizza box, opened my front door, and left.

Uh.

Was he coming back?

The door opened. Trevor sauntered in, minus the pizza.

He sat down again.

"I gave it to the driver. We can order food delivery and you pick whatever you want."

That was…thoughtful.

"You didn't have to do that."

"Yeah, I did. It's your home." He tapped away on his phone. "Here's the app. Order whatever you want. Groceries, whatever."

He slid the cell across the drum.

"Thanks."

Snowball meowed with approval and curled up next to him.

"Do you mind if I have this?" He pointed to the can of beer he'd brought.

"Yeah, no problem."

The can hissed as he opened it. I used to love that sound when I drank soda in my past. The good ole days.

I perused the app and ordered a Greek salad. I gave him the phone.

"I'll order the same. Done."

"Let me tell you what happened."

I finally relayed the details of my trip as he petted Snowball. She purred.

"The good news is you did travel to where you intended. Kai was right. You're a natural."

"The bad news is after I was expelled, I threw out everything, including my notebooks. I'm starting to recall some of the material. In the class, we were studying Maxwell's equations. They describe the behavior of the electromagnetic field. Then I remembered that we learned about the Lorentz force right before I was expelled."

"What's that?"

"Imagine a charged particle—say, a person—moving with speed through an electromagnetic field. Doesn't that sound familiar?"

"I'm not sure."

"A Time Machine. That could be exactly how it works. A person travels at an insanely fast speed through an electromagnetic field to somewhere else. We'd have to see the Machine up close and have more than a millisecond to examine it."

"We know that Jay hooks himself up to his chakras. How does that work? Wouldn't he have to get in the box?"

I shook my head. "Yeah, this is where I'm lost. He's using and manipulating the laws of physics. It's impressive."

Trevor smirked. "Are you jealous?"

"A little."

More than a little. In theory, Jayden scientifically accomplished a feat that was beyond my wildest dreams. It was beyond the Nobel Prize…and beyond dangerous.

"He had these little drawings in his notebook. I couldn't get close enough to see."

Trevor said, "I wonder if they were the beginnings of the drawings I saw?"

"Could be."

He took a sip of beer.

"Where do we go from here?" I asked.

"I guess we eat our salads and figure it out."

I yawned. "I wish it were that simple. My brain is fried. You?"

"It might be good to sleep on it."

"Exactly. It's past midnight and I have a trip tomorrow."

Trevor checked his phone. "That's okay if you're kicking me out, because the salad order was cancelled. This isn't the city. Not much is open this late." He grabbed his beer. "I'll take this for the road, since I'm not driving."

"I have a flight tomorrow from Teterboro to London. I'll attempt time-traveling and can hopefully find answers then. Can you travel too? Try to go into your past and find something about Jayden that will help us?"

"Yeah, I will. Who are you flying tomorrow? Us jet owners, we all know each other from Bedford to the city."

"Amanda Karrington."

He whistled. "She's psycho. Good luck."

Her reputation preceded her. Good to know.

He walked over to the door, opened it, and paused. "I wish I knew you in high school, Indy. It would've been different."

"Nah, you and your friends wouldn't have given me the time of day."

"Maybe. That's why I'm glad we're friends now. Good night."

As he shut the door, I thought, *are Trevor Stone and I really friends*?

Only time would tell.

CHAPTER ELEVEN

This morning, I had woken up late. All this traveling across time and space made me hungry, tired, and *horny*. The last one came as a shock, especially how I had to immediately take care of it to move on with my day. That part of me hadn't been aroused in a while.

Now, I was on the jet and dressed in my FA uniform: a black suit-dress and cardigan, nude compression thigh-highs, and plain, black flats. I had to learn to be a time traveler plus do my job, feed my cat, and pay taxes and shit. I was only on day three of this new meta-human lifestyle and it was already exhausting. How did Claire Fraser and The Terminator do it?

"Indy, *Indy*?"

The dyed-blond version of Satan stood in front of me.

"Yes, Amanda?"

I was in the aft galley of Amanda Karrington's G4 or Gulfstream 400. I had filled the cabin with every kind of food a person could imagine, such as sushi and sashimi from Nobu to lobster tail and caviar to petit fours and three kinds of cakes. It was enough food for sixteen pax, yet there was only one.

Blond Satan had told me that she liked "to look at all of it." Very Marie Antoinette—actually, it was very Kai too. The irony was she merely nibbled on a piece of donut here or sushi there. When flying on a private jet, it wasn't allowed to bring food from one country into another. I always had to throw out her ridiculous buffet when we arrived at the destination. It broke my heart every time.

I hadn't noticed her strolling to the aft of the plane. That wasn't like me.

"Would you please move? I have to use the lav."

"Of course," I said and stepped aside.

She threw me a faux smile, slid past, then opened and shut the lav door. I heard the unmistakable sound of a drawer opening. I wondered if she was taking her usual upper or downer? Hopefully a downer.

The door squeaked open. I grabbed a fork and microfiber cloth and pretended to polish.

As she exited the lav, she said, "I added a passenger a few minutes ago. I'm picking up my friend in New Hampshire before we go to London."

She snatched a petit four from the tray, bit into it, and spit it into a napkin.

"This is *totally* not up to my standards or even a dog's standards. Where did you get them?"

"L'orange."

Exactly where I've ordered them from the last ten times, and you and your friends loved them. L'orange made the best petit fours in the city. It was like buying them in Paris.

She scrunched her nose. "Find another place. They suck now…and I'm moving to a Keto diet tomorrow…and so are the other passengers on the return leg. We're all doing this together and seeing if we can lose a few before the big wedding. If you've already ordered the food for the return trip, cancel it and change it all to Keto. Thanks."

She sauntered over to her inflated jet bed, slipped under the covers, and picked up a glossy magazine.

Whatever. I searched my email for the updated trip sheet with the new pax to find any preferences. It hadn't come through yet. My phone chimed.

The captain texted: "We're re-routing to LEB in New Hampshire. P/u 1 pax and headed to Luton. Trip sheet coming soon."

I gave the text a thumbs-up.

Unfortunately, Blond Satan had taken an upper, because she violently flipped through each page of the magazine. Her eyes darted left to right.

Oh boy.

I was in for a long-ass trip to London.

I quickly wrapped and stored all the food and secured the cabin for landing. Amanda stayed in bed for landing, which of course was illegal, but that was the difference between flying commercial and charter versus owning a PJ. Owners set the rules, and the pilots and flight attendants couldn't override them.

After we landed at LEB, the pilots told me that I had the unusual request to meet the pax in the FBO. I wondered which one of Amanda's twat-like friends it would be.

I took off my flats and slipped on my heels to greet them. I then deplaned and hurried across the tarmac. While walking through the FBO sliding doors, I really hoped that this friend wasn't as high maintenance as Blond Satan. I couldn't take another one today, and this request already made them seem annoying.

An insanely beautiful, statuesque young woman with blondish-brown highlights so perfect they almost looked real rushed toward me. At her feet was…a cat…on a leash. A meow escaped from its mouth.

"Indy!" she said with actual enthusiasm.

Who was this?

"You don't recognize me?"

I narrowed my eyes. "No."

"Oh," she said and giggled. "Sorry, I'm coming on too strong. You will recognize me soon."

The look on my face must have conveyed pure and utter confusion.

"I'm your passenger today! Yay!"

Yay.

"Have you had sex with my brother yet? I've heard he's not bad in the sack." She scanned my face. "Okay, you seriously don't know who I am?"

I shook my head.

"Hello, it's me! Serenity Stone."

A gasp caught in my throat. What was Trevor's sister doing on this trip?

She examined me. "Yep, close to what I remember. Great tits, good teeth, and beautiful hair." She sighed. "If you were into women, you'd be mine—*not* my brother's. I like 'em small and dark." She winked.

Her sheer gall left me at a loss for words. This had to be, hands down, the most inappropriate conversation I'd ever had with a pax.

And how did she know me like that? *"I remember?"* She remembered what? I had a million questions, yet all I could manage to say was:

"You're friends with Amanda Karrington?"

She laughed and tossed her hair. "Yeah. We go way back to the WASP nursery. She's one of the most horrible human beings I've ever met, but I'm kinda fascinated by that. You know?" She paused. "Uh oh. That bitch is on the steps waving. We've gotta go."

We walked toward the aircraft. Serenity's Russian blue cat plodded along.

"That's Frank. You've met him before. Franky, say hi to Indy."

He looked up and meowed.

Very cute.

"We don't have much time. Treat me like a regular passenger. I'll keep Amanda occupied with the usual bullshit. You need to do your thing and figure out how we've met before."

I stopped walking and said with a raised voice, "What do you mean?"

"We don't have time for this. Amanda is staring at us."

I began walking again, but this time it was a march of annoyance. "Fine. Then tell me how can I travel to where we've supposedly met before?"

"I can't time-travel, like you and Trevor. I wish. But I've researched a lot and I have extraordinary abilities for a human. I've coached Trevor. Just put the energy out there of where you want to be and voila!"

She quickened her pace. "BTW, I originally met you at my house. We'll talk after the flight. Bye."

Serenity scooped up Frank, bounced up the aircraft stairs, and said, "Hi bitch!" and hugged Blond Satan.

I blinked in utter disbelief and asked myself, *what the hell is going on?*

#

My stomach flipped and flopped, and this time it wasn't the UC. Like Trevor had said, I was a natural, but how much of a natural?

Serenity said "her house" but which house was that? The one she lived in now, the one in which she grew up?

I sat in a club seat in the aft cabin for takeoff and thought about the fact I could end up anywhere. I mean *anywhere*, which was scary to me. Blond Satan and Serenity giggled and sipped champagne at the front of the cabin. God, I wished this plane had a crew rest.

I closed my eyes, took a deep breath, and exhaled. The wheels lifted off the runway; we were in flight. I could do my thing.

What were Kai's instructions?

Oh yeah.

Silence my mind and focus on where I'd like to return. Visualize every detail.

My eyes popped open as I realized I didn't know where I was going. I'm supposed to travel back to when Serenity and I met? We'd never met. How can I visualize the details of a place that didn't exist?

Instead, I invoked Serenity's advice of: *put the energy out there and go.*

I shuttered my eyelids and asked the Universe to take me to where Serenity and I had met for the Highest Good—that last part I improvised.

Suddenly, I felt a dull ache in my tailbone. Then it jumped to my hips of all places. A warm sensation encircled this area, and I saw a bright orange color wrap around it and climb steadily to my solar plexus. I received the image of a sun bursting and exploding with such force that I gripped the armrests.

I felt powerful, radiant, and brave.

Not the human idea of bravery, but a courage directly sent from Source. Tranquility enshrouded me.

Angelic light beamed, and the purple lightning hummed in my third eye. I sped through time and space until I was falling onto pavement.

Someone caught me. We tumbled onto the cement together. Trevor.

"Are you okay?" I asked, while lying on top of him.

"It's a good thing you're small."

As I was about to push myself off the pavement, I stared into his eyes. Amber surrounded the outside of his pupils and then a bluish-yellow filled the irises. The combination fascinated me. I couldn't look away.

"Are you gonna get up?"

"Oh! Yeah." I rolled my body off of his.

He stood up first and brushed the dirt from his school uniform pants. I did the same as I realized I was wearing my favorite pair of faded jeans from when I was seventeen years old and a puffy winter jacket.

Snow cascaded all around us and the air smelled like the first snowfall of the year. My teeth chattered. *Next trip, I swear I'm going back to a warm time in my life.*

Trevor was never in my past, not in any significant way. We never talked—not that I could ever remember. He was just there, in the background, in the hall, class, or the courtyard at lunch. We had no contact, so how was he in my past?

"How am I in your past?" he asked, as if reading my mind.

"I dunno."

He patted down his uniform and touched his face and hair in disbelief. "I'm in your past as my eighteen-year-old self."

I shrugged.

"This is my house. You've never been here."

"Trevor, I have no idea."

I touched my puffy jacket and those boot-cut jeans that I always wore around the house during the time I was grounded.

Trevor looked exactly as I remembered him. He didn't have the weight of company drama on his shoulders. In physical appearance, he was young and fresh like a teenager with his entire life ahead of him. A life filled with money, good times, and few worries.

His eyes widened as he scanned the surroundings. The Trevor Stone I always knew appeared outwardly confident. I had to muster some form of compassion and understanding if we were to get through this trip and find answers.

I took his hand in mine and squeezed.

He turned to me, smiled faintly, and squeezed it back.

I dropped his hand gently. Better not hold it too long and have things become awkward.

I gazed upward at his house. All I could see was a gigantic wall that enclosed a home of the wealthy. "I guess we go in."

Trevor led the way as we ambled down the Brookline street and rounded a corner. A narrow black gate appeared.

"Do you know the code?"

"I snuck out this door when I was younger. Let me focus—gate code, gate code." He punched in a set of numbers. The door clicked and buzzed. He pushed the gate open.

Trevor's house wasn't a house; it was an actual castle. With a tower and multimillion-dollar landscaping.

"We all live here in different parts of the house. Grandpa and Grandma in one wing. Mom and Dad in theirs, Serenity in hers when she visits, and me in mine."

"You live at home? That sounds like torture."

"It's not so bad. I have my own quarters and don't pay a dime."

"I couldn't live with my parents. There would be a murder on day one."

He laughed. "Yeah, I know what you mean. That's why Serenity went to Tuck instead of HBS. Close enough to work at the company when she can, yet far enough away to have her own life."

"Was Serenity showing up on Amanda's plane your idea?"

"No, it was Serenity's. She said she had met you in the past before."

"Do you remember Serenity meeting me in the past?"

"No, but she claims she did and we have to see it for ourselves. That's why we're here."

We continued along the path onto the grounds. Uh, what were those hedges—wait, nope—topiaries?

"I know, it's weird. My mom has a thing for *Alice in Wonderland*."

She recreated the chess board with topiary characters from the book, including the White Rabbit with his clock, and a humongous grinning Cheshire Cat.

"That is the creepiest fucking thing I've ever seen."

"Tell me about it."

As we walked along the snow-covered path, the *Alice* scenes ended. The castle extended far and wide with muted brown brick, a wing here, and dozens of windows there. Finally, we reached an ornate side door, where Trevor punched in another code.

"This one I know because it's the door I use in the present."

"You haven't changed the code in thirteen years?"

"Nah." He stopped himself. "Valid point. I'll change it later."

He opened the door and stepped inside. Of course, the entryway was spectacular. Ceilings that touched the sky like the Sistine Chapel minus the painting, and muted beiges and cream-colored walls. You could take one painting off the wall, sell it, and feed a small country.

Heels echoed off the marble floor.

A woman rounded the corner. She was tall and blond like Serenity. She plumped her face with Botox and fillers. She looked young, around thirty-five, but her skin was lumpy from all the work. She maintained a model figure wrapped in an ivory pantsuit.

Kiki Stone from the *Housewives of Boston*. I'd only seen a flash of a promo here and there on YouTube; she looked the same in person. I smelled Clinique Happy on her. This was ironic, because the scent was bright and joyful, consisting of zesty citrus and light florals—and she seemed to be the complete opposite. It was an odd choice too, because it was a perfume even I could afford.

"Trevor, I thought you were busy after school. Who is this?"

He hesitated, "This is Veronica, Mom."

Huh.

"Nice to meet you, Mrs. Stone."

She upped and downed me. "Aren't you polite, and tiny! Trevor, I've never seen you with such a petite young lady before. I see you're switching things up." She winked.

What parent would say that…aloud?

Oh yeah, my mom would totally say that aloud.

Her smile boasted porcelain veneers. "It's nice to meet you, Veronica." She turned to her son. "Trevor, make sure you're around for dinner tonight. Your dad's business colleagues are here from London, and unfortunately, it's our turn to entertain. God, they're so boring. Anyway, I apologize, Veronica, but you can*not* stay for dinner."

She snatched her bubblegum-colored Birkin and exited through another hallway.

I read the embarrassed expression on Trevor's face. "I'm sorry about that. She is…blunt."

You think?

He said, "I know you're thinking she didn't like you because of social status, but she doesn't like anyone."

"He's right."

We both turned around.

"Serenity! Jesus. You scared the crap out of us."

There she was. In "her house" exactly as she said. She was a girl of about ten years old who was balancing on one leg. The other leg formed a low tree pose, with her toe touching the floor. Long, wool socks covered her calves, and she wore a school uniform. Her tousled, blond hair was spun into a messy, lopsided bun. She resembled a J Crew model.

"I'm Serenity. Who are you, really?" she said with a smirk. "I know when Trevor is lying."

He sighed. "This is Indy. I couldn't tell Mom her real name—"

"I've seen Pyro Girl."

Suckerpunched…by a child.

"Serenity! It's all a misunderstanding, and it's *none* of your business."

"Mom isn't dumb. Pyro Girl is all over the internet."

My face blazed. I was the talk of elementary schools too.

"Then the press picked up the story, even though you're a minor, Indy. You got screwed."

"I got royally screwed."

She giggled. "Anyway, Trev, I'm sure Mom recognized her. That's why she doesn't like her. It's probably because she's poor too."

Trevor said, "For Chrissake, she's not poor. She's middle class."

Could this conversation get any worse?

"Any-who," Serenity said as she twirled around with clumsy ballet moves. "This conversation is boring, so I'm off to do something exciting like cut the head off The White Rabbit. Or stick one of Grandpa's antique swords down the Cheshire Cat's throat? I don't know. So much time, so much to do. See ya losers."

So this was Serenity Stone. I didn't like the Pyro Girl recognition, but for some reason, I liked her. I couldn't hold a grudge against her for speaking the truth as she knew it.

"She was a funny kid, huh?" Trevor asked.

"Yeah. And she still has personality today."

"I apologize about what she said, you know, about the fire."

"She was just saying what everyone else was thinking."

"Yeah, I guess." He craned his neck to peer around the corner. "Coast is clear. Let's go to the kitchen. Only Maria should be there, and I'm the only person in my family who cooks."

As we walked down a hallway, the judgmental eyes of the Stone ancestors glared at me from the old-fashioned paintings. These people must have originated from the Mayflower, because this was by far the WASP-iest museum of portraits I'd ever seen.

We rounded the corner as a middle-aged man on his cell walked toward us.

SJ Stone. The man who helped frame me. I fumed inside.

He finally looked up, waved, and pressed a button to hang up the call.

"Hey Dad, this is…Indy Kash."

SJ's smile disappeared. He was tall with graying blond hair—were all the Stones Vikings?—and wore an expensive black suit. The lines and contours of his face created a map of distinction, each crease etched with experience and marked by authority. His eyes filled with worry.

"Indy," he said in a gentle voice. "I'm sorry for what happened. I've heard you're a nice young lady."

He had to cover his ass. He couldn't come out and say, "Sorry we all went along with framing you and kept the secret despite ruining your life." This was the best apology I'd ever receive from the people who took so much from me, but I refused to accept it.

Instead, I glared at him.

He looked away and turned to his son. "I have to get going. See you at dinner, Trevor."

He continued down the hallway.

Trevor said, "I'm sorry again. This place is a fucking landmine."

We finally entered the kitchen. An older woman wringing a dishtowel nodded at us.

"This is my second mom—actually my first mom a lot of the time. Indy, meet Maria."

We smiled at each other. Trevor explained that she had been the family's housekeeper for many years. He reached around her stout body and hugged her. She giggled and then looked straight into his eyes.

"You seem different. Not yourself."

He pulled away. "Oh c'mon Maria. You've had too many margaritas."

"I don't drink."

"Uh, I know. I was teasing. I—uh"—It was fascinating to see the untouchable Trevor Stone falter— "It's me, Maria. See?" He picked her up and swung her around.

She chuckled and tapped him to put her down, which he did.

Crisis averted. For now.

The kitchen was yet another reflection of the Stone wealth with its massive size and ornate décor. I couldn't even find the refrigerator until Maria opened what looked like a huge cabinet. She set down guacamole, chips, and two Cokes in front of us.

Could I eat in my past what I couldn't eat in my present?

The Coke—that dark, syrupy, fizzy liquid taunted me in my favorite: a glass bottle…I couldn't resist. I tipped the old cold carbonated goodness to my lips and drank. It hit my taste buds and glands and slid with ease down my throat. I savored every drop. I was so happy I was practically in tears.

A text rumbled in my coat, interrupting my food vacation. I reached into my pocket and pulled out my old Nokia. Mom lifted the phone ban when she worked late in case of emergencies.

"Good night, doodoo. I'll be home around 8:30 in the morning. Be good."

I texted: "Have a good shift. Love you."

That should stave off any concern for my whereabouts.

There was a knock at the kitchen door. Maria in her heavily accented English said, "Who would come over when it's snowing this much?"

Trevor shrugged. We kept eating and drinking as Maria opened the door and then said, "Oh! What are you doing here in this weather?"

Then I heard, "Hey, Maria." Trevor heard it too because we looked at each other, eyes wide.

"That's Jayden!" I whispered.

"You can't be here."

"No shit."

His eyes searched as he thought quickly. "It must be around late February? He's here to tutor me for midterms. Shit. He'll be here for a while."

Maria said, "It's so cold. Come in, Jayden, come in."

Out of nowhere, a tiny hand grabbed my wrist. "I'll take her."

Serenity.

She quickly led me into the pantry, which was the size of a normal person's living room, and kept the door cracked.

Just then, an older man rushed into the kitchen.

"That's Grandpa," Serenity whispered.

Steven Stone, the Green Goblin.

"Oh!" Steven said. "I didn't realize it would be Grand Central in here. Trevor, I thought you were busy after school? Jayden, good to see you. Thank you for coming."

"Jayden's here to tutor me. No need to thank him. Mom and Dad pay him well."

"Of course!" Steven laughed nervously. "But actually, Jayden is here to see me."

Silence.

"Why?" Trevor blurted.

Jayden said, "Remember I asked you about that high-school internship program at Stone Corp? I'm applying and interviewing with Mr. Stone today. A little snow doesn't stop me." He winked and followed Steven out of the kitchen. He turned back to say, "Trev, don't worry. We'll hit the books later. I got you."

I saw Trevor's shocked face. I knew he was wondering, *did this actually happen in the past?*

Trevor beckoned me and Serenity. Maria looked incredibly confused, poor woman.

I said, "Where are Jayden and Steven most likely having this meeting?"

"Grandpa's study."

Serenity asked me, "Why couldn't Jayden know you're here?"

Trevor answered, "It's complicated, Seri. Both you and Maria—" He glanced in her direction. "You cannot tell Jay that Indy's here. It's important."

They both nodded. Serenity declared, "I'm coming with you."

"No you're not."

She grimaced. I could tell she wasn't used to being told no. "But I want to."

"Not this time. Sorry. And no following us."

We left the kitchen and rushed through the hallways from wing to wing.

He said, "This is the hallway to Grandpa's study."

"Wait!"

"What?"

"Take off your shoes. They make too much noise."

We removed our shoes, tiptoed in our socks, and reached the door. It was closed. I could hear them talking inside but couldn't make out a word. I grasped the knob with both hands and closed my eyes, praying the door wouldn't creak if I opened it ever so slightly. It worked. I breathed a quiet sigh of relief.

As we peered inside, I saw Jayden on the couch and Steven on the chair.

"You're an inventor, Jayden. I admire that, and you have a *great* future ahead of you, but not at Stone Corp. Not right now."

I wasn't expecting that.

"Why?" Jayden asked with an undertone of anger.

"Easy there, kid. Remember who is boss and who's still in high school."

Jayden shifted on the couch.

"Like I said, I admire your ambition, but you're impatient. You need to go out into the world, go to college and graduate school, get some experience, and then we can talk."

"Zuckerberg didn't need all that school. Jobs didn't either."

Steven roared with laughter. "You do have confidence. I'll give you that, but you are *not* Mark Zuckerberg or Steve Jobs."

Jayden's face twisted into a scowl, but then he transformed into the Jayden Mokashu everyone knew and loved. He gave Steven that signature grin.

"Can you tell me what you don't like about my invention?"

"It's not that I don't like it. I find the idea, well, far-fetched," Steven replied while squirming in his seat. "It's not possible."

I wished we had heard the beginning of this conversation. Were they referring to the Time Machine? Had Jayden invented it this early?

"I can work out the details."

"Over time. But for now, Jayden, the answer is no. I will not be investing in your invention."

"That's okay, Mr. Stone. I don't give up that easily. Next time, you'll say yes."

He stood up and they shook hands.

"We've gotta move and get our shoes," I said.

Steven and Jayden conversed for a minute, which allowed me to silently close the door. We scurried down the hallway, grabbed our shoes, and fast-walked into another wing.

Trevor stopped and nodded to a room. We entered a guest bedroom, I assumed, with hotel bedding and not much else.

"No one comes in here," he said. "Jayden never asked me about a 'high-school internship program' and there isn't one. Stone Corp only allowed interns from Harvard, Stanford—all those places. I think I remember this tutoring session; it was snowing and Jay seemed a bit agitated but maintained his cool."

"Can we talk to Steven and get some answers?"

"We can try. No guarantees."

Someone burst through the door.

"Serenity! Jesus! You're old enough to knock."

"Why? Were you guys having sex?"

"Does it look like we're having sex?"

She shrugged. "I have no idea. I'm just a child. Why are you asking me about sex?"

He shook his head. "Why are you following us?"

"I wasn't. I ran into you here."

"Uh huh. Sure."

"It's snowing pretty hard outside."

We peered out the large window. The lights illuminated the fluffy snowflakes that poured from the evening sky.

"Where do you live?" she asked.

"Lower Allston."

"LA. What a crap hole."

I laughed. "Yep."

"You can't Uber home with the icy roads, and our driver won't take you either. Trev, she has to sleep over."

"No, no. I'm fine. I'll figure it out."

"Mom will be *pissed* if she finds you sleeping in a guestroom. You can sleep in my room, and I'll sneak you out in the morning."

"Shit. I have to do this study session with Jayden," Trevor said. "I'll come find you afterward. I won't be long."

Serenity giggled, took my hand, and zoomed me through the house as I carried my shoes. Then we stopped in front of a door. She pushed it open.

This wasn't a ten-year-old's bedroom; it was a condo. A couch and loveseats surrounded a wooden coffee table. The size of the bed looked like two kings put together. A desk and chairs, a huge flat screen, and wow, a mini fridge stocked with water, soda, and juice. The only semblance of a child was all the awards and trophies on a credenza. Duke University Talent Identification Program, National Young Scholars, and a Mensa Foundation Award. What everyone had said about her was true. She was wicked smart.

What was that smell? A litter box?

Serenity observed my sniffing. "I have a secret kitten. No one knows—well, Maria does, because she cleans the box. Mom *hates* cat hair." In a cutesy voice, she said, "Come here, Frank."

There he was in all his kitten glory. He slinked out from underneath the bed, and she picked him up. He purred loudly and nuzzled her.

She hugged him. "He's sweet and cute and I love him. You'll keep him a secret, right?"

"Yes, I will."

She nodded toward the litter box smell. "That's the bathroom." She placed Frank on the oversized window seat. He curled into a ball and tucked his face under his leg—exactly like Snowball. I missed her.

Serenity radiated a feeling that I knew all too well: loneliness. At only ten years of age, with everything at her disposal, she was alone in this huge condominium setup where her parents didn't even notice she was hiding a kitten. This bedroom was bland—white, cream, beige, off-white. It displayed no character or personality, of which Serenity had so much.

Despite all the wealth and luxury, I felt sorry for her. A child should have her parents' undivided love and attention at all times. I could relate. My parents were always off working or having affairs or whatever else they did. I knew exactly what she was missing and that this perpetual feeling of loneliness would follow her into adulthood and create more problems.

She interrupted my thoughts by saying, "Do you wanna watch a movie?"

Before I could utter a word, I was already spinning into the blackness.

CHAPTER TWELVE

Oxygen masks dangled in front of me. My eyes flickered to Serenity and Blond Satan who each pressed a mask to their face. Poor Frank looked frozen with fear in Serenity's arms.

I winced at the pain throbbing inside my head. There was a manageable amount of turbulence and I could breathe normally…so far. I unbuckled, steadied myself, got up, steadied myself again, and stumbled to the front of the plane to figure out what was going on.

The coldest rush of air I'd ever felt then swept through the front of the cabin…like I was standing inside a meat locker, but worse. The outside air was rushing inside—fuck—and we were descending. We should be near LEB; we had just taken off when I traveled. More time must've passed because the air-show screen read we were at an altitude of 20,000 feet.

I looked behind me. The women's eyes rounded with the sheer terror that only an impending plane crash could illicit. Blond Satan was sitting up in the jet bed. She needed to be in a seat and buckled. Now.

I marched into the cabin and demanded, "Amanda, get into a seat *now* and put on your seatbelt."

She shook her head no.

I crouched down and got right in that bitch's face. "Get in your seat now and put on your fucking seatbelt."

She dropped the mask, quickly got up, plunked down in a club seat, strapped in, and pressed the dangling mask to her face.

Good. I didn't have time for her bullshit. What I had to do now was take my own advice: sit down, buckle up, put on a mask, and watch over the pax.

As I was tottering toward an empty seat, the plane miraculously leveled out and the cold air dissipated. The pain between my temples subsided and everything returned to normal—except for the pax who would never forget this horrifying experience.

I wouldn't either, considering my last flight could've been working for someone so vile. To end my life like that? No way. It was like getting in a fatal car accident while listening to a cheesy boy band. Not fucking worth it.

I then headed into the cockpit to check on the pilots.

The captain pulled the mic away from his mouth and said, "We have to head back to Teterboro for repairs. Pressurization issue, obviously. It's safe to fly at 15,000 feet. Please tell Amanda that Ron is brokering with another company to charter a plane to take her and her guest to London. Ron said to tell you that that charter company only uses in-house FAs, so you can't do the trip. The upside is you will be paid in full for the trip and now you have a few days off. Please let Amanda know the situation. Thank you."

I nodded and returned to the cabin to deliver the message. To receive paid days-off was nice—if this were a normal situation. Instead, I had to, you know, fight evil.

At least we were alive.

I told Blond Satan everything, who in typical prima-donna fashion, complained of a "terrible" headache, even though I knew better. I rustled around in the snack basket and found peppermint gum. I told her: "the chewing gum will help." I actually had no fucking idea. I'd never dealt with loss of pressurization before, but it sounded good. Serenity grinned.

I did a walk-through of the aircraft to ensure that nothing came loose—which thankfully, nothing did. Blond Satan, of course, returned to lying on her jet bed and flipping through gossip magazines as she chattered away. I refused to set out any food for this flight if we were having safety issues. If she complained, I'd have the pilots back me up.

I began the lengthy process of wrapping each mask and re-stowing it in its proper compartment over each seat.

Serenity came bouncing over to me, champagne in hand and with a much calmer Frank in tow. "That was *so* hot how you screamed at Amanda. You're a fucking legend. I have to pee. More champagne, please." She continued to the lav.

As I was about to reach for the champagne bottle, my phone chimed with a text from Trevor. "Serenity told me you're headed back to TEB. We've heard Grandpa has a big announcement coming today and we don't know what it is. Can you meet me in the city?"

I texted: "Let's meet in Central Park, at Wollman Rink."

He responded: "I'll send a car to the FBO."

I gave the text a thumbs-up and typed: "I'll text you when I'm on my way."

#

New York City bustled with traffic. Police and ambulance sirens blared. The racket of jackhammers, drills, and other never-ending city construction rattled through me. We drove through neighborhoods that once had mom-and-pop shops but now had big box stores and grocery chains. Every new skyscraper felt like an erasure, replacing memories with glass and steel. This was the city, unchanged yet ever-changing…beautiful and majestic, while at the same time ugly and claustrophobic.

The driver navigated the streets toward Columbus Circle, and traffic crawled as we turned onto Central Park South. I marveled at the hues of the sparse remaining leaves—luminous golden, deep red and orange, and vibrant green.

It had been an unusual fall. On a normal year, the leaves would have been long gone for the season. This autumn had been warm; there was an absence of gusty storms to blow the leaves off the trees. Here in the city, the holdovers glimmered in the sun.

The driver said, "I'm gonna drop you off right up here."

I hopped out, closed the door, crossed the busy street, and then traversed the path to Wollman. It was already a pool of frozen ice with twirling tourists and children shuffling around on skating trainers.

The wind had picked up. Good thing I wore a long fall coat. I stuck my hands in my pockets and continued to walk.

I heard a whistle.

"Looking good, Indy Kash," Trevor said as he snuck up from behind me.

Even in a potential world-ending crisis, he could find the positive.

He wore a black coat that cost thousands, khaki pants, and black ankle boots. A white dress shirt peeked out of his coat. His dark blond hair looked washed and shiny, and he was clean-shaven. A dimple indented his chin.

I hadn't noticed it before.

"Glad to see you showered."

He smirked. "That does happen sometimes." Then his face darkened. "Serenity and I have been calling everyone, but Grandpa is nowhere to be found. Serenity already landed at the helipad and is in a car to our house."

"Did she talk to SJ?"

"No. We can't find him either. I called my mom but she's filming."

We continued along the path.

"What do you think Steven's up to?"

"I know he has to name a successor. There's a guy who's been his right-hand man for years, and we're pretty sure he's going to name him. If he does, that's not good. The guy's pretty conservative and won't look good for optics. But he would be Grandpa's first choice."

"Do you want to be first choice?"

"My ego likes the idea of being Chief Excruciating Officer." He paused for a laugh at his *really* bad dad joke. "But I'm not cut out for it. Serenity would be the best choice by far. I'd throw my support behind her, but I doubt the board would ever choose a woman."

His phone beeped with a text.

"Serenity sent me a link."

"Open it."

He did and said, "What is this?"

"Let's sit."

We sat down on a green, slatted bench. Trevor turned his phone landscape so that I could see too.

It was a video—no—a livestream that said "Channel 7 News" with a stage and a podium. Behind it was the choppy blue sea and bouncing sailing vessels in Boston Harbor.

Steven appeared on the screen as he walked onto the stage. He looked all of his eighty-four years. I assumed that the woman who followed and stood behind him was Trevor's grandmother.

I glanced at Trevor, who was holding his breath. I touched his shoulder and said, "It's going to be okay."

Steven said, "We are happy to announce that Stone Corp has taken a new direction. At the helm will be a young, innovative entrepreneur who is a rising star."

Serenity was certainly young, but was she considered an "entrepreneur"?

"We are proud to announce our new CEO, Jayden Mokashu."

Air shot into my lungs like I'd been punched.

Trevor's mouth fell open. We watched in horror as Steven, his wife, and the scant audience clapped. Out of nowhere, Jayden bounced up the stairs and onto the stage. He shook Steven's hand and adjusted the microphone.

"Thank you so much, Steven. I am honored to carry on the Stone Corp legacy."

That shit-eating grin. I wanted to slap it off his face.

"Moving forward, we have challenges to overcome and lofty goals to achieve. We strive to be a leader in diversity and inclusion. I am from Roxbury. I grew up in a low-income family raised by my grandmother—"

Here we go. The sob story. Right on par for Jayden. When the reality was in high school, he was riding on his friends' private jets to all-expense-paid vacations in Aspen or Ibiza. I doubted he would mention *that* part of his childhood.

"Stone Corp's first investment in diversity and inclusion will be a foundation to educate a diverse group of Boston youth for leadership positions in business. We are excited to announce our lead mentor, Ty Collins of the New England Colonials. Ty, please come up to the stage and introduce our exciting new organization, Boston Youth First, or BYF."

Trevor clicked out of the livestream. He stared straight ahead and did not speak. His phone beeped with messages. He switched it off and shoved it in his pocket. I let him absorb this horrible news that a true monster was about to take over his family's corporation.

How did he manage to pull this off? If I knew Jayden as well as I thought, his style was an Epstein-ian combination of damning information he collected on each board member with a sprinkle of framing, like he did to me. I bet he blackmailed Steven, too. I wasn't a corporate America expert, but I'd listened to enough podcasts to know board members, chairpersons, CEOs, and the highest-level executives weren't choir boys.

Jayden had won.

Trevor finally spoke. "This is bad."

"Yeah."

"He has something on Grandpa. He has to."

"Yeah. All the board members, too." I gave him a moment and then said, "Worst of all, he has the Time Machine. The Spirit Council's premonition…" My voice faded. "We have to stop Jayden now."

"How? It's over, Indy."

"I don't know, but we'll figure it out. 'The future has not been written.' *Terminator* reference. It's not over 'til it's over."

More bad news. I drank Coke in my past, and now my current-day digestive system was *not* happy. My stomach howled and swished like a washing machine on permanent press. It was either the soda, or the stress of everything that had been thrown at me.

I knew nothing about corporate takedowns, except for binging *Succession* and *Billions*.

What was I thinking?

The look on Trevor's face, though. I couldn't help it. A human who appeared that sad and lost…I couldn't turn my back on him, or the Earth. The Universe put me in this position for a reason, and I would damn well try my best.

CHAPTER THIRTEEN

Mrs. Albright had called. She had an emergency that involved her sister up in Maine and said she couldn't take care of Snowball for several days. Ugh. I had to deal with this on top of everything else. So I Uber-ed to the FBO to pick up my car and then to my apartment to throw a few things in a bag and get her.

I winded my convertible through the New York City streets with Trevor in the passenger seat holding Snowball. He mindlessly stroked her head.

Trevor came along but barely uttered a word.

I broke the silence. "Trevor, don't the board members live in Boston?"

"Some. Some live here. You can live anywhere in the world and be a board member." That snapped him out of his daze. "The more powerful and connected ones live here. They know Grandpa, but they also know me. I've been to their Christmas Eve parties, kids' weddings, and other boring social events. They'll talk to me."

Let's hope.

My phone rang; it was Lily calling.

"Hey Lily."

"Indy, I had to call to say congratulations!"

"For what?"

She giggled. "Seriously, GIRL, you're so funny sometimes! You're like *the* corporate flight attendant celebrity! On the trip today, even Mr. Jacobs pointed out your photo in the *Boston Globe*—great pic, by the way. We did a quick trip to Bedford and back to Teterboro."

Just pretend like you know what she's talking about, I thought. My voice rose an octave. "Oh thanks so much, Lil! I appreciate the call."

"No problem! We have a trip coming up soon that I'd love for you to cover. It's a good one. I'll email you next week. Enjoy your time off!"

"Thanks. Bye,"

What the fuck?

"What was that?" Trevor asked.

"I have no idea, but I'm about to find out."

"I'll search. You drive."

He typed and clicked until his thumbs stopped. He took a long pause and said, "Uh oh."

"Tell me. Now."

He read:

Newly Christened Stone Corp CEO Names BYF Mentors

At a press conference earlier today, Jayden Mokashu was named CEO of Stone Corp—blah, blah, blah—Mokashu chose mentors from various industries including engineering, technology, fashion design, and even aviation to name several. Mokashu said he selected the mentors based on merit, morality, and excellence in their respective fields. "The mentors can live anywhere in the New England area and New York, but their roots must be Bostonian." When asked who of the mentors in particular were standouts, Mokashu said, "I have been most impressed by a woman named India Jean Kash—

"AAAAAAAAAAAAAAAAAAAHHHHHHHHHHHHHHH HHHHHHHHHHHHHHHHHHHHHHHH!!!!" I screamed so loud Trevor jumped and Snowball meowed.

He continued, "We briefly attended the same high school, where she overcame hardship and stigma. I have watched her flourish in corporate aviation as a leader in her field with numerous awards from the National Business Aviation Association and her stellar volunteer record. I am excited to see how she takes another young woman under her wing and helps mold her into an aviation leader and beyond."

I AM GOING TO KILL JAYDEN. Steam might have actually come out of my ears. My knuckles blanched as I clamped the wheel.

"What the hell is his angle?!"

"Oh boy," he mumbled.

"What do you mean 'oh boy'? Trevor, what do you mean 'OH BOY'?"

"Uh, well, the media connected you to, um, Pyro Girl."

"FUCK! I fucking hate the media!" I banged my palm on the steering wheel.

My cell rang again. It was Ron. I gritted my teeth and said, "Hey Ron."

"Indy, congrats on your award—or whatever it is! A newspaper in Boston called me and wanted a quote on how great you are. Of course, I said good things, just wanted you to know that."

This was insanity. "Thanks Ron, I appreciate it."

"Congrats again on the honor, and I'll be calling you soon. Nothing for this weekend so far, but next month looks busy. Gotta go, bye!"

I was seeing red. Thank God I couldn't go more than ten miles per hour or I'd be crashing into every single Tesla and Mercedes.

"Why would Jayden put me on this list…and hello, how am I a business leader and *successful*?! I'm a flight attendant for fuck's sake. I serve the people on this list for a living. I mean, *really*?"

I glanced at Trevor who was skimming the article.

He said, "Yeah, you're not curing cancer like the doctor from Dana-Farber or developing spacecraft for NASA like the professor from MIT—"

"Or you know, doing important shit."

Jayden invented yet another way to horrify me. It was unbelievable the level of psychopath of this guy. What was next? Waterboarding or an actual burning at the stake like a Salem witch?

Trevor said, "I like all the stuff the *Globe* printed about you. You really created a program so kids with cancer can fly on private jets to St. Michael's Hospital? And you helped build a school in Mali and volunteered at an elephant sanctuary?"

I shrugged. "Yeah."

"Jesus, you should run for office."

I loosened my grip on the wheel. "After all the court-ordered community service, I became more involved in volunteering. I was never any good at making friends after what happened, so I figured I might as well do something."

"You're impressive. Jayden wasn't exaggerating. You belong on this list."

I turned my head and said, "Thanks." That little dimple on his chin…

"Eyes on the road. I have a lot of live for."

Even in a potential world-ending crisis, Trevor Stone could bring a smile to my face.

"I'm on the list too. As a 'young entrepreneurs' mentor. I guess Jayden couldn't think of anything else."

My phone chimed with a text. It was from an unknown number with a Boston area code.

Trevor nodded to the screen and said, "Let's listen."

I clicked on the text and it read: "Hi India. This is Tameka Mokashu."

"WHAT?!" I yelled.

The text continued: "I'm one of the BYF mentors for fashion design. I'm in NYC all the time for work. I'd love to meet up? Jayden, my husband, who you know, has said many nice things about you. I've been thinking of designing a flight attendant-inspired line. I'd love your input? Thanks!"

Why was this all happening? I was barely holding it together, and now more was piled on. I couldn't make any sense of it all.

"I mean, of all the people who would text me, Jayden's wife?! Jayden 'has said many *nice* things about' me?!"

This was becoming more psychotic by the minute.

"This is fucked," Trevor said. "Another block and we'll be at the parking structure for my building."

I breathed in and out to calm myself. Then I asked, "What's Tameka like?"

"You've seen her."

"Not up close."

"She's a former model and was doing pretty well in her career until she hooked up with Jay and married him. They were the power couple everyone wanted to be, but then he changed."

"But what is *she* like?"

"Tameka? Take the next right. It's the first parking garage on the left."

"You have an apartment on Central Park West?"

He passed me the card to swipe, which I did. The arm lifted and I drove into the garage.

"Yeah, I bought it after my trust fund kicked in. I figured it was a good investment."

Spoken like a true trust-fund baby.

"Park there. That's my space."

I parked my car, which looked so out of place among the McLarens, BMWs, more Teslas, and at least two Bentleys.

"You never answered about Tameka," I said as I twisted the key to shut off the engine.

"I thought she was a wild card when Jay met her. Obviously smoking hot—"

My cheeks burned with…was that jealousy? I hadn't felt that in quite some time.

"She didn't come from the Brookline upbringing. Jay picked up the Queen's English, but she was from a different part of town. I always liked her. She's smart, quick, and used to keep Jay in his place. He said he met her after a runway show and that was it. He kept her a secret in the early days of their dating and then she just showed up one day. No one questioned it, and she was accepted into our friend group."

My mind flashed to the night of the fire. Jayden stood in the middle of a group of parents and classmates laughing. Always the center of attention. He was able to engage and relate to the elite. He didn't hide his life in Roxbury but didn't bore his wealthy friends with the details either. As another scholarship kid, if we both hadn't fit in, I could've understood that. But one of us did, and one didn't…and that hurt. It was a constant reminder that I didn't have that natural "it" factor, where I could fit into any group or situation. I wasn't magnetic or charismatic or appealing to anyone. No wonder Snowball was my best friend.

"Why did everyone at Brookline like Jayden so much?"

He shifted in the cloth seat. "Back then, man, he was a breath of fresh air. We meet the same people at the same events. All. The. Time. Even visiting my cousin down in New York, after a few weekends of partying in the city, I knew all the private school royalty there too. Imagine here in Boston, which is much smaller, and then the microcosm, which is Brookline Prep. Jayden made things fun and different."

"Did he talk about his life in Roxbury?"

He scratched behind one of Snowball's ears. "Nah. He was just funny, talking about guy stuff or rowing or his take on all the events or school. He has game when it comes to people. That's the only way I can explain it."

"So he was basically entertainment for you?"

"He was a brother to me."

Sadness crept into his voice. Jayden really destroyed any relationship he could.

Trevor cleared his throat and handed me Snowball. "What's our plan?"

Okay, he refused to become emotional—understandably so. There was so much to get emotional about, but we didn't have the time. We had to focus on our goal: stopping Jayden.

"You're going to talk with the board members."

He nodded.

"Meanwhile, I'm going to sit at a coffee shop and search on my phone for anything I can find to help us. Anything about Tameka or why I'm a BYF mentor…I don't know. I'm hoping the Universe will guide me."

He laughed. "That's the dream. You can't bring Snowball into a coffee shop. Use my apartment."

She purred in my lap. He was right.

"Thanks."

#

With Snowball in my arms, I stepped into the elevator. The doorman, dressed in a crisp blue uniform, was beside me. With the swipe of his keycard, he summoned the ascent and then pressed a button with a gloved finger. From a hidden compartment, he pulled out a chilled bottle of water and offered it to me. I declined. Here I was, suspended in effortless privilege, and foreign to this situation, I squirmed in its presence.

I prayed for this elevator ride to end, yet it seemed to last forever. I glanced at the doorman. I was typically the one providing the service. What did he think of me? Could he ascertain from my clothing that I wasn't in the Stone echelon nor did I exude an overly-confident air like Trevor, who had been privileged his entire life?

The elevator *finally* dinged and we exited onto Trevor's upper-level floor.

He then opened the door to one of the most stunning apartments I'd ever seen. It actually took my breath away. Window walls overlooked Central Park. It was a feast for my *Architectural Digest*-reading eyes. There were seating areas of leather couches that I was sure felt like butter. Cashmere throws, Moroccan pillows, sconces, art, textured wallpaper, dark walnut floors.

Snowball squirmed in my arms, so I let her go. She jumped to the floor, rubbed her tiny body against a couch leg, and meandered through the new space.

My stomach grumbled, reminding me that I had hardly eaten today.

I texted him: "I'm starving. I'm raiding your kitchen."

He texted back: "Go for it."

I rummaged through drawers and cabinets of processed snacks and ramen noodles, and in the freezer, fish sticks and popsicles. I thought Trevor said he cooked? I opened the refrigerator to thankfully see fresh raspberries, blueberries, strawberries, sliced melon, and plain Greek yogurt. The smell of stale pizza wafted to my nose. He needed baking soda and more healthy options. I took out the yogurt.

As I peeled back the lid, I heard something drop in the bedroom. I froze.

What the fuck was that?!

Was it a random supermodel waiting for Trevor naked on the bed…and she dropped her humongous vibrator? Or had Serenity returned early and no one had alerted me? Was it Kai?

"Kai?"

Nothing.

"Serenity?"

Footsteps came closer.

Should I hide or find a blunt object or—what the hell should I do?

I *refused* to die opening a container of mediocre yogurt. It wasn't even organic.

"Hi India."

Steven Stone.

Eww. I instinctively recoiled, like seeing a rat scurry across the subway tracks.

Without thinking, I blurted, "How did you get in here?"

"I own this building."

So Trevor buying here wasn't exactly an "investment decision" the way he made it sound. The top one percent owned everything. There was nowhere to run and hide.

"I bet Trevor got a good deal on this place."

He stared coldly. "I'm still a businessman, and I don't care to be talked to like that. Remember, you're just a flight attendant."

What a douche. I wasn't at work, and honestly, what could he take away from me, my shitty apartment in Hackensack and Snowball? Okay, I'd be upset about Snowy, but other than that he could fuck off.

"I don't care to be talked down to like I'm a moron, despite what you think of corporate flight attendants."

"Oh I'm well aware. You've done an admirable job of worming your way into Trevor's world. Such an admirable job, in fact, I've come to ask a favor of you."

Speaking to me the way he just did, I didn't believe him. However, I wanted to play the game. "Why me?"

"You're an outsider, and if you help me out, I will make it worth your while."

It was always money with these people.

"How much?"

"I'll talk numbers *after* we discuss terms."

Now that I had a clear view of him, I saw a man who resembled more of a power player than the actual power itself. I would mistake him for a lawyer from the Southern District or a senior vice-president of a major company—an exec, not the chairman of the board. His style of dress was a bit frumpy with a lopsided tie and sports coat that hung past his wrists. It was more than the eccentric billionaire type; it was someone who was too impatient to stand for the tailor.

"What do you want?"

"I had no choice but to give my company to Jayden."

I bit my tongue. It was best to play my cards close to the vest.

"You gave him Stone Corp hours ago. What's happened since then?"

"He's planning something big. Something I never saw coming."

"Big? Like what?"

"I'm not entirely sure. He's already trying to reallocate half a billion dollars for a secret project. No one knows what it is. It could be a nuclear weapon for all I know."

"Aren't you still the chairman? You could override him."

"You don't understand. He has information on all of us…everyone on the board is scared."

Translation: Steven Stone was scared.

"Jayden is a brilliant mind. I underestimated him. He could destroy everything."

What he meant was Jayden could destroy his company that he worked so hard to rebuild and his family's generational wealth.

Time to put Steven to the test.

"Maybe Jayden is the right person for the job? He's young, energetic, different."

"Young lady, don't BS me. I'm well aware of how he framed you in high school. You hate him, which is why I'm surprised by you dating my grandson"—whoa, I was *what*?— "but then, I examined your meager life and bank accounts. Now I understand why."

What a lovely way to insult my entire life and the savings for which I had worked so hard.

"I think, well I hope, the way to get through to Jayden is Tameka. If she can talk to him, that's a start."

"How do I factor into your plan?"

"You know her. You went to school with her."

Huh?

"Not Brookline Prep. That subpar public school in Lower Allston."

I scanned my brain. Tameka, Tameka. I didn't know anyone by that name, and that high school was huge, more like a college.

Wait.

There was a tall, gawky girl named Tammy in the grade above me. Tammy was quiet; I recalled her eating lunch alone with her nose buried in a book. I had noticed her because I had done the same thing. What was her last name?

"Was her maiden name Harris?"

He nodded. "That sounds right."

"We weren't friends. I saw her in the cafeteria at lunch and that was the extent of it."

"That doesn't matter. You come from the same background, and you can relate to her. I certainly cannot and neither can my family or anyone I know. Right now, she's in a bad place with her husband, and Jayden wasn't good to you either. You have much in common."

I saw his point, but I couldn't help but to wonder, "Why do you trust me?"

"I do everything by instinct. That's why I've done well in business. I have the instinct to trust you."

He shifted his eyes. I had the instinct to know that Steven wasn't telling the whole truth.

"What's in it for me?"

"I will give you a job at my new company that is creating a fleet of environmentally-friendly private jets."

"That has nothing to do with me. I don't design planes or fly them."

He grimaced. "I'm getting to that. I've heard you did very well in STEM at Brookline Prep—at least for the short time you were there. You don't have a degree. *I* could put you in charge of designing the aircraft interior. It's not engineering, but it's a step above what you're doing."

I felt a spark of electricity in my heart center.

"You would work your own hours and be the boss."

Intriguing offer. He had done his research. It was something I would seriously consider—I mean, this was an opportunity anyone in my position would jump at. Alas, I had to get it together and remember the rat standing in front of me.

I led him on for fun. "I don't know FAA standards, the nuances of the safety equipment—"

"You're thinking too small, India. You can pay people to do all of that. As an executive, you would have a salary, bonuses, stock options, and the best part?"

He raised his eyebrows. I unintentionally leaned in a bit.

"We have a tuition reimbursement program. With *me* writing *you* a letter of recommendation and pulling a few strings, you would be accepted into any university you desire."

A large butterfly spreading its wings was wreaking havoc inside the middle of my chest. Trevor had offered this, but I hadn't wanted to engage with him. I hadn't fully believed him either. But with Steven Stone making the offer...

"Sound good, India? You could make *real* money and finally buy that house for which you've been saving—and it could be a house worth showing people."

What an arrogant prick.

Like I had thought before, I'd be making a deal with the actual devil. However, my intuition told me to agree with him. I knew that I wasn't getting the whole story. In my heart, I was certain I could never work for a megalomaniac like Steven, but I had to stop Jayden. If that meant appeasing this asshole, I would. For now.

"Fine, we have a deal."

"Good. The details are as follows: Tameka recently moved to Harlem. This is her address." He fished in his pocket and handed me a piece of paper. "My sources tell me she and Jayden are separated. Apparently, Tameka loves Harlem and wanted a pied-à-terre when she visited, although they already have a penthouse in Chelsea. She's been spending a lot more time there than in Boston. Talk to her and see what you can find. Can you do that, India?"

I had no idea. "Sure."

He ambled to the door. "We have a verbal agreement."

As he was about to leave, I asked, "Should I tell Trevor?"

"As long as the job gets done, I don't care," he said and closed the heavy door.

Snowball slinked out from underneath the couch. She was staring at a corner of the apartment, and there was glowing.

Kai.

Her eyes gleamed with a fiery intensity. She moved with her usual weightless grace.

The ingredients for her PSL appeared, and she said, "Your travel technique is clunky. We have to work on that."

She pointed to the ingredients and I began to make the drink.

"I know. I was hurling onto the sidewalk. Luckily, Trevor caught me."

"I saw that. And you can't control when you leave the past."

"Will I ever?"

"It takes time and patience."

Trevor had said the same thing.

She sniffed as I added the vanilla extract. "For your first time intentionally traveling, you did an okay job."

"Gee, thanks."

"If I give you a compliment, you deserve it, which is why it rarely happens."

No kidding.

"I'd like whipped cream today." A canister appeared.

I snapped off the top and pressed the button. The cream swirled out, while Kai watched with wide, neon-green eyes.

"Yummy."

She enveloped the drink in her hands and brought it under her nostrils. She brushed the tip of her nose against the whipped cream and giggled. "It's so fluffy."

When did this become my life?

She looked up and asked, "Do you trust the Stones?"

"I trust Trevor and Serenity enough to stop Jayden."

"Good."

"What I don't understand is how I traveled to a past that wasn't my original past. "

"This is confusing to the guides too. We are seeing changed pasts among other human time travelers as well. The only explanation is it was an alternate version of your past—a version where Serenity had met you."

Hmmm.

"I can't say more about your changed past because I don't know more. Everything is happening so rapidly now on Earth and in the spirit realm. At the very least, that past showed you that Serenity is a good human. You can trust her."

"But not Steven Stone."

I relayed the details of the conversation between him and me.

She nodded. "That sounds like a corporate raider human *and* he has the gift as well."

Yes. Trevor said he inherited traveling from his paternal side of the family.

I asked, "Have you met Steven like you've met Trevor?"

"No."

"Do you think Steven knows or senses that I have the gift?"

"I don't know. One thing I've learned is that corporate humans can disguise themselves well. I've seen some of the most corporate types be the most metaphysical."

Interesting.

"Look at Trevor and Serenity. Remember how he knew exactly where your tea mugs were?"

I nodded.

"That's because intuiting to him is like breathing. He doesn't even think about it.

"Serenity's always been top of her class, so her intellect combined with her developing intuition makes her an exceptional human."

"Same with Jayden."

"Unfortunately, yes." She frowned and placed her mug on the counter. "On a better note, I found your protection. In order to receive it, we must travel to The Meadow."

In a flash, we were floating in a cotton-candy space with the scents of lavender, rose, and honey. Below me was an opulent stream of lights, but not of light beings. Instead, these were sparkling gems of all varieties. Ruby, garnet, emerald, topaz, diamond, pearl, yellow citrine, amethyst—like the purple cave crystal on my nightstand—and so many more I couldn't identify. It reminded me of the aerial views of the twisting tulip fields of the Netherlands.

We landed right in the middle.

There we stood among the shimmering crystals, which did not poke or prod. They morphed into formless stones that glittered up to my knees. Their energy pulsed and welcomed, all calling out in telepathic voices, "Pick me!" I felt a profound sense of connection that awakened a flicker of courage. A gentle warmth blossomed in my chest and filled me with belonging and wonder.

"Quiet!" Kai yelled.

The voices stopped.

"Now you can focus. I'm using crystals for your protection. You must decide which ones. Feel into the experience and see which ones resonate with you."

I strolled around the field, gazing at the brilliance and taking in the scenery. Kai followed. There seemed to be an infinite number of choices, all of which gleamed in my direction. At my feet, the stones tingled as if I were receiving a delightful massage. Everything felt right and possible. I was on a high, like shopping at Harry Winston for the Hope Diamond.

"Don't get lost in the glitz and glamour, Indy."

As I refocused and continued my search, Kai explained, "You will use these crystals to protect you against the dark forces. If you're in trouble, they will create an energy field of safety and protection."

Beyond my control, my feet halted. A black stone glowed so bright that it dimmed the others. A second stone—a clear white quartz—repeated this pattern. These two crystals overpowered the entire field of the more beautiful, exotic, and exciting ones.

I looked at Kai. "The other crystals are more brilliant. Why am I choosing these boring ones?"

"Don't let them hear you say that."

"Oh—sorry."

"You're not choosing with your logical human mind. Your soul chooses."

My soul sounded basic.

"You've made your choice. I will get the gem carver out here to crack off a couple of pieces. When your protection is ready, I'll give it to you."

I breathed in the clean air. "I don't want to leave The Meadow. I feel so at peace."

She beamed. "The Meadow has that effect on humans and even light beings. It's good to have a break sometimes."

"It is."

"I have to get you back to Earth to continue your mission."

Kai transported me to Trevor's apartment, where I was left staring at a canister of whipped cream and an empty mug. The dullness of the human world had returned. It felt uninspiring and too grounded, clunky and dense. I already missed the sweet warmth of The Meadow.

#

Trevor hadn't texted in hours; I assumed he was getting answers and couldn't be disturbed. Serenity texted that she was staying in Boston to talk with the board members there. She kept hitting a dead end. Between her and Trevor, they had to uncover at least one piece of…well, something useful.

It had started to rain, so I took an Uber up to Harlem. I stepped out of the car onto the wet street. In the evening light, Tameka's building exuded the literary and artistic Harlem Renaissance. Langston Hughes, Zora Neale Hurston, Moms Mabley—they all could've lived on this street. It gave me chills, but there was no time to fan girl out. I got lucky because a person was exiting the building and held the door for me. I thanked him and slipped inside.

Apartment 6A. I got lucky again because the doorman must've been on break. I rode the elevator up to the sixth floor, walked to her door, took a breath, and rang the bell.

An older woman who appeared out of sorts said, "You lookin' for Tameka? She's down in the cafe, where she always is, writin' on a napkin."

Helpful.

"Don't worry, you can't miss her."

I thanked her and left.

There was only a diner, not a cafe. That had to be what the old woman meant.

I entered and spotted an absolutely gorgeous young woman with the silkiest black skin I'd ever seen, almost the color of night. She was a waif with cheekbone structure any woman would envy. My memory of her from high school was different. Tammy Harris was a gawky, nerdy teenager with frizzy hair and thick glasses. This duckling had indeed grown into a swan.

Unlike the last time I saw her in Trevor's past, she donned a bald head, which worked for her because she didn't need hair. It would distract from her sensual dark eyes and eyelashes, full ruby lips, and symmetrical, well, everything. If there were a modern Helen of Troy, this would be her. She scribbled on a napkin.

I walked over to her table. "Tameka Mokashu?"

"Yes" she said, narrowing her eyes in suspicion

"My name is Indy Kash. I tried texting you, but you didn't answer."

Her eyebrows raised. "You came all the way here? We could've set up a dinner or coffee."

"I know. Sorry to disturb you, but I was in the area."

"You looked up my address and came to where I live?"

Yeah, this looked bad. Using the excuse of *really* wanting to discuss flight attendant fashion wasn't going to cut it.

"I fly all the time, so my schedule changes constantly. I was in the area, so I figured why not? Sometimes you've gotta take a risk, right?"

She stared at me. Finally, she replied, "Sit down."

I noticed that her napkin was full of words and doodles. She quickly folded it and placed it to the side.

I pulled out the chair and sat. "I apologize for coming here without any warning. I went to school with your husband, as you know, and with you in LA."

Her eyes pierced. "Okay."

"I was a grade below you. I didn't remember you at first, but then I remembered, like me, you always read in the cafeteria at lunch. I did the same thing."

Her eyes flashed with recognition. "You're Pyro Girl!"

That hit like a bullet.

"Oh! I'm sorry. I didn't mean it that way. I—I—"

My voice softened. "It's okay."

"I'm sorry. That must've sucked."

"It still does."

Tameka remained silent for a while.

I scanned the restaurant. A server dumped silverware into a bucket, another laughed with a customer, and there were many empty chairs and booths. The city never recovered after the height of the pandemic. People had moved out in droves, never to return to the hustle and bustle, urine-soaked streets, and skyrocketing costs. A diner near us slurped a thick, chocolatey milkshake through a straw. I quietly seethed with jealousy.

Tameka finally said, "Why are you here? It's not for a fashion emergency. So say it."

She was already on the defensive, and I understood why. I was coming off like Joe from *You*. My only choice was to be honest.

"When you said that Jayden had said 'nice things' about me, was that true?"

"Maybe."

"It wasn't, right? Otherwise, you would've known I was Pyro Girl right away. You and Jayden never talked about me. If you had, he would've said many *not*-so-nice things. You read the *Globe* article and contacted me?"

She looked away.

"Your husband framed me for arson in high school. Did he tell you that?"

Her eyes met mine.

"I'm sorry, Tameka, but I think you know your husband isn't a good man. That's why you're living here and he's in Boston. If you do get into a nasty divorce, I can't imagine what he'll do to you. It could be much worse than what he did to me."

"Why do you care?"

"Because Jayden is building something big, and I know that you know. He may use it in a destructive way. We have to stop him before he does."

She broke into a laughing fit. "Wait, wait," she said while waving her hand. "Is this a joke? From Shirley, right? That girl is mental."

"No, it's not a joke. I'm coming to you because I need your help and you'll need mine if things get worse with Jayden."

I sounded like Trevor when he first tried talking with me in the FBO parking lot.

She stopped laughing. "All I know is you're a flight attendant. All this other stuff you've been saying, I think you're mental. You know nothing about me or my marriage. You think you'd come here because we're from the same hood? I moved to LA in high school. I was raised in Dorchester. LA was a *vacation* for me and the lifestyle I have now, all this—" She gestured with her palms. "—is because of my husband. You bloggers or social media people have come at me before. You're pathetic. Get out of my way, Pyro Girl."

She picked up her pen and napkin and stormed out of the diner.

I failed miserably…but at least I was consistent at something. My mind replayed the moment again and again. Each repetition sharpened and seared even more until I wished I could claw it out of my mind. I had really fucked up.

I hadn't known that she grew up in Dorchester. When Tameka was there, parts of it were very rough, where, yeah, I couldn't relate to her childhood. It was a small world over there too—Dorchester, Roxbury, Jamaica Plain. I knew this because I had volunteered in JP to fulfill my community service requirements.

I forced myself to order an Uber to Trevor's apartment. The entire way I thought of what a mess I had made. I had exposed myself even more to Jayden. If Tameka talked with him, which she might, he would be after me by tomorrow morning.

Shit!

Why had I acted so rashly?

I emerged from the car and dashed into Trevor's building to avoid rain on my hair. Then I nodded to the doormen and continued to Trevor's apartment. I rang the bell and heard a meow.

He opened the door holding oven mitts in one hand and Snowball standing by his side. "Welcome home, honey. How was your day?"

I cracked a smile. "Pretty shitty. Yours?"

Did I smell meatloaf? How *Ina Garten* of him.

"You cook?"

"I told you I did."

A glazed meatloaf rested on the countertop.

"Impressive."

"The secret is to baste it with ketchup on all sides. Why was your day shitty?"

"I met with Tameka, completely fucked it up, and now I'm exposed to Jayden. Can you top that?"

"Jayden visited me."

Whoa. He topped that all right.

"Tell me."

"I can do better than that."

When Time Flies by Jennifer Moreno (Ciotta)

He threw the oven mitts on the entry table, grabbed my hand, closed his eyes, and proceeded to walk through his front door. We raced through time and space and then we were back in the past.

#

We traveled to earlier that day at Trevor's apartment. The sun beamed through the windows, indicating it was late morning. The smell of meatloaf still lingered. Snowball curled herself into a ball on a couch and napped.

I was alone, observing his past, while Trevor must've jumped into his past body.

He was sitting on a couch, hunched over his phone like the rest of the world. Someone knocked at the front door. He rose and answered it. On the other side was Jayden.

I wasn't sure I was invisible, so I looked around for a place to hide. I scurried to the hallway bathroom and quietly snapped my fingers for Snowy to come, which she did. Perhaps Jayden would grow suspicious if he saw an unknown pet. I cracked the door. I really hoped that Jayden didn't need to pee or worse take a dump. That would be traumatizing.

Jayden said, "Hey man, can I come in?"

Trevor nodded.

"It smells good in here, Trev. I like to see you're still burning it down."

"I've always liked to cook."

Jayden grinned. "Yeah you have. Can we sit?"

Once they were sitting across from each other, each to a couch, Jayden said, "Trev, man, we go back a long way, and I know what happened earlier today was shocking. That's why I took the company jet down here to see you." He coughed a few times. I was sure he was hacking up evil. "There's no good way to say this: Stone Corp needed a change. Steven saw me as the best man for the job, and I took it."

Trevor glared.

"Sorry man. I know you or your dad or even Serenity wanted the job." He paused. "Listen," he said as he placed five fingers on his heart. "I want you to know there's a place for you at the company, but we have to make sure certain things are right, like diversity and hiring more women. I'll take care of you, but you have to be patient."

I was sure Trevor knew that Jayden thought of him as a moron. The entire world thought that of Trevor, just like me with Pyro Girl.

"What about my father?"

Jayden shook his head. "I don't know, man. SJ is…well, he's not that business savvy." His eyes darkened. "I'll take care of him somehow."

I could sense Trevor's fury about to spill over, like he was about to physically attack Jayden. As if I were Trevor myself, I could feel the heat rising in my body. How could he keep doing this to people and get away with it?

Trevor finally responded, "I understand."

Jayden flashed his signature grin. "Thanks man. I appreciate the support." He looked around. "Plus, you're doing all right, Trev. You're definitely not poor and starving." He stood up and buttoned his suit jacket. "I have to go to a meeting before I leave the city—oh, by the way, did you see the list of BYF mentors? You're on there under 'young entrepreneurs.' I figure I'd leave it open-ended and let you decide. You've always been good at marketing and networking, so the kids can learn those skills from you. They're important."

Trevor ignored the bullshit and said, "Hey before you go, out of curiosity, what about Indy Kash? Why's she on the list?"

Jayden turned. "She's a woman of color who's not too fond of us. That night," his voice trailed off. "What happened was unfortunate and the video shows all the evidence, but we can't have another person come forward with any type of potential scandal. A woman of color's disempowered voice is heard these days. I had my private eye do research. She's had a stellar record since high school. She's pretty, looks good in a flight attendant uniform, and has an interesting career that other girls can aspire to. She's a tiny, brown Barbie."

The proverbial pot had spilled over. I was fuming.

He grabbed the door handle. "Gotta think of everything, Trev. Now that she has some prestige, what can she say? That we're the villains? Nah. If she's smart, she'll launch this into a brand, make money, and stay gracious. What recourse does she have? Refuse to mentor the kids from her old neighborhood?" He scoffed. "C'mon. She's smart. Lunch next week when we're home?"

Then he glanced at the powder room where I was hiding.

My body froze.

His gaze lingered. A little too long.

Trevor said, "Sure."

Did Jayden know I was there?

Alas, he turned around and left.

#

Trevor led us through the doorway and we returned to the present. The aroma of meatloaf filled the apartment.

I asked, "He looked at the bathroom. Do you think he knew I was in there?"

"I don't know."

"The Spirit Council said Jayden has extraordinary meta abilities. He could've sensed me."

Trevor frowned. "He could have. I've been noticing that things are changed when I revisit my original past. Look at what happened when we traveled to your past."

"Yeah, it's all…off." I chose my next words carefully. "You did a good job by going along with Jayden. That was smart."

"Most people think I'm stupid, so I appreciate that."

"I hate to admit it, but after getting to know you, you're not as dumb as I thought."

He laughed. "Thanks, but there's more that happened after Jayden left."

We traveled to his past again. This time I was sitting on the couch with Trevor.

"Why am I my present self who observes my past sometimes, but not others? Sometimes I'm my past self, and other times I stay my present self?" I asked.

"I guess it depends on the situation."

"Does that happen with you?"

"Usually, I'm an observer. It's been switching lately."

The oven timer dinged, as did the alarm on Trevor's cell phone. He wore his plaid mitts and cracked open the oven door. He slid out the baking dish of meatloaf and placed it atop the stove. I couldn't believe he was such a homemaker. I would imagine a typical weekday would include porn stars, Instagram models, and orgies. Instead, I was watching a single, thirty-one-year-old man with all the money in the world cook his own meatloaf and listen to a true crime podcast.

There was a knock at the door.

"Come in," he shouted.

In walked a gorgeous, maybe nineteen-year-old, blond, tall drink of water who was a cross between a *Sports Illustrated* swimsuit cover and a fantasy woman on OnlyFans. She glided over to Trevor as if it were a runway and threw her arms around him.

My face reddened. My last boyfriend had a personality that was like watching paint dry. I didn't have strong feelings for him either way. But Trevor Stone…really?

I hadn't been close to a man in a while, so perhaps it was the proximity? Or was it that we were in this heightened, all-encompassing situation together? Or was there something more. A connection? Did Trevor feel it too?

She pressed her body against his. Then she glanced at me on the couch and wrinkled her nose. "Who is that?" she asked in an Eastern European accent.

"That's my friend. We're working on a project together."

"Oh," she said with disinterest.

A buzzer sounded. He and the woman untangled.

"I wasn't expecting anyone," he said. He hit the intercom on the wall. "Hi Jacque, who is it?"

"Mr. Stone, it is bike messenger."

A couple minutes later, a young man appeared at the door wearing a bike helmet with an envelope in hand.

Trevor said, "Hey there! You have something for me?"

"Are you Jayden Mokashu, sir?"

Without missing a beat, Trevor replied, "Oh man, he just stepped in the bathroom. I think he ate some bad oysters or something. Might be a while, man."

He flashed his signature grin. The messenger was no match for Trevor's charm and the powerful energy he emanated when he was fully confident. The young man smiled shyly and handed him the slip, to which Trevor signed and gave him a wad of cash. The messenger passed the envelope to him, said thanks, and left.

The door closed. He glanced at the woman, who was rifling through his fridge. He tore open the manila envelope, removed the papers, and flipped through each stapled sheet as he skimmed.

"Shit," he mumbled.

"What Trevvie?" the woman said.

"Sorry Anna, but I have to be somewhere."

She closed the fridge and slinked over to him. She wrapped her arms around his neck and purred like a kitten in his ear, "No play time?"

She was good. Even I might've been turned on.

"Not right now. Let's meet for a drink later."

"Later, I walk in show. You come see me. You my biggest fan, yes?"

"Sure. Sounds good. Later."

We traveled to the present, but this time, Trevor plunked us down on the area rug. Snowball looked up from grooming herself. It wasn't a soft fall; it wasn't hard either.

"Man, I was getting better at landings. I don't know what happened?"

I sat up and threw my hands in the air. "What's in the papers?"

"The worst thing possible."

CHAPTER FOURTEEN

"The board members told me that Jay has allocated half a billion dollars to a secret project."

Exactly what Steven had said.

"Okay, but what's in the *papers*, Trevor?"

"From what I could piece together, I think he's trying to take the Time Machine public. Like sell it or something."

A wild mix of dread and awe crashed through me. "Are we talking mass production here?"

"Could be."

No, this couldn't be happening. "How would he do it?"

"We'll have to figure that out, too. He must have a working prototype."

A Time Machine for sale. Such a cruel novelty.

"Why couldn't you've just told me about the papers? Why did we have to return to your past? I sat there while some girl pawed you."

He smirked. "Jealous?"

I rolled my eyes. "Whatever. Let's go back to Jayden. Let me see those papers."

"I bike-messengered them over to our New York headquarters. Otherwise, he would've been suspicious. Do you think he planted those papers to throw us off?"

"Did you take any screenshots?"

"A couple. A lot of it was corporate jargon."

"Let me see, and then I can give you an answer."

He unlocked his phone and handed it to me. I viewed the last two screenshots. One was corporate jargon, but I got the gist. Jayden wanted to sell a "service" to the public. It was vague. He alluded to SpaceX and Virgin Galactic. The next screenshot was of a study that referenced Nikola Tesla. The title of the page was Tesla's famous quote: "I could see the past, the present, and the future at the same time." It discussed Tesla's time-travel experiment in his lab with his assistant, and a snippet concerning the wrongdoing of the Philadelphia Experiment.

I halted breathing for a second. If Jayden took anything from Tesla's experiment, this would be a bloodbath the world couldn't fathom.

After I finished reading, I said, "He's telling you something. Sending you a message. With the whole BYF thing, Jayden's not only onto you but me as well. He's telling us to back off. Has he texted you to ask if the papers he messengered showed up here?"

"No."

"That's definitely a message. The way he looked at the bathroom before he left, he knew I was in there. I'm sure of it. Shit."

The unknown loomed so large. This was a game I had never played and certainly didn't understand. I had mistakenly thought Jayden and I would be competitors in school. Now, I wasn't sure anyone could compete with Jayden—human or otherwise.

Trevor stood up and moved over to the couch. I did the same. Rain was coming down harder now. It beat against the windows.

I asked, "Why would Jayden go through all the trouble of messengering papers and playing this whole game? Why wouldn't he come out and say, 'back off'?"

"Because that's him. He thrives on mind games. Think about what he did to you in high school. It was a big production, right?"

I nodded.

"Yeah, that's his thing. He has a flair for the dramatic."

"Same ole Jayden."

"Yeah."

"What did the board say?"

"Nothing that helped. I've known these people forever and they were too scared to talk."

"What about SJ? He's on the board, right? But you and Serenity aren't?"

"Yeah. Jayden's maneuvering where everyone else has been blackmailed with the exception of my dad, but who knows? He's been quiet and chooses to stay out of it. Any vote will go in Jayden's favor."

"Why do you think your dad isn't being blackmailed?"

"He's a pretty innocuous guy. With the exception of what he did to you, Dad doesn't ruffle feathers."

I wasn't so sure of that. If SJ could destroy my life without a care in the world, who's to say he's innocuous? He was just like any other billionaire, willing to step on the little guy.

"Have you gotten ahold of SJ?"

"Serenity ran into him at the house. She tried to ask him what was going on. He muttered something about 'stay out of this mess,' and left."

I threw him a hard look.

"Yeah okay. My dad's response doesn't sound good, but I really don't think he's involved."

It was too convenient that SJ was removed from everything. I let it go for now. After all, it was Trevor's and Serenity's father. I had to tread lightly.

Trevor asked, "Did you understand the stuff about the Philadelphia Experiment?"

I actually did. At some point during the AP physics class, I had stumbled upon Tesla's experiment while searching electromagnetic fields online.

"I do. Tesla allegedly teleported a U.S. naval ship. The ship disappeared and teleported from Philadelphia to Norfolk, Virginia and then reappeared in Philadelphia. Many of the sailors became fused together with the ship; their limbs were sealed to the metal. Other sailors developed severe mental disorders or other mysterious illnesses."

"That's gruesome. Is it true?"

"Honestly, I don't know for sure." I wondered aloud, "It's even worse that Jayden is citing it. Has he used the Time Machine to experiment on other people?" I shuddered at the thought. "I'm not sure how much he's achieved. If he's citing the Philadelphia Experiment, that's teleportation, which is different than time travel. Teleportation doesn't affect the physical space, but time travel is where we move through physical space and warp it in a way."

"I know I'm a time traveler, but this is a bit over my head."

"Teleportation is like the transporter machine on *Star Trek*. 'Beam me up, Scotty,' you know?"

"How do you know so much about this stuff?"

"I watched *Star Trek* when I was grounded, and I know how to use the internet."

In my head, I mulled over the details of Tesla's invention then spoke them aloud to Trevor. "Two sailors had been down in the generator room of the *USS Eldridge*, the ship of the Philadelphia Experiment, and the steel beams had protected them from the gruesome result. They time-traveled to 1983 to Montauk Air Force Base, but even forty years into the future, scientists couldn't stop the Philadelphia Experiment. So, the sailors traveled back to 1943 and shut down the generator. However, the damage was done and the energy that released from the generator could not be destroyed."

"What a shitshow," he said.

"Yeah. The electromagnetic field—created to make the ship invisible to the enemy—had spun out of control. The actual physical object, the generator, had unleashed mass chaos but didn't wreak havoc alone. Its partner was the unharnessed energy that released from it.

"If the Time Machine were to go rogue, it would be *the energy* from the Time Machine that would be the genie that couldn't be put back in the bottle."

"Damn."

I said, "Following the arson event when I practically lived in my room, I had watched a series on quantum physics. In one episode, a scientist had discussed—what was it called?—oh yeah, *negative energy density* and how it was necessary for energy teleportation…and that energy teleportation acted similar to an electromagnetic field.

"Energy could be teleported, like on *Star Trek*.

"An electromagnetic field could be created."

This idea reminded me of something I couldn't quite put my finger on. The deep recesses of my brain lit up. I wandered and routed around the spiritual memories of pasting magazine photos on a vision board—never to be repeated again—and a trauma therapist singing to my colon. No, that wasn't it. Then I remembered those hands. The magical hands that beamed energy at me from across time and space through a computer screen.

"Long-distance reiki," I said. "That is energy teleportation."

"I know what that is. I've watched a couple of YouTube videos on it."

The reiki healer did it with her mind, and at the session's end, she raised her hands and shot powerful energy through the video conference screen. She did help me. Alas, my mindset corrupted any form of healing, and a week later, I had returned to my miserable self.

"There's something about this idea of teleportation and reiki, but it's not coming together. Anything for you?"

He shook his head.

Man, I wished I had read more, researched more, hell, stayed at private school to learn more. Jayden was so brilliant, and here I was completely stumped, unable to nail down this possible start of a theory.

Trevor interrupted, "Listen, I'm sorry about you having to see the Anna thing. I'm not into her. We use each other to pass the time."

"She seemed *pretty* into you."

"We've hooked up a few times, but she's high maintenance. All I am to her is a green card with money attached. She'll move on to another billionaire's grandson tomorrow."

That was probably true.

Trevor Stone could get any woman he wanted. I couldn't imagine the amount of women who dated him for money alone. It must be hard to tell who was real and who wasn't. Same with friends too. Look at what happened with Jayden.

I certainly didn't have his money "problems," but I did understand the inability to trust others. Rich or middle-class, at times, people sucked.

Trevor went into the kitchen and opened a bottle of expensive whiskey. "Want some?"

"No, thanks."

"You never told me about your day."

I relayed the surprise meeting with Steven, Kai's visit, and the miserable fail with Tameka.

He poured the whiskey in a low-ball glass and sipped. "Damn. Grandpa's hiding something. And Kai is seeing these changed pasts among other travelers—what's that about?"

I shrugged.

"With Tameka, you've got her thinking. I don't think she'll tell Jay right now. They're in a bad place, and he's consumed with the Time Machine. Where do we go from here?"

"We have to find that Machine and the plans and destroy both."

"Even if we do, what's to stop Jay from building it again? He could travel back in time and copy the plans, right?"

Fuck me.

"You're right, Trevor. We don't have the time to figure this out. We know the Machine exists, and all we can do right now is destroy it."

I glanced at my phone. It was getting late. "I'm taking Snowball and driving home. Let's get some sleep and meet here early tomorrow morning."

"We haven't had dinner yet. I looked up what 'inflammatory bowel disease' is and cooked a meatloaf with ingredients I think you can eat."

My head whipped over to him. "You did?"

"Yeah, it was easy."

That was the nicest thing anyone had done for me in a long time.

To my surprise, my heart began to expand and ache as if I were in deep meditation. The color green spiraled through the center of my chest. The feeling was immense, as if my heart had grown wings and filled the entire sky with pure love. The sensation rushed down my spine instead of its usual upward motion—from the heart to the solar plexus to the sacral chakra, where it stopped and hovered. I felt a vibrant orange and an explosion of…intense sexual desire.

Whoa there, tiger.

"It's pouring out there. I don't think you should drive. I have a guestroom."

I was so caught off guard and my sacrum was practically jumping out of my body. "I don't have pajamas."

"You can borrow anything you want. I sleep naked anyway."

He winked.

That was *not* helping my situation.

He seemed like a partier. Perhaps he would drink most of the whiskey and pass out, and that would be the end of it. Either way, I had to get out of this room.

"Thank you so much for the meatloaf. Really. I'll eat it in the morning. Where's the guestroom?"

His face fell. "You don't want any?"

Oh boy.

He was looking extremely cute and disappointed. My vagina throbbed. I decided to lie.

"No, I'm sorry. I'm really tired."

He pointed. "Right there with its own bathroom. That's where the litter box is too. I keep it there when Frank visits. Extra clothes are in the dresser."

I looked down at Snowball. She must be starving. "Crap. I forgot to feed Snowball."

"I gave her a small piece of meatloaf earlier. She's fine."

He thought of everything. "Thank you, Trevor. Night."

"Night."

In the bathroom, Snowball stepped into the litter box and did her business. I removed my clothes. Underneath, I had a soft, almost translucent tee shirt, minus a bra. Why wear one when my tits were this perky? I'd start when I was thirty-one.

I walked out to the bedroom, opened a dresser drawer, and selected a hoodie. I pulled it over my head.

Then in the bathroom again, I gazed into the mirror and said, "There." I was officially unattractive to someone like Trevor, who was used to La Perla and Coco de Mer.

I had to wipe off my makeup, yet if I was spending the night in a man's apartment—*whoa*, I had to check myself. It *had* been a while since I'd had sex, but with Trevor that would possibly destroy the sort of friendship we were trying to build. If we solved this crisis—and that was a big if—he'd forget about me anyway.

He *had* given me his jacket when I was cold, prepared a nice meal for me, and kind of flirted with me. On the other hand, he was cozy with another woman hours ago. On the other hand, again, this was a unique situation and my feelings weren't in my head. On the last hand—apparently I was the goddess Durga with all the arms—I hadn't been with a man that excited me…well, ever. Were his gestures friendship, kindness, or something more?

No. Nope. I should be thinking about the Time Machine and how we can destroy it.

I heard him stride down the hallway and enter his bedroom. He didn't shut the door.

Dammit! I could go back and forth all night long and still not come to an answer. All I knew was that my sacral chakra was on fire, or at least it felt that way. My solar plexus began to rev up too. It called for me to claim my personal power and go fuck the shit out of Trevor.

I emerged from the bathroom and marched straight into Trevor's bedroom. No knocking. He was sitting up on the bed with a pillow between him and the headboard. He was consumed with his phone.

He looked up. "Yes?"

His shirt, pants, and socks were strewn across the oversized chair. I didn't see underwear of any kind, so he must be wearing them, and I noticed he was shirtless—and that he was in good, actually, great shape. Thin but he had small muscles and a sculpted chest.

Without thinking, I blurted, "Trevor, do you have feelings for me?"

Rain pelted against the window wall.

"You surprised me." He paused. "What about you? Do you have feelings for me?"

I peered at my feet. "I hate admitting it, but maybe. All this time we've spent together, and I didn't realize how lonely I was until we started hanging out. I don't know."

I felt like a little girl wearing a hoodie and hoping my crush said that he liked me back.

He twisted his body to face me. "I say 'I'm not sure' because you're different than the other women from my past." His voice softened. "India, look at me."

I couldn't. I was so humiliated.

"Please."

I met his eyes, which seemed to radiate sincerity. Or was he a really good actor who had yet to win an Oscar?

"I've never really been friends with a woman before dating her. We're friends, so—"

The way he gazed at me and upped and downed my body, even while I was wearing sweats, signaled that he was interested. We both were. My eyes shifted to the nightstand where his glass of whiskey rested. It had the same amount as when he was in the kitchen. He wasn't drunk.

When Time Flies by Jennifer Moreno (Ciotta)

I remembered my mom's words: *Be open to the possibility…*

This was an unusual time to take her advice.

Okay, fuck it.

I removed my hoodie and exposed my almost sheer tee shirt. My nipples hardened and poked at the fabric. He stared intensely. I crawled onto the bed as he watched my every move and positioned myself on his lap to straddle him. He grabbed my hips, guiding me closer. I hadn't had anyone touch me like this in a long time. Pleasant electric shocks danced in my hips, pelvis, and vaginal area, deep inside my body. He slid his hands to my lower back and I leaned in to kiss him.

"Wait," he interrupted.

"Jesus!" I said, inches away from his face. I guess we were putting on the brakes.

"I want to make sure you really want to do this. I don't want you to regret anything."

"I want to do this. Do you?"

"Hell yes."

I leaned in once more and parted my lips and kissed him. Once I did, I couldn't stop. Our mouths, tongues, lips all synced together and I tasted the whiskey on his breath. He tugged at my shirt, and I lifted my arms for him to remove it. He happily groaned when he saw my exposed breasts. I leaned back as he kissed down my neck, to my nipples. His kisses and how he caressed my lower back lit a fire in me I hadn't felt…ever. He cupped my ass and then took one hand and rubbed my clitoris. *Oh God, that feels good.*

"You're so wet."

I shifted myself off his lap, tugged at his boxer briefs, and threw them on the floor. He was hard and ready. He reached for his wallet on the nightstand, fished out a condom, and rolled it on. I straddled him again and let him inside. *God that feels amazing.*

I rode him until we both moaned, gasped, and shook. I came harder than I ever had. I caught my breath as he flipped me onto my back and thrust in and out until he couldn't hold it anymore. He let out a prolonged yell.

To my surprise, after we were done, he pulled me close to him, and I lay in the nook between his shoulder and chest. Like our friendship, we didn't mindlessly chatter or say things we didn't mean. We were both figuring out what our relationship was, amidst all the confusion and our individual worlds.

As I traced his chest, I sighed with relief.

"What's wrong?"

Oh, the sigh must've sent the wrong message. "Nothing. I'm good. I was thinking about how I'm on birth control. That feeling of relief made me sigh."

"Me too," he said and kissed the top of my head.

I got up to use the bathroom, because I was old enough to know to pee after sex.

I examined myself naked in the bathroom mirror, and for some reason I felt like I was seeing what Trevor saw. Smooth brown skin, messy hair, and a glow that only followed good sex.

The world hummed around me. Everything seemed perfect in this moment. I allowed myself to let my guard down and connect to someone. I'd never done that before, even with my exes and one-night stands.

With Trevor, I felt the heat between us, the deep connection, and the chemistry. Something was definitely there, which I'd been fighting. I could just *be*.

Is this love?

I stared into the rectangular mirror. I wasn't sure yet if this was love, but I knew that I cared about him, and that I finally cared about myself enough to let someone else into my world.

God, all of these epiphanies from sex?

#

I woke up in the morning no longer on the high from last night. In fact, I was feeling…awkward. I was in bed with a man whom I'd always detested. To him, I was sure that I was yet another notch on his belt.

I looked down at myself. There I was in a see-through tee shirt that barely covered my ass, and in front of Trevor?

Well, I *did* sleep with him.

I heard water running and smelled eggs cooking…in butter? I threw on the hoodie and walked into the kitchen. Snowball was curled up on a pillow. I sat down next to her, kissed her nose, and stroked her head.

"Morning," Trevor said as he scrambled eggs in a pan. "Did you sleep okay?"

I yawned. "I think so."

"I had eggs and sourdough bread delivered. I read online that sourdough doesn't have much gluten."

"Oh." He kept surprising me. "That's perfect. That's so nice of you."

Should I throw my arms around him and kiss him on the neck as he cooked?

Maybe.

I was sensing more of a friend vibe from him, so I stayed put.

Sunlight blared through the window. I checked my phone. "It's seven o'clock. Have you heard from anyone?"

"Not yet."

"We need to find that Machine. Where do we start?"

"We start with a quick breakfast. I've hardly eaten in two days."

"Same with me. I'm starving."

"Good sex will do that."

Okay, definitely not a friend vibe. Phew.

Crap. My sacral chakra was heating up again.

Yes, finding and destroying the Time Machine and its plans was top priority, but my libido was a *very* close second.

"Cooking can wait."

My pointer finger motioned "come here." I placed Snowball on the rug, who pranced away with an annoyed swish of the tail. Trevor shut off the burner and came over.

I grabbed his face and kissed him. He moved his lips down to my neck. I couldn't help but smile. He removed my clothes, and then his. He caressed my body all over and kissed my shoulders, breasts, stomach, and then my clitoris. I moaned.

The next thing I knew I was kneeling on an oversized couch cushion and he was thrusting in and out as he rubbed my clit. It was *so* fucking hot. He continued rubbing and thrusting until I squirted all over.

I turned over and lay on the couch, dripping on the expensive leather. I was sure it had been dripped on before, so I wasn't worried.

As I caught my breath, I said, "Okay, I'm good. We can have breakfast."

He burst out laughing.

BOOM! BOOM! BOOM!

We jumped. Snowball meowed from across the room.

"Who the hell is knocking like that?"

Trevor threw on his clothes and I did the same with my tee shirt and hoodie. I scurried to the guest bathroom, lowered the toilet seat, and peed. Then I found my underwear and jeans from yesterday, slid them on, and exited the room to find…

Serenity and Frank.

"Hey gorgeous! It's me, your favorite passenger!"

"Serenity, hey. Hi Franky," I said in a baby voice. He meowed. I noticed Snowball hiding behind the kitchen counter and peeking her head out.

"Holy shit, that flight, right?! I thought we were for sure going to die!"

Trevor said, "What?"

I quickly explained how we almost joined the Mile-Under Club.

"Scary. I've never had that happen on a PJ."

Serenity eyed Trevor and then me. "You both have that after-sex glow!"

"Serenity, Jesus!"

I walked over to Frank and bent down. "Look at you. You're such a big boy." He purred as I petted his head. "You'd make a good boyfriend for Snowball. She likes older men."

"Who's Snowball?" Serenity asked.

"My cat."

"Is she cute? Frank only goes for cute."

"She's the cutest. She's over there," I said and pointed. Snowball was hiding. "Well, she *was* over there."

Serenity bent down and said to Frank, "Oh Franky, would you like to meet Miss Snowball?" He meowed. "Of course you would. We just have to wait for Miss Snowball to come out of hiding." She stood up and turned to me. "Where do you live? Here on the Upper West Side?"

"No, in Hackensack."

She made a face. "Gross—oh sorry, I'm a Sagittarius. I'm too blunt; it's my worst quality. You were living in Lower

Allston when I met you. You went from one shithole to another!" She put her hand over her mouth.

I really did.

"I'm saving for a house."

"Oh that's nice. Where?"

Man, she loved to dig.

"Serenity, enough with the questioning. Indy has a great apartment. She decorated it herself; you'd like all the crystals and woo-woo shit."

Go Trevor.

A squeal escaped from her mouth. "Really?! We have *so much* in common!"

I doubted that. She seemed pretty enthusiastic about…everything. Did she take Blond Satan's uppers? I examined her pupils.

"Why are you looking at me like that? Trevor, why is she looking at me like that?"

"You seem like you're high. I'm checking."

"What's your assessment?"

"You're sober."

She roared with laughter. "Holy shit. Trevor, your girlfriend is funny as fuck."

I braced myself for "she's not my girlfriend" or "we're not dating" or an embarrassed expression across his face, but nothing changed.

Serenity then pointed to the glossy couch cushion that Trevor must've quickly wiped. "I knew it smelled like sex in here."

"Ser, please—"

"I mean tiny woman," she said as she upped and downed me. "I get it. Oversized cushion under the knees, doggy style?"

"SERENITY ENOUGH!"

She smirked. "Sorry, Trev. Just living vicariously."

Before Trevor could open his mouth again, she said, "You need to get dressed—in a suit. Grandpa called an emergency meeting. He's in the city. I don't know what it's about. I tried texting and calling, but you had your phone on Do Not Disturb." She sniffed him. "Shower fast. You smell like vagina."

"If our board members knew about your mouth—"

"Oh trust me, they know. Go! Now!" She shooed him away.

"Before I shower, Indy tell her about your day yesterday."

I quickly gave her the synopsis.

"Why wouldn't Grandpa ask me to speak with Tameka? We *are* friends after all."

Trevor scoffed. "No you're not."

"I went to her bridal shower *and* bachelorette party for Chrissake."

"That doesn't count and you know it. Those are business obligations. I don't even think she likes you."

She narrowed her eyes. "Everyone likes me."

Snowball then appeared out of nowhere. She crept up to us and let out a huge meow. We broke into laughter. She and Frank hissed, leapt, and swatted until they realized each other was harmless and a fun playmate.

Serenity glanced at her phone. "Shit, we have to go. Trevor, shower."

He threw up his hands as if to say *what am I gonna do but listen* and I gave him an affirming smile.

"Let's take a seat, well, not there," she said as she pointed to the sex spot.

Instead of sitting, she stood in front of a window wall and gazed out to the Park. The back side of her body was as annoyingly perfect as the front. But there was more to her than looks. The way she commanded her brother and how she switched from teasing sister to boss bitch in a matter of seconds. She had so many layers to peel.

"I knew you'd be back someday," she said. "So did Frank." He swished his tail and she picked him up for a cuddle. "Trevor, he's a work in progress. You gotta stick with him and mold him. He's loyal, chill, smart in his own way, but he doesn't give a shit about business stuff. Yes, he went to business school and it's in his blood, but he's not a natural. Our dad's the same. Both disappointments to Grandpa."

Why was she telling me this? I'd thought we'd talk about the trip with Blond Satan or Tameka or stopping Jayden from world domination. I didn't know how to respond.

She set Frank on the floor. "When I was ten years old, I watched you vaporize and disappear with my own eyes. Frank saw it too. Isn't that right, Franky-poo?" He purred. "Before then, I'd been hearing voices and seeing things. I thought I was losing it, until I realized that, nope, it's just that I can connect with the Spirit World. That's how I connected with your guide, Kai."

Where was this going?

"As a child, she saw me, a lonely little girl and gave me a sense of peace. Maybe not in words, but I could always feel her presence and unconditional love."

"I tried going into Trevor's past with him, but the Universe wouldn't allow it. I stood there while Trevor faded away. That was the saddest day of my life, realizing that I had a glass ceiling and I'd hit it."

Serenity Stone had everything a human could want: beauty and intelligence of the highest degree, money, a world-class education, but the one thing she wanted was out of her reach. I had it. So did Trevor.

"You have gifts too, Serenity. Money, power, intelligence, and intuitive abilities. We'll need all of our gifts to stop Jayden."

She turned around. "Yes, we will. Let's get this fucker."

CHAPTER FIFTEEN

Serenity and Trevor had left in a flurry of gestures and trailing words. My phone chimed five minutes later. It was a link to, oh, *Boston Celebs Podcast*. The title of the episode was: "Breaking News! A Breakup Worse Than Brad & Jen!" I pressed play.

"As you all know, I usually don't drop an episode today…but I received some juicy news early this morning! A little birdie close to the Mokashus told me they're officially splitting! We've all heard the rumors, but this anonymous source had confirmation that Tameka Mokashu had purchased an apartment in New York City—with her own funds. She and her husband Jayden, now CEO of Stone Corp, have not been seen together in ages. They were last spotted at The Bunny Hop fundraiser in April. Now we're in November, approaching the holidays.

"The source also said that Jayden has retained the absolute shark of divorce attorneys: Abe Cohen. We all know Cohen is the modern version of Roy Cohn, which is terrifying. Tameka should be shaking in her designer boots. Good luck girl, because if Jayden talked to all the best lawyers in town and in New York, then she can't hire them due to attorney-client consult privilege.

"We'll keep you posted as more information comes our way. Until then, sit tight because it's about to get medieval."

I was sure that Serenity leaked this to the press. That way, Tameka would be put in a vulnerable position and looking for allies. She had to know that anyone connected to her husband's world would take his side. He wielded too much power.

I sighed.

I knew how this would end for Tameka. Once Jayden found his target, he was ruthless. He would dismantle her life piece by piece. I couldn't let him do that to one more person, especially one more woman.

Boston Celebs Podcast had been useful so far. I clicked through the episode list and downloaded a few. After that, I decided to clean the couch so Serenity wouldn't make another comment. I placed the oversized cushion back on the correct sofa and then wiped the other leather cushion. There. She couldn't utter a word. But who was I kidding?

I finished scrambling the eggs that Trevor had started to cook for me. I had two eggs, a slice of meatloaf, a piece of toast, and sliced myself an avocado with a side of blueberries. I'd hardly eaten lately, and who knew when I would eat again with everything happening so fast.

Snowball meowed. Frank rounded the corner and looked hungry too. I opened and closed cabinets in a desperate search for cat food. I found two cans. I peeled back the lids and dumped them into bowls. Snowball devoured hers, while Frank ate demurely. Yesterday, Trevor had put a large water bowl on the floor near the refrigerator. It still had plenty for both cats. I'd have to clean the litter box later.

I sat at the kitchen counter and ate my breakfast while I listened to one episode then the next. The meatloaf was really good. I mostly ate the inside because I didn't want all that sugary ketchup.

There wasn't much useful information in the episodes, except for the host recounting the list of models that Trevor had boned. I just *loved* hearing that. I was about to press play on the third when Trevor and Serenity burst through the door.

"We've got something. We think we may know where Jayden's hiding the Time Machine."

My face whipped around toward them as my phone nearly slipped from my hand. Whoa, I couldn't believe they found out something this fast. "How?"

She continued, "Grandpa had this meeting to tell us he wants to immediately form his new company so Jayden doesn't have his hands all over it."

"The green private jet company?"

"Yep. He purchased a property upstate where he could demolish buildings and build a runway, factory, and hangars. It's a fifteen-minute flight from the city."

"Where?"

"The old insane asylum," Trevor said.

Oh. *There.*

I recalled the gory history. The rich dumped their "undesirables" there to be tortured, experimented on, and cast aside. "Undesirables" including people with Down syndrome, autism, and those causing "domestic trouble." Doctors performed frontal lobotomies, insulin shock therapy, and electroshock therapy.

The world was a fucked-up place.

Serenity typed on her phone and said, "Okay, I've got something. It says: 'As the hospital dwindled into nothingness by the 1990s, many of the buildings became dilapidated as wildlife, plant life, mold, and asbestos overran them. A developer bought the almost *900 acres'*—geez, nice purchase, Grandpa—'and eighty buildings, but he vastly underestimated the scope of the project, and it fell through. A Christian college tried again, only to violate building codes and see its project also come to a standstill.' I guess it's not public info that Grandpa bought it yet."

I said, "You think Jayden would have the balls to put a secret laboratory on Steven's property?"

They both gave me an *are you kidding me* expression. "Duh. Sorry."

Trevor said, "It's perfect. Indy, you saw his old lab. It was an abandoned building. If he's CEO of Stone Corp, no one would question him on the property, especially if he keeps out of sight. Plus, it's *nine-hundred* acres and eighty buildings in a remote area."

"That is a lot for security to guard."

"It's impossible unless there's a SWAT team there 24-7."

I thought aloud, "That place must be haunted."

"Totally!" Serenity lit up. "Next year, I'm doing a paranormal investigation there on Halloween night. I have the EVP equipment and can hire my parapsychologist friend—he's great. You both have to come."

The eve of All Saints' Day, the one night of the year the veil between the human and Spirit World thinned. That was a hard pass. The last thing I needed was an unwanted entity who made itself comfy in my apartment.

"Nope."

"Suit yourself," she said, reading my expression. "We have to get up there *now*. Jayden wouldn't keep anything on his phone either. The board *hates* him, and he's made no friends since taking over. They would've gotten together and hired an expert to break into his technology. I'm sure they already did and found nothing."

Trevor nodded. "When he was developing his original app, he was smart enough to keep his plans off the Cloud. He always had physical office space to draw out his plans, which he kept under lock and key. Drawing things out must be how his brain works."

I asked, "Why can't he 'draw things out' in one of his properties? I'm sure they're big enough for privacy."

"Not if you have a wife snooping to find shit against you for a divorce, and a cleaning crew, a housekeeper, a chef—"

"Got it." I paused. "Were you able to talk with Steven?"

"He keeps dodging us. The meeting finished and he left among a flurry of assistants."

Serenity typed on her phone. "I texted Kiki that we're helping Steven and asked if we can use the jet today. She actually said yes. No fight. Wow." She shrugged. "She must be filming at the house or throwing a private event there. That's the only time she doesn't care. I've already texted the pilots, and they'll be ready in Teterboro in an hour."

"Wait," I said.

They both looked up.

"What's wrong?" Trevor asked.

"Us taking the jet and landing it at Stewart…Jayden will find out."

"We can do the helicopter instead."

"We can't, Serenity. The private side of Stewart Airport is *small*, and if we took the helicopter to Sky Acres, that's even smaller. If Jayden has even one contact at either place, he'll know."

"You're right," Trevor said.

"I'll go. You two should stay here and be visible to Jayden so he doesn't get more suspicious. Who knows? He may have a PI tailing both of you."

"He may have one tailing you too."

"Maybe, but that's a risk I have to take." I sniffed myself. I hadn't rolled on deodorant in, well, too long. "I don't know when I'll be able to wash myself and change clothes again. Let me take a quick shower and I'll drive up there."

Trevor opened his mouth, but I stopped him. "I know it's dangerous, but I'll be in contact with you the whole time. See?" I held up my phone. "Technology is great."

"Not if you don't have a signal."

Okay, he was right.

"I have to get going." I started to walk down the hall when I stopped and said, "By the way we need cat food, beef bone broth—organic, grass-fed only—for my stomach, and someone needs to clean out the litter box."

As I twisted the shower faucet and waited for the water to heat, I heard them order delivery for cat food and bone broth. Why grocery shop in a crisis—or ever if you were the Stones? Then Serenity told Trevor to call the cleaning lady and have her take care of the litter box.

I shook my head, the absurdity pressing down like a weight.

What could possibly go wrong?

Oh right—everything.

#

As I pulled off The Hutch and onto 684, I realized that I was wearing dirty underwear.

God forbid I got into an accident and the EMTs had to pry two-day-old panties off my body.

There was no time.

If I found the answers we needed at the old psychiatric hospital, I could drive home, change, and pick up more things.

My phone rang. It was Ron. I pushed the answer button on my car screen.

"Indy, I have a trip for you—"

My stomach tightened.

"It popped up this morning. It's actually bringing Amanda Karrington and her pax from London. She extended her stay. You would commercial out there on Monday and fly back with her on Tuesday. You'd be paid for two days."

Only a couple days away. Technically, I was a contractor with Ron's company. I could refuse trips whenever I wanted, but I never did. This was my livelihood, I was saving up for a house, and I hadn't been tasked with rescuing humankind up to this point, so why not work all the time?

As a knee-jerk reaction, I blurted out, "Sounds good."

When Time Flies by Jennifer Moreno (Ciotta)

Oops.

"Great. I'll be in touch with you about your airline ticket, first-class for international, and send the trip sheet when it's ready."

"Thanks Ron. Bye," I said and pushed End.

Frustration needled through me. I would have to find a way out of it later.

The rest of my drive involved weaving through traffic among the weekend warriors heading upstate. There must have been storms up here, because all the leaves on the trees had fallen.

I arrived at the old psychiatric hospital and parked in the lot at the Harlem Valley train station across the street.

As I got out of my car, I felt the energy already flowing as I approached the property. It was creepy. Spiritual bodies crawled around me, and it felt as though they attempted to hollow out my soul. I shuddered. I had to get in, get the info, and get the hell out.

Recalling a soul healing workshop I had attended, I shielded myself in white light and muttered an awkward prayer of protection:

Please Universe, Source, protect me from any evil and make sure the evil does not stick to me in any way. The white light protects me, as does your love. I do not want to bring home any negative entities, or poltergeist and demons. And please help me find whatever Jayden is hiding. Amen.

I hadn't seen this place in a very long time. It was still the same.

The overgrown plant life surrounded the red brick buildings. Someone had attempted to clean up the property; the trees and bushes were pruned, then all work had ceased. The buildings loomed over a vast area, a spooky reminder of the past—and this was during the daytime. Serenity wanted to do a paranormal investigation at night?

Nope.

I checked that no one was around. I knew the town was wary of ghost hunters who trespassed, and I didn't want to raise any alarm bells. It was empty. The cold air blew through my damp curls. I shivered.

"How am I supposed to find where he set up shop on 900 acres?" I said aloud.

"And eighty buildings."

I jumped. Glowing next to me was Kai.

"Hi. No time for a PSL today. Jayden has blocked me from his energy field, and that includes this place. That means his energy either is here or has strongly been here."

"Which means I'm headed in the right direction?"

"It seems like it."

We both gazed up at the entry building.

"You can do this, Indy."

I wasn't so sure.

There was no time like the present. I looked straight ahead and took a step, about to begin my journey into the real unknown.

"Wait!" Kai said.

"What?"

When I turned around, I noticed two crystals hanging on a flesh-colored string around her neck. They sparkled. Kai removed the necklace in one swift motion. "Take this," she said and dropped it onto my open hand.

I recognized the gems—one black, one clear.

"The black tourmaline will protect you from negative energy and dark forces, while the clear quartz magnifies any stone with which it's paired. The Spirit Council blessed them specifically for your soul and energy. They will not work for anyone else." She flashed a loving smile. "I'm proud of you, Indy. Keep going."

I fastened it around my neck. The warm stones rested on my clavicle. My throat chakra instantly lit up and spun like a tiny fan inside my larynx. My energy center for self-assurance and expression had begun to open. I felt lighter and more secure in what I was about to do. Any feelings of my old, uncertain self faded away.

I turned around once more, my spirit guide and the world I'd always recognized at my back.

I took a deep breath, put one foot in front of the other, and walked into a space of possible no return.

CHAPTER SIXTEEN

The first building was a damp and musty refuge for mold. Water dripped from the ceiling, and with minimal sunlight, it was the type of cold that permeated my skin. I heard, saw, and felt nothing of importance, which made me realize: I couldn't do it this way.

I touched the crystals as I said aloud, "Please Source, guide me to where I need to go."

Nothing.

Try #2: "Please Source, allow my intuition to guide me to where I am supposed to be on this campus to stop Jayden. Please permit me to find the Time Machine or his plans…for the good of humanity. Thank you."

I waited.

Nope.

This was ridiculous.

Think Indy, think.

As I touched the crystals, I thought about how to use the sensory details of where I wanted to go and how to will myself to travel there. That wouldn't work here, because this wasn't my past and I had no idea where to go on this campus.

The crystals warmed more and tickled my skin.

Suddenly, I remembered Immanuel Kant's idea of physical space. He said that physical reality or space was a framework that the mind imposed upon the person, while the person had a sensory experience. He believed that space was the human way of understanding our sensory experiences and organizing them.

How could I, Indy Kash, cut through space in order to find what I needed?

Instinct guided me to put my hand on the center of my chest. I began to hum as if I were stimulating my vagus nerve—which I did for bouts of acid reflux.

The crystals heated more. I recalled Schelling's concept of "intellectual intuition." It was a higher form of perceiving that focused on the interconnectedness of all things. The person became aware of herself not as an object she perceives, but as a living act of consciousness itself. In other words, the act of knowing and being are one.

When Time Flies by Jennifer Moreno (Ciotta)

My heart was tugging at me to explore deeper—and not with the surface meditations I'd done many times. Not when I almost walked out on a Buddhist monk during an hour-long meditation class because it was so boring.

I had to focus like I never had before.

An inner knowing called for me to slow down and engage my five senses. From all the metaphysical stuff I had done, I knew one way to gain presence was to be in nature.

I remembered the Cher-touching-surfaces exercise too, but I didn't want to touch anything in this place.

I walked out the nearest door, down the steps, and stood behind the building. I peered at the grass. I reminded myself that this wasn't Chernobyl; it was an old psychiatric ward where people had suffered. Okay, that was bad too, but it wasn't radioactive. I removed my shoes and socks and stood on a patch of grass. The cement was filthy. Steven had quite the job ahead of him—*okay, stop!*

I wiggled my naked toes to still my mind and center myself. I began to chant "Ommmmm."

All I could think about was my cold feet…and how stupid I felt, again.

I inhaled, exhaled, and tried again. "Ommmmm."

This shit wasn't working.

I had to "go within." Yeah, I knew that, and I'd "gone within" before on a surface level, but how could I reach the depths of my soul? The core of my being? The center of my…center?

Where were psychedelics when you needed them?

I closed my eyes and held the crystals. I breathed in and out and focused on the slight breeze, the chirping birds, and the smell of autumn. The soft fabric of my tee shirt swaddled me, and the coziness of my light sweater brushed my forearms. My lips parted. My third eye began that electrical humming, while purple buzzed between my eyebrows.

My eyelids flew open.

All of a sudden, my feet started to walk, as if an invisible force were pushing me.

I hesitated.

I broke the spell.

The idea of walking on this dirty cement with glass shards and tetanus…

Dammit.

I put on my socks and shoes and did the whole process over until…I was wandering through the physical space of the area.

I wandered for quite a while. My calves ached. All the buildings loomed with their massive size, from the power plant to the main hospital. Then my feet halted in front of another downtrodden building with an ornate, teal-colored door. I took the psychic cue and attempted to pull it open.

It wouldn't budge.

I grabbed the knob with both hands and pulled with all my might. It sprang open and I stumbled backward onto the concrete.

I got up, dusted myself off, sneezed, and walked inside. I had lost a bit of the magic spell, so I caressed the crystals until the deep meditative state returned. Instinctively, I felt that I should protect the stones, so I tucked them under my sweater. I fished out my phone from inside my pocket and turned on the flashlight.

The interior was similar to the entrance building with its mustiness. In addition, there were items that I found…disturbing.

Large barber chairs with restraints sat in one room, while in another room, two chairs had a headrest with a metal skullcap attached and a chin strap. On the floor was a wire harness that led to a footrest monitor.

I shuddered.

In my research of this place, a long time ago, I recalled that it was rumored to have been used during the Cold War. For experiments on anyone the government considered "subversive" or "unpatriotic."

I had read about the underground tunnels and a laboratory for testing monkeys. It was a different time and people were scared shitless of everything in those days. Still, it was hard to understand the cruelty. I saw the connecting walkways where patients and staff must have somberly traipsed back and forth.

The feeling was beyond ominous. If Serenity did an investigation here, she might not be able to get herself out. The same would go for me if I didn't leave soon.

Even so, Jayden's energy was here…or some equivalent. Not his actual physical self, but he was here or had been. When his photo had appeared on my phone, it possessed the same dark energy: menacing with a side of maniacal.

I shut off the phone flashlight and stuffed it in my pocket. I decided to invoke a meditation I hadn't done in a while: "powering up." I zoomed each chakra color, starting with red for the root chakra, up my body until I ended with the purple color of the crown. I breathed in each color as it raced up like a vibrant rainbow of light from within.

My phone rang. I had cell service?

It was Mom.

"Hello?"

"Hi, doodoo."

"Mom, I'm busy. Can we talk later?"

"You're echoing. Where are you?"

"Uh. In a parking garage."

"Indy, we need to talk."

"Okay, but listen Mom, I seriously have to—"

"Kai visited me. She didn't explain much"—That sounded like Kai—"just that you may need support. What have you gotten yourself into, India?"

How could I even begin to answer that?

"There's something you should know—"

The line went dead.

"Mom? Mom?"

I tried calling her back to no avail. The one time I actually felt like talking to my mom, and I couldn't get through. *Figures*.

Was it my imagination or was the space around me widening? The walls and ceiling stretched and groaned. Everything became vast and endless.

I felt like I was on shrooms times ten. The edges of everything melted, and this new blur made my heart lurch. I was a thread in an endless tapestry, trembling with the awareness of how fragile I was.

My five senses dimmed to nonexistence. Keener senses replaced them. Everything was clearer, crisper—as if someone had turned the world's contrast up a notch. Edges gleamed, sounds had color, and time breathed. My body was a vessel pulsing in rhythm with something vast and wordless. Consciousness unfolded like an origami universe. I was both the paper and the fold.

My entire body had shifted into what I presumed was an altered state of awareness. I was guided to see and hear through my third eye.

The mustiness vanished. If I could smell the beams of the sun on a perfect spring day, that was the aroma and taste.

I'd tripped balls on Ayahuasca before, so I warned myself that the enjoyment could quickly take a dark turn. When I did Ayahuasca, I had one good memory of playing in the sandbox, then it turned into me reliving my childhood anger and puking and shitting in a bucket for hours.

Disorientation was the next sensation.

The room disappeared.

My entire being dismantled. Everything that bred familiarity, even my identity, shattered. I could separate truth from illusion in a millisecond.

I was not human anymore.

I was not me.

Did I exist any longer?

I had no idea.

What I did know was everything had changed at warp speed.

My energy then floated and bounced throughout the room. It raced around corners, zoomed through hallways, and rebounded off each stair as I ascended to what I could only perceive as an attic.

As soon the experience came, it went.

I was left standing on yet another grimy floor.

I touched all over my body. Yes, I was still here. I was back in my body.

What the fuck just happened?

My phone rang again.

It was Trevor this time. "You've been gone for hours. What's going on?"

"What time is it?"

"Just after four. The sun's about to set. Did you find anything?"

"No but I had a life-changing metaphysical experience."

"Cool. Get out of there."

I heard Serenity in the background say, "Did she contact any spirits? Ask her."

"I made contact with something, but I don't think it was a spirit." I paused. "I'm staying here until the job gets done. I'll text you when I find something. Don't worry. Bye."

I hung up. It was sweet that he was worried about me…or was I misreading everything and was he actually concerned about the dire situation at hand? He could be worried about both, and that was okay.

Something caught my eye.

I walked over to a closet with a missing door and swiped on my phone flashlight. The shelves had fallen onto themselves. Brown and clear glass bottles with rotting labels were piled in a heap. The few labels I could read showed medicines from an older time period. Lithium carbonate. Thorazine.

I peered in farther.

One shelf had been completely removed. My flashlight illuminated the space where it originally connected into the wall. I reached my hand inside to find…papers.

I shined the flashlight on them and tore through each one.

Sadly, they were pages from what looked like the diary of a juvenile prisoner. He discussed his crime in detail: killing a girl because she wouldn't pay attention to him. It was dated 1994. As I quickly skimmed it, I realized it was a suicide note.

Something told me to keep reaching farther into the space.

Bottles clanked as I wedged my body deeper into the closet. It reminded me of when a pax would lose their phone in the "hole of death," the open space from where I pulled out the tray table.

Dust entered my nostrils and I sneezed. My eyes began to water. All this exposure to mold, dust, and asbestos was *not* good for my health.

I felt a small, rectangular notebook and pulled it out. Bottles clanked more as I maneuvered out of the closet.

I wiped the dust off the little book and held my light over it. It had a solid black cover. I opened the pages and skimmed. It was gibberish to me, like Trevor had described when he found Jayden's papers.

When Time Flies by Jennifer Moreno (Ciotta)

It was Jayden's book for sure; I felt his dark and thick energy all over it. Then I saw a drawing of the Time Machine. It showed the metal box and eight wires, with one winding to the top of the page, the eighth chakra. The text was in a language I didn't recognize. It had a lot of the word "ta" and symbols and drawings.

Did they resemble what I could barely see of Jayden's notebook in the physics class?

I heard a noise. Footsteps.

"There's no trespassing on this property. Come out now and we'll go easy on you," a man yelled.

I froze.

As I peered out the window, I realized that, yep, this was definitely the attic. I couldn't jump or crawl out of a window. The sun was dropping fast. I had to get out of here.

The footsteps came closer.

I stuffed the notebook in my coat pocket and tiptoed out to the hallway.

I didn't hear the footsteps approaching. They must have been stopping in every room and searching each crevice. Then I saw flashlights.

I shut off my phone flashlight and was practically navigating blind. I used my third eye instead to intuit my steps.

The voices were down the hall at the other end. I darted my head left then right and ran as quietly as I could, like a ballerina on the balls of her feet.

A stairwell!

The footsteps sounded in the hallway. I ducked into another room—the one right next to the stairs. Almost free.

One yelled, "Where are you? There's nowhere to hide. Come out to play-yay."

Geez, quoting *The Warriors*. Loser.

I held my breath as the footsteps quickened toward me. They stomped into a room. Bottles crashed.

I bolted to the hallway, out the door, and down the stairwell as quietly and as quickly as I could.

If I survive this, I need to increase my cardio.

Finally at the bottom, I pushed open the door to the outside. The cold air rushed me. I stopped and looked up at the building. Flashlights moved floor by floor.

They'd heard me…and saw me.

The train station was across the street. Though the property was humungous and I thought I'd walked for miles, I'd actually been walking in circles. I ran as fast as I could to the station. From a short distance, the train was approaching. I looked over my shoulder to see the security guards scrambling to the last floor.

I held my breath and sprinted across the tracks.

Merely seconds after, the train pulled into the station. My chest heaved. The train doors opened and commuters poured out. I blended in with the others and strolled to my car. The train chugged onto its next stop.

I got into my car and pulled out of the spot. As I was driving away, I saw two men searching the crowd.

If the security guards saw what I looked like, I surely had a target on my back. I touched the little black book in my pocket and said aloud, "I hope you're worth it," and began my drive to the city.

CHAPTER SEVENTEEN

I sat on Trevor's couch sipping bone broth for my aching colon, while the softest Hermès blanket enveloped my body. I held the soup at a distance, because we had these blankets on the jets so I knew they cost $2,500 a pop. Snowball and Frank perched atop the couch opposite me happily swishing their tails.

During my car ride back to Trevor's, I tried calling my mom. She didn't answer. I wondered what her cryptic "there's something you should know" was all about? I texted her. She hadn't responded. I tried to stuff down the uneasiness I was feeling from not hearing from her. I couldn't.

Between sips, I told Trevor and Serenity what had happened at the psychiatric hospital. They paced in front of me, and Trevor held the Little Black Book. Then he plopped down next to me, opened it, and studied. "That was brave of you, Indy, but if Jayden finds this missing—"

"I know. Trust me, I know. What does it look like to you?"

He flipped through slowly as Serenity peered over his shoulder.

"It looks similar to his plans I saw from the abandoned warehouse in Boston, but these symbols I'm not familiar with."

"I am!" Serenity piped up. "It's called light language. It's the language of the soul; anyone who is tuned in can speak it and understand it. I would draw it as a kid, and I speak it too. It has meaning and can be translated, but only the recipient can understand the message—it's magical this way." She pointed to words that read *ta, ta, ta*, and said, "I recognize that."

I looked at Trevor. "We're time travelers. How do we not know about this?"

She said, "It's a different thing. You can time-travel; I know light language."

She moved to the couch opposite us and lowered herself onto it. Her face morphed into a blank stare. "*Oru ta ta ta, moo moo, oru papapapa*," she said, as the words flew out of her mouth. It sounded like the creatures speaking at the bar in *Star*

Wars. Rapid, cute, and bubbly. Frank began to sway his furry body and swish his tail even more.

She stopped. "Franky loves light language. Most animals do."

"Where did you learn it?" I asked.

"I had a teacher who beat a drum and helped get it out of me, and I've been speaking and drawing it my whole life."

Why did it sound vaguely familiar as she was speaking it?

My mind returned to a group meditation I did years ago. The spiritual healer leading it burped and spoke in a funny language, but hers sounded more sinister and eerie. It was slower, and she annunciated each word.

"Does light language have dialects?"

"Yes."

"I've heard it once before."

Serenity pointed to the book. "The '*ta ta ta*' usually signals happiness. I don't know what's so happy in that book, but that's what it universally means."

"Do you think you can translate it?"

"Let me look again."

Trevor handed her the book.

"I can only make out the '*ta ta ta*.' The rest is a dialect I don't speak or the message is only pertinent to Jayden himself." She flipped through the pages. "Did you see this drawing?"

She squished herself between Trevor and me. I put the broth on the side table and examined the drawing. I never thought that reading all those science magazines would actually pay off some day. I furrowed my brow.

"What's wrong?" Trevor asked.

"Nothing." Like my cardio, I needed to work on my poker face. "I think I may know what this is."

"Really?"

The drawing was of a three-dimensional circle on top of a large coil. At the end was a see-through chamber to enclose an object, I was guessing. Two tiny wires connected the circle to an "oscillator," the words Jayden had actually written out.

"What is it?" Serenity asked.

"I think it's a cyclotron. I read about them in an article. Think of a cyclotron as a round, oval track with magnetic fields. Particles are charged through there. When the track spins, these charged particles are accelerated into high energy."

Trevor whistled. "I'm lost."

"Shit, I'm pretty smart, and I'm lost too," Serenity said.

"Remember the movie *Ghostbusters*?"

They nodded.

"In the proton pack they use to bust ghosts, there was a cyclotron. It spun to a high speed and gave the proton pack its energy."

Serenity said, "So it's a source of power."

"Kinda. From my basic knowledge, an insane amount of energy would be needed to time-travel, and it would have to be very fast. Think of Doc using the lightning bolt as energy in *Back to the Future*, and how they drove the DeLorean ridiculously fast in order to time-travel. It would be like that. Jayden would need the highest energy and the highest speed possible, hence the cyclotron. That's my guess. Let's keep going."

Serenity turned a page.

The drawing was a nondescript, square object. Jayden had written the word "transporter" beside it.

I asked, "Remember what I said before? *Beam me up, Scotty.*"

"Right. *Star Trek* had the transporter. They would stand on a big platform and be teleported to somewhere else." He typed into his phone and read: "'A transporter takes matter, breaks it down into energy, transfers that energy from Point A to Point B at a high speed, and then reassembles it back together.'"

I said, "Exactly like the way I time-traveled at the very beginning. My traveling body became particles and then they formed into my human self again." I examined the drawing. "The transporter is inside the Time Machine. That means the metal box is the transporter that breaks down matter and transfers it at a high speed to another time and space. The cyclotron must create that requisite energy, but where is it?"

We flipped through the pages and couldn't find anything except for more light language and indecipherable drawings.

Serenity spoke up, "I don't read or watch a lot about time travel, but from the little I've seen, doesn't the time traveler have to get *inside* of something in order to travel?"

Exactly as Trevor had said in our first conversation about the Time Machine.

"The chakras," he said. "Jayden figured out a way to harness the energy of each chakra and as they spin, they're eight cyclotrons."

"That's brilliant, Trev!" Serenity said. "You aren't useless after all!"

I was speechless that he figured that out so fast. I reached out and squeezed his hand. He beamed.

"Serenity's right. That's impressive." I thought for a moment. "There is something about that eighth chakra. Jayden has found a way to manipulate the chakras, but the soul star, the eighth chakra, is often regarded as the most powerful and must serve as the main cyclotron. The transporter would need to teleport at an insane speed, but for the cyclotron, I would imagine Jayden would need an even higher velocity than that. Beyond the speed of light? If so, he would need the strongest otherworldly energy, and that's the soul star."

Serenity said, "Jayden figured out how to harness the energy of the chakras to time-travel. That's fucking genius."

Though I hated to admit it, it really was.

Trevor and Serenity began to comb through each page. The cats napped on the carpet; it was nice that Snowball had a friend.

I glanced at Trevor and Serenity and felt the same way. Even if we saved humanity and never spoke again, I was ready to let others into my life. And…I never thought I would *ever* say this…I hoped that Trevor and I would stay close.

Serenity handed the book to me.

"Did you guys find anything else?"

"Just the words 'phase shift,' written in tiny print," Serenity replied.

"Me too."

I said, "That's all I found as well. The words are next to what looks like a drawing of a ship. If it's what I think it is, that shit is terrifying."

"How?"

"Remember the Philadelphia Experiment?"

Trevor nodded.

"Yeah, I know it." Serenity said.

"If Jayden implemented the idea of phase-shifting, people could end up in extremely gory situations. Death would be a mercy compared to that." I paused. "The other shitty thing about the Philadelphia Experiment is the navy kicked out Tesla once they *thought* they understood his technology. He warned them that if they didn't get their power settings right, it would spiral out of control. So of course the navy turns the dial up to the highest degree and it goes down in history as the Philadelphia Experiment, which wasn't Tesla's fault."

"The navy was operating out of the realm of science, like Jayden," Serenity said.

"Yep. Jayden's in over his head."

I thought about the second photo that had appeared on my phone. I was hooked up to the Time Machine.

Was this a prophecy?

Would I phase-shift, and excruciatingly melt into a blob of human jelly?

A cold wave rippled through me. A mixture of terror, rage, and vulnerability tangled together.

Both Trevor's and Serenity's phones chimed.

"It's an email from Jayden to all the main players of the company. His ears must be burning. Jesus," Serenity said. "It's instructing us to sign into the VPN for a crucial message. Trev, let's use your iPad so we can all see it."

He snatched it off the kitchen counter, logged in, and set it up on the coffee table.

Jayden popped on the screen.

I wrinkled my nose. Gross.

Trevor pushed play on the video. Jayden said:

"Good evening, I hope you're enjoying this lovely fall weekend"—*seriously?*—"As you know by now, I have received the half-a-billion-dollar funding that I requested. Thank you so much for that wise decision. I am releasing a radical invention on behalf of Stone Corp come Monday morning. It will revolutionize the way we think of time and space, and bring *trillions* of dollars to the company. The average person will be able to erase the mistakes of their past and create the perfect life. My name for it? Timeline Tourism. Enjoy the rest of your weekend and see you on Monday."

The three of us stared at the screen that froze on his wide grin.

He was releasing the Time Machine *this fast* to the public? I mean, yes, I knew it would be fast and everything was time-sensitive, but in less than two days?! Didn't he need more prototypes, more experimentation, more something?!

"We are fucked," Serenity muttered.

How was he going to drop something like this and convince the public he wasn't losing his mind?

Because he clearly was.

I was sure Jayden had strategized a marketing plan for that too. Was it going to be: "It only costs $300,000 a pop. Take a spin in my Time Machine and change your life"? Or would he actually be selling machines to the public?

Either scenario was bone-chilling.

Serenity broke the silence. "Jayden understands that a public Time Machine would be disastrous, possibly to him as well. So what's his real angle?"

"That's a good point," I said. "He has to be doing this for another reason. There's something we don't know. Trevor, you've spent the most time with him. Any ideas?"

He pondered my question. "Nothing comes to mind. I'll think about it."

"We all will."

Once the Time Machine would be released to the public for profit, no one could close that Pandora's box. It would make the Philadelphia Experiment look like child's play. All the altered timelines, and humans randomly showing up in places they shouldn't be…

I couldn't live in that world.

Not to mention, there wouldn't be a world in which to live.

CHAPTER EIGHTEEN

The members of the Stone Corp board and the higher-ups were furiously texting both Trevor and Serenity.

"What are they saying?" I asked.

"Uh," Trevor said as he scrolled through his texts. "They are utterly confused. They're asking if it's a space program thing. One did ask if Jayden is 'off his rocker.' I haven't heard that in a long time."

Serenity said, "They're pretty hung up on 'erase the mistakes of your past,' as they should be. 'Timeline Tourism' is keeping them busy, too. Of course, Jayden isn't responding to them."

"Will they go to the media with this or leak it to the public?"

"Between the blackmail and the NDA Jayden made everyone sign, I doubt it. They won't be able to figure it out either. It's way too vague. I mean, whose mind would jump to time travel?"

"Totes," a voice said.

We turned around. Kai had appeared. Both Snowball and Frank were mesmerized, swishing their tails even faster.

Serenity gasped. "I can see you! I can finally see you!" She ran to envelop Kai in a bear hug. "You feel so warm and ethereal, like hugging a star."

That was the perfect analogy.

"Let me look at you," Serenity said. "You're the most beautiful thing I've ever seen." Tears welled up in her eyes. "I've always felt you and saw a version of you in meditation, but this is the real you. How is it possible I'm seeing you with my own two eyes?"

"You're strengthening your skills. You've immersed yourself in Trevor's and Indy's energies, and that elevated your consciousness." Kai hesitated. "How much time do we have?"

We told her about Jayden's plans.

Then I asked her, "Do you know what his ulterior motive could be?"

"No."

"Neither do we."

She made a *tsk* sound. "Only a human day and two nights to come up with a solution. That's not much time even for the spirit world."

She walked over to Snowball and Frank and petted them. They looked as if they were about to jump out their skin with delight. I'd never heard such loud purring.

She said, "From what we know, Jayden sees time travel as a commercial venture. Having a controlled metaphysical service that assists humanity is one thing, but what Jayden is doing—" She shook her head. "At least we have more insight into the inner workings of the Time Machine."

I replied, "Getting to the Machine is our priority. Let's put out this fire *first* and then move onto the next."

"Do you know where the Time Machine is?" Kai asked.

"No, but we know someone who might."

#

I was at the diner again, the one in Harlem by Tameka's apartment building. I sat down at a small table and ordered a mixed green salad with avocado slices on the side, olive oil for dressing, and a baked potato. I nibbled as I watched people come in and out.

Today was a Saturday night, so Tameka's schedule could've changed. The wafting smell of chicken fingers and French fries enticed me to the point I was about to give up and leave. Then I spotted Tameka's neighbor, the old woman, hobble into the diner. She was around 4'10, frail, and missing several teeth. She wore a purple dress and an old-fashioned bonnet on her head.

I left my dinner and approached her. "Hi, ma'am. Have you seen Tameka?"

"Oh that girl's makin' so much noise! That's why I came down here. It's a racket up there. All those lights. You young people."

Lights?

"Can you get me inside your building so I can check on her?"

"Let's go," she grumbled.

I quickly handed some cash to the person at the register, pointed to my food, and said thank you. I followed the old lady, as she shuffled one tiny step at a time.

It was like following a turtle on vacation.

She jingled keys in her pocket, then slowly removed one from the ring and handed it to me.

"This is for T's place."

We finally entered the building. The neighbor said to the doorman, who was busy on his phone, "She's visiting T." He nodded and didn't even look up. Good security.

"You go up. I have to get my mail."

I said thank you and ran up the stairs. As I reached her floor, I heard a strange sound, like a swishing…or many swishes at once. They were loud. From underneath Tameka's door, colorful lasers beamed out into the hallway.

I heard a roar.

My parents and I had vacationed close to a zoo and once a day the lion would roar. It resounded throughout the area. That was close to what this sounded like, except it wasn't from an animal. It was something…mechanical.

As I inched closer to the door, I smelled burning.

What the fuck was going on in there?

I touched the door handle; it was cool. The burning smell strengthened. I didn't see any smoke under the door.

I put the key in the lock, and thank God, it opened. I pushed it farther to find…

Tameka connected to the Time Machine.

The look on her face was one of a zombie. It was pale, like a vampire had sucked the life out of her. The sound of the lasers blared to a deafening level. I instinctively covered my ears.

Her body levitated several inches off the ground in the pose of the Vitruvian Man.

Horror rooted me in place. I clutched my hands to my chest as if to shield myself from something I couldn't unsee. My lips parted, but there were no words. Only my trembling gasp hung in the air.

The burning…was it coming from her chakras?!

The wires suspended her in air and connected to each chakra. All eight smoldered. Her crown chakra was by far the most hideous sight to which I retched. The top of her head was steaming. I could now smell what I presumed was burning flesh.

What the fuck was I supposed to do?!

I snapped out of my daze and yelled out, "Tameka!"

Her eyes shifted to me. She was still in there. I didn't know how that was humanly possible, but she was, and she was silently begging for help.

Out of nowhere, Jayden stepped into view.

My heart almost stopped.

He ran full speed at me.

I lunged toward the eighth chakra wire and touched it with my finger.

My entire body jolted and crashed to the floor. The most excruciating pain shot through my skin and coursed my bones, my organs, and into my blood. It felt like a hot poker slicing every inch of me.

When I was a little girl, I had wedged scissors into an electrical outlet and the shock blasted through me and put me in tears. This was a gazillion times worse.

I could not move.

A white light surrounded my body. This was it. The famous white light, and then everything was in slow motion.

#

When I awoke, my head was throbbing and my ears were ringing. I lay there for a while and then attempted to move my legs.

I couldn't.

My heart raced and my intestines screamed. My breath quickened to the point of no control. I was now hyperventilating, yet I couldn't hear myself.

Everything was muffled.

There I was, on the floor like a starfish lying on my stomach, paralyzed.

I was able to move my pointer finger on my right hand. The bending of it made me wince. The lower left side of my back tinged with pain. My left arm and hand slowly reached down to touch it. *Ouch!* It felt hot.

Pretend this is a plane crash, Indy. What would you do?

I would recognize that while I couldn't move right now, my brain seemed intact. I had to relax my muscles as best I could. If I shit and pissed myself, oh well. I did the breath work, the 3-3-3 rule, and counted backward. The ringing lessened.

My right foot twitched and then my left as my lower half was brought back to life. The sensation crawled from my feet, up my legs, and to my hips.

Was it safe?

I was still lying on my stomach and attempted to push myself off the hallway floor…to no avail. I noticed an absence of lasers, swishing sounds, and anything that reverberated like a lion's roar. There was only deafening silence.

My head dropped to the floor for rest. I had to get myself out of here.

I reached for my cell in my coat pocket. As soon as I touched it, my hand jumped. The phone was smoking. It had melted into the fabric of the pocket.

Shit.

I raised my head again. The shock had blasted me into the hallway. I was lying across the threshold of Tameka's door. Inside the apartment, there was nothing except for furniture pushed to the sides of the room. No Tameka, Jayden, or Time Machine. From what I could see, not a trace of what had occurred was left.

How was this possible?

There was no way Jayden would've let me go. It must've been out of his control.

"Oh my, you lookin' bad, girl."

The neighbor loomed over me. Nude pantyhose covered her tiny legs, and she wore old-fashioned loafers. She stood next to my head.

"At least that dang party is over."

CHAPTER NINETEEN

My eyes fluttered as I rubbed away the crust, then they widened.

How had I ended up in Trevor's apartment? In his bed. The fabric that encased my body was silky and soft like cashmere. I gazed toward the window wall. It was night.

The crystals rested on my throat. After all that had happened, they remained.

As I wiggled my toes and shook my legs, tears of relief formed. I blinked them away.

My instinct was to reach for my phone on the nightstand, then I remembered it had melted inside my pocket.

Footsteps padded into the room.

"You're awake."

A chair scraped across the hardwood floor. Trevor sat down. He took my hand and stared at me.

"You gave us a major scare."

For the moment, all I could utter was, "You were worried about me?"

"All of us were. Me, Serenity, Kai, even Snowball and Frank."

I noticed Frank outstretched on the oversized chair, and Snowball curled under the blankets by my side.

"Don't do that again," he said.

My head pounded, and my breath was shallow. Minute electrical charges pricked all over my body. I glanced at my right pointer finger which had a burn where I had touched the eighth chakra wire. The lower left side of my back throbbed. I rolled my body onto my side and pressed it.

"What are you doing?" Trevor asked.

I cleared my throat and gained some semblance of my voice. "It's like I'm a survivor of a lightning strike. I have the entry and exit wounds."

I showed him.

"That's what the doctor said."

Wait. "I saw a doctor? How did I get here? What happened?"

"While we were in the emergency board meeting, Serenity intuited that you were in serious trouble. I found Tameka's address in Harlem and took a car up there. I paid off the doorman and ran up the stairs to discover you unconscious.

"I talked with the neighbor. She was *interesting*. She didn't say much and walked into her apartment. I guess she didn't care that you were lying on the floor passed out."

"That sounds like her."

"I carried you down the stairs into the car service. You'd woken up a few times and then you were unconscious again. I decided to call our concierge doctor and have her meet us here. Dr. Munk is on call 24-7 for our family."

"Why didn't you go to the hospital?"

He shrugged. "This is how our family's always done it, unless someone's not breathing or their heart's stopped. Plus, I didn't want to attract Jayden's attention."

A memory crept into my mind. A middle-aged woman with brown eyes studied mine with a small light.

"Dr. Munk said it looked like you'd been struck by lightning, too. She asked to see your clothing and shoes. The soles are tinged with burn marks. Your phone melted to your coat, and like you said, you have the classic entry and exit wounds. She said you are extremely lucky. Most victims are severely burned and their brains are, well…fried."

Tameka. My heart plummeted.

"Dr. Munk wants to take an MRI of your brain when the shocks subside. I didn't know how to explain your symptoms. Luckily, she knows to ask just enough. We pay her plenty to keep quiet. Why do you look so sad?"

Before I could say anything, Serenity traipsed into the room.

"You're awake! You look pretty good despite all the shit you've been through."

She sat on the bed and petted Snowball. Frank meowed with jealousy.

"How do you feel?"

"Like I've been struck by lightning."

"Well, you basically have. While you were sleeping, I read that fishermen are the people most struck by lightning. They refuse to get off their boats when it's storming. Morons."

Though it hurt, I laughed.

She pointed to my necklace. "Black tourmaline and clear quartz? Kai gave them to you for protection, right?"

I nodded.

Trevor pulled out an identical necklace from under his shirt. "Erik took me to The Meadow too and then had it calibrated to my soul's frequency. When I returned from the board meeting, I saw it on my nightstand with a note."

"He took me too!" Serenity said. "It was so surreal. Like eating mint chocolate chip ice cream and masturbating at the same time."

What the fuck? We both looked at her.

"Hey, you have your kinky shit. I have mine."

I let that one go.

"BTW, where is *my* necklace?" she asked.

"Oh he left one for you too."

Trevor dug it out of his pocket. Hers had a rose quartz and black tourmaline. Love…and protection from evil. Nice.

She snatched it from him and fastened it around her neck.

"I feel official." She paused. "Is this calibrated to my soul's frequency too?"

"Yes."

"Word." She whipped out a rectangular box. "And a present for you, Indy. Your new phone. If you give me your ID and passcode, I can set it up tonight."

The Stones were efficient.

"I brought you pajamas. I see you don't wear bras. You should start. Saggy tits aren't pretty. Right, Trev?"

He rolled his eyes.

She said, "I changed your burned clothes and dressed you in the cashmere pajamas."

"Thank you, Serenity. I appreciate it."

I could not hide the despair in my voice as I thought about Tameka.

"What's wrong, Indy?" she asked.

I relayed the details of what I could remember despite the hammering and searing in my head. My mouth was so dry. I reached for the glass of water on the nightstand and gulped the room-temperature liquid between my words.

Trevor whispered, "Tameka. Fuck."

"Gone. Vanished with Jayden and the Time Machine." I paused. "The only good news—if you can call it that—is that I saw the Time Machine in action. It's horrifying. God knows where Tameka is. I can't imagine her surviving an electrocution of that degree."

"We should let you rest," Serenity said. "But before we do, do you remember anything else? By morning we'll have less than twenty-four hours before Jayden releases mayhem on the world."

I wracked my brain.

"Nothing…" I said slowly. "But I do have the ability to take Trevor into my past." I looked at Serenity. "I wish you could come too."

She shrugged one shoulder, trying not to look as hurt as she probably felt.

"We can see if we notice anything as silent observers."

"How do we know we'll be 'silent observers'? Anything could happen. We've been lucky so far, but you never know."

"It's a huge risk, but that's our only hope. You've gotta get me on your family jet."

"This isn't a good idea, Indy. There has to be another way," he said.

"There's not. We all know it. Maybe if we had more time, but we don't. We have to find that Time Machine and my past is our only hope."

I moved to get up.

"Whoa! It's the middle of the night. Get more sleep and we'll go first thing in the morning. I promise."

"I can do it now," I demanded.

Serenity said, "Even if you can, the jet won't be ready. I'll make all the preparations, and it'll be ready by early morning."

They both gave me a look that said: "it's settled."

"ID and passcode?" She pointed to the box. "You back up to the Cloud, right?"

I nodded yes, told her the information, and thanked her.

As she jotted down everything, I asked, "When are *you* going to sleep?"

"When I'm dead."

Trevor threw her a stern glance.

"Sorry. Bad joke. Sleep well." She hurried out of the room.

I remembered their meeting. "What happened with the board and the execs?"

"Not much. It was a cluster of them yelling at each other, at Grandpa. He didn't have much to say except he would be in touch."

"With Jayden calling it 'Timeline Tourism,' Steven has to know Jayden followed through on the Time Machine that he originally pitched him."

"Yeah, and for the first time in Grandpa's life, he doesn't know how to save the company."

"I was hoping we'd find something."

"I know. Do you need anything else before we let you rest?"

I thought. "Actually—"

"Anything."

"I need a change of clothes, a coat, and apparently socks and shoes."

"Will do."

He started to get up and follow Serenity out of the room. "Trevor?"

"Yes?"

"And some clean underwear."

#

As we boarded the Stone Corp private jet, all I could think was *I'm the pax for once.*

The three jet engines of the Falcon 8X hummed, and the pilots were ready in the cockpit. An FA did not greet us, because Trevor and Serenity wanted full privacy. Serenity gave the pilots the destination of Newark Airport. It was a very short trip—only fifteen minutes at most. The private aviation side of Newark had jets flying in and out constantly. We'd hopefully be lost in the shuffle, and Jayden wouldn't be alerted.

We took our seats in the cabin. Trevor and I sat in the forward-facing power seats, while Serenity was in front of Trevor, facing aft. I unbuttoned my new designer coat—thank you, Serenity—and removed my new phone from my pocket and stuffed it into a new handbag. I had to admit, even in a crisis, I kinda liked feeling spoiled.

When Time Flies by Jennifer Moreno (Ciotta)

When I awoke this morning, my head thumped less than before. The electrical charges still prickled inside my body, but they weren't as fierce. I patted the crystals that hung around my neck. They had protected me from harm. I quietly thanked Kai and the Spirit Council.

This morning, I had also awoken to clothes, socks, shoes, underwear—thank you, Trevor—and a bra sprawled at the foot of the ginormous bed. The latter had a Post-it saying: "Your tits will thank me — S."

Serenity had guessed my size; everything fit. So far time-traveling was a cold endeavor; I truly appreciated her buying me this warm coat. She'd thought of everything, because stuffed deep inside the pockets were leather gloves.

"I can't believe I can't go with you," Serenity pouted.

Kai appeared in the seat facing me.

"Serenity, don't whine. Indy, where are you looking to return?"

I told her about Tameka and the Time Machine.

"We have to get you to the correct time. No stumbling around."

"During my last trip, I managed to travel to the correct time to the physics class and then left unintentionally."

"We don't have time to work on the exit. That takes a lot of practice."

"Yeah it does," Trevor said. "In the beginning, my forehead was one gigantic purple bruise because I tried leaving through doorways that wouldn't open. I swear my brain is permanently damaged."

"Yeah but not from that," Serenity replied with a smirk.

He chuckled.

"You have the crystals. They will help you. Once we're airborne, touch them and do what you did before."

I reached for Trevor's hand and grasped it.

I shifted in the club seat and closed my eyes.

The plane taxied the runway. It came to a stop, turned, and stopped again. The pilots were ready for takeoff. The jet zoomed and the wheels lifted off the ground.

Butterflies flitted in my solar plexus. This was go time. It was the bottom of the eighth—or was it the ninth?—with two outs and I was at bat. I had to swing and hit a homerun.

It was now or never.

My heart pounded.

I thought about the scene in my head. A sour wave rolled through my stomach. My insides twisted, feeling hollow and heavy at the same time. I breathed in and out, detailing the sensory aspects of the event, as unfortunate as they were.

I touched the crystals.

My third eye rumbled. It didn't hum as usual. The purple color was absent, and the crystals remained cool. A sheen of sweat dampened my skin.

There I was, on the Stone jet holding Trevor's hand.

I concentrated again…

And again and again.

I felt so much pressure to be *on* in this moment. Emotionally, I had been transported to the night of the fire, the plea bargain, and the second night of the fire where I desperately tried to locate the door. My breath quickened.

I tried invoking the sensory details, the immersion of the physical space…none of it was working.

Tears welled up. "Fuck!" I screamed and dropped Trevor's hand.

The wheels bounced on the runway. The flight was over.

"I can't do it!"

Kai said, "Indy, relax. Yes, you can, but you're under too much pressure."

"It's okay, Indy," Serenity said. "We can have the pilots do a longer flight. We can fly until we have to get fuel."

Kai added, "If she's this upset, it won't work. And we're running out of time."

"Can't you help her?"

"I wish I could."

Trevor said, "Kai's right. When you're too frustrated it won't happen. At least for me, it won't."

My insides burned with anger. Why was this happening *now*?

Okay, all right.

I just had to calm down.

My chest heaved and the liquid inside my colon splashed.

Trevor examined me and turned to Serenity. "We'll go into the FBO and take a minute. Time for Plan B."

The story of my life.

#

I now empathized with men who had "performance" anxiety.

Trevor and Serenity tried to cheer me up by saying "we'll stop Jayden another way," and I appreciated that, but it hurt. I ended up letting everyone down, especially myself.

After we landed, Kai had returned to the astral plane.

Trevor, Serenity, and I sat around a conference table in a private room at the FBO.

The pressure of saving humanity loomed. I rubbed the crystals; they lay cold and lifeless on my throat.

The door of the conference room swung open.

It was Steven Stone.

I recoiled instinctively. The threshold framed his unwelcome face. As powerful as he was and as surprised as I was to see him here, I stood my ground.

"Grandpa!" Trevor jumped up.

"We need to talk," Serenity said.

She rose from her chair and shut the conference room door.

"Why are you here? You've been avoiding us for days."

"I've been busy."

"You've been avoiding us," she said. "Why are you here?"

He stared her down. She wasn't having it and crossed her arms. "We're waiting."

"I need *my* jet. My assistant contacted the pilot, and to my surprise, he says you have the jet in Newark. Considering it's the property of Stone Corp, I'll assume you're conducting business and it's not a joyride." Steven then glowered at me. "She can't be here. She's not family."

Trevor said, "Yes she can, she's family now"— Did Trevor say *family*? My heart chakra spun—"*and* she's a traveler like us."

Steven's mouth fell open. He immediately shut it. "We all like to travel. It's a good hobby."

"You know we mean *time* travel. Indy does it too," Serenity said.

He simply replied, "Oh."

"Grandpa, we're under the gun here. Jayden's 'Timeline Tourism' idea is sinister. I'm sure you know that he's built a—"

"Time Machine. He pitched me on a Time Machine when he was in high school."

So that *was* Steven's original past.

Serenity asked, "When he allocated money for his secret project, you didn't think it was a Time Machine?"

"Why would I? There were no hints that it was a Time Machine, and frankly, it was an impossible feat. I thought he was young, it was a whim, and that he had dropped it. I was wrong."

"Why didn't you talk to me or Dad about it?" Trevor asked.

"Or me!" Serenity said.

"It was an event that came and went. Then I saw the video. All this time-travel nonsense…" He sighed. "I've always wanted to shut off the ability. I stand there as an observer, witnessing arbitrary things, such as a past lunch or playing squash at the club. It doesn't help my business or further my financial gain, so I deal with the trips when they come and hope they're short-lived. It's only been as of late that I've jumped into my past body. That's new. I don't like it."

"What about Dad?" Serenity asked.

"SJ never embraced it. It terrifies him. I told him it would happen when he turned thirty and he laughed it off, calling me 'nuts.' Just after his thirtieth birthday, it happened. I tried to discuss it with him, but he shut me out."

"I wish our family talked. We wouldn't be in the position we're in now," Trevor said.

"Perhaps." Steven's voice lowered. "I've lost control of Stone Corp because…Jayden has something on me like the rest of the board and higher-ups. It's bad."

"How bad?" Trevor asked.

"I've had many extramarital affairs."

Serenity replied, "So what? This isn't the Bill Clinton 90s. Admit it and move on."

"The affairs were with men."

I glanced at Trevor and Serenity who looked genuinely shocked. I couldn't stop my own eyebrows from raising too.

"Young men."

"How young, Grandpa?"

"They were over eighteen."

"You sure about that?"

"They were vetted sex workers."

Well shit.

I didn't think the old guy had it in him.

Trevor whistled and Serenity smirked.

"The board and shareholders are conservative. I can't hold a press conference and expect this to blow over. I'll be ruined and sentenced to a life of playing golf at the club."

He had it so good he didn't even know it. A "sentence" like that sounded pretty damn good to me.

He turned in my direction. "What happened with Tameka?"

I told him.

"Goodness. Poor girl."

I thought aloud. "If Jayden's known about traveling since high school, someone had to prepare him. His dad or another relative."

"That is very possible," Steven said. "Before heading to Boston and trying to solve this mess, I have to fly to Wingdale to check on the property."

"Why? It's Sunday morning," Serenity inquired.

"The guards called me. They'd encountered a disturbance. It was the second time they'd had one in the last two days."

Uh oh.

"Yesterday they chased a woman off the property. They didn't get a good look at her."

My plan had worked. "It was me. I trespassed and found Jayden's book of plans for the Time Machine."

He raised one eyebrow. "Impressive, India."

"It was all of us. We haven't found the Time Machine yet."

"Do you have an idea where it is?"

"No. It disappeared along with Jayden after Tameka's electrocution. You said your guards encountered a second disturbance?"

"They called me a couple of hours ago and said they saw a flash of something and then a sound like—it's so strange; it's preposterous to even say aloud—like a roaring lion."

I gasped.

"That's the Time Machine. We have to go."

CHAPTER TWENTY

We stood on the grass. Trevor, Serenity, and me.

Steven chose to remain in the car service. Pussy.

In front of us was the teal door.

I inhaled deeply. The Time Machine was here. I was sure of it.

The crystals lay motionless. I had no time for self-doubt or anxiety, so I exhaled and looked to Trevor then Serenity. They nodded.

We were ready.

I took my first step into the danger zone.

Screaming erupted.

Tameka burst through the door, fell to the ground, and shrieked, "Help me! Someone please!"

I could smell burning. Her clothes were partially singed, and her skin was smoldering. Trevor removed his coat in a flash and covered her with it. She took shallow breaths.

He said, "Hold on, Tameka. We've got you. Stay with us."

He bent down and gently patted his coat all over her body. She cried in pain. He said, "Ssh. It's okay. Just a little more and you'll feel better."

She passed out on the concrete.

He turned her over and put his ear against her chest. "We have to do CPR."

"I know how to do it from flight attendant training."

Serenity bent down and said, "We know too. Emergency training for jet owners. We do it every six months."

Trevor started the compressions.

I said, "You have to take turns. You'll become exhausted."

"We know!" Serenity said. "I'll call an ambulance."

Trevor was doing CPR correctly. Serenity whipped out her phone, dialed 911, and told the most benign version of the story she could. "My friend got electrocuted. I don't know how. We're at the old psychiatric hospital in Wingdale. Come fast. We're doing CPR."

She ended the call before giving any more information and said to me, "Indy, go! It's now or never. I've got to tell Grandpa."

She then sprinted—shockingly fast.

Trevor was completely focused on saving Tameka. I couldn't disturb him.

I dashed up the crumbling steps and halted at the teal door. I had to get into the right headspace. *It's okay, Indy*, I thought. The usual breathing techniques, focusing on a brown spot on the door, and visualizing the rainbow colors for the power-up exercise was how I was able to re-center myself. Then I rubbed the crystals.

They did not heat or flutter.

What was going *on*?

The next I knew Trevor was beside me.

"What's happening with Tameka?"

"Serenity found the guards and they have it covered. The ambulance is on its way. You seem…stuck. You've been in this spot for a little while."

Had it been *that* long?

"I'm here with you. We'll get through this together."

I pulled open the teal door and reached for Trevor's hand.

Before he could say another word, we were traveling.

#

Was this…an abandoned FBO?

Normally, a private jet terminal would've been bustling with line people hoisting designer suitcases onto luggage carts. No one stood behind the long desk with the marble countertop. The automatic doors did not slide, and the popcorn in the machine didn't pop. Heels, metal carts full of food, and heavy boots didn't reverberate off the engineered wood floor. The ultra comfortable chairs and love seats remained untouched, as did the large rack of aviation and luxury magazines. I did not hear voices, walkie-talkies, or anyone answering phones.

Silence pressed in, thick and wrong. Even my own breathing felt intrusive. The rhythm of it stuttered, matching the jitter of my pulse.

Outside, aircrafts of varying size and expense were parked on the tarmac. The sun crept over the hangar in the east. Its tangerine hue beautified the scene over the otherwise plain, nondescript buildings.

A large FBO in a major hub was always open 24-7. Yet this one was closed. At least a line person or two would've been here for the overnight shift.

This was creepy.

Wait.

This was an FBO I recognized.

Aire Aviation.

When I served lunch to Trevor, Jayden, and their colleagues on the Citation X, it was here.

I peered over to Trevor, who was taking in the scene. "What do you think?"

"It's the FBO where we met. We're our present selves."

"I thought you had to set an intention and close your eyes to travel?"

"Things have been wonky lately."

They sure have.

Just then, something heavy dropped. I turned my head. It came from the direction of the hangar. Clanking, the whizz of a drill, and the sound of…was that a laser?

Trevor's eyes bulged, which proved I wasn't hearing things.

We followed the sounds and tried to open the hangar door. We needed an entry card. I peeked inside the little window and all I saw was another hallway that led to another door.

"How do we get in?" Trevor asked.

I scanned the area. "I bet they have a card at the front desk. Let's look."

We opened and shut every cabinet and drawer and perused the counter space.

Nothing.

Behind the front desk was the backroom. The refrigerators hummed, though no catering boxes were inside of them, and the long table used for checking their contents was bare. Near the ice and coffee machines, there was a newspaper stand with empty tiers. The line office had windows that overlooked the tarmac. I checked the desk there.

Damn.

The bright yellow vest of a line person hung over the desk chair. I reached into the pockets—bingo!—and pulled out a card and read it. Today I would be: FBO manager, Brian Ryan. Really? His parents named him "Brian Ryan"?

Trevor gave me a thumbs-up.

We raced across the FBO and swiped the card. The reader beeped and turned green. I breathed a sigh of relief and hurried through with Trevor in tow. The mechanical noises increased as I swiped to get through the next door.

A team of workers was deconstructing or constructing a plane. This type of work typically wasn't done in an FBO hangar. I had never seen a plane gutted to this level. Yes, of course, mechanics did maintenance on site, but anything major was usually taken to a service center.

Wires, parts, pieces of metal—pieces of jet—were strewn on the hangar floor. I couldn't tell what type of plane it had been. A small, rectangular window sat amongst the debris. It wasn't a large Gulfstream or a Boeing Business Jet. It had to be a smaller PJ.

Closer to us stood a large jet. We crouched and hid behind its wheel. I saw an engine painted white that read: Citation X.

The aircraft that Jayden was looking to buy.

I heard a man's distant voice. It wasn't Jayden's.

Trevor whispered, "Is that—*no*, it can't be."

"Who is it?"

"Wait.

The voice shouted orders. I couldn't quite understand what he was saying, but he was emphatic. I peeked out from behind the wheel.

I knew that flat tone.

"Oh my God. *Dad*?!" Trevor whispered.

A tall man emerged from behind the other side of the aircraft.

Yep.

SJ Stone.

My intuition was *always* right. I knew SJ wasn't "innocuous."

SJ kicked a piece of metal and pointed to something. A worker scurried away. He then picked up a long black wire with a silver thing on the end. I recognized it from the Time Machine. He held it up to a piece of metal. It attached. "Yes!" he said.

That looked identical to the wires connected to the Time Machine—although a black wire was pretty common.

He shouted more orders. Workers scrambled.

I saw a metal piece that had to be a side panel of the Time Machine. My eyes darted everywhere. I spotted a round piece that could be used as the base for the cyclotron and a loose coil that could go underneath.

I whispered, "He's breaking down this plane to build the Time Machine."

"Dad's working with Jayden."

Once Jayden had SJ convinced of his idea, he must've promised him the world. That made sense, because SJ wasn't respected in his family company. However, SJ *was* terrified of time travel. Perhaps they struck a deal where he didn't have to use the Machine itself; he only had to help build it.

He was ruthless like Jayden.

I scoffed.

"Fuck, fuck!" Trevor whisper-yelled.

I touched his shoulder. "We have to stay quiet."

He nodded. His eyes glistened with tears.

At that moment, I realized where we had traveled. It was when Aire Aviation hadn't yet opened. It looked new. It made sense that I only found Brian Ryan's tag, because he would've been responsible for setup.

That lunch meeting was about purchasing a jet to break down for parts. If anyone researched SJ's recent purchases, I was sure they would find an older plane or two. It was SJ who had the deep pockets, not Jayden.

Another piece of metal clanged on the hangar floor.

SJ was inspecting parts and conversing with the workers. Every time he talked with someone else, he moved closer to our hiding spot.

We had to get the hell out of here.

I grabbed Trevor and we ran to the door. I swiped the card, sprinted down the hallway, and swiped again until we traveled…not back to the psych ward. Instead, we were still at the FBO…except it was busy.

Two front desk personnel chatted with pax. A woman in a vicuña coat scooped popcorn out of the machine. Pilots walked around with cups of coffee, and I craned my neck to peek in the backroom. An FA was rummaging through a catering box.

It was the normal hubbub of Sunday afternoon at Teterboro.

I didn't know what was more unsettling, the creepy quiet or being thrown back into normality. Was anything "normal" anymore?

Reading my mind, Trevor fished his phone out of his pocket and looked. "We're back to present day. We only left for a couple of minutes. Why didn't we return to the blue door at the psych ward? Jesus, things are fucked."

That was an understatement.

His phone chimed with a text.

In a somber tone, he said, "Serenity wants us to meet her at the hospital."

That didn't sound promising. Right now, nothing did.

CHAPTER TWENTY-ONE

"The doctors are questioning us and it's not good," Serenity said.

We sat in the waiting room of the burn unit, in the corner so we wouldn't be disturbed.

It was a typical waiting room with cloth chairs in wooden frames. It smelled like a hospital with that distinct combination of *antibacterial-meets-eau-de-sick* person.

"The doctors are questioning you how?" I asked.

"They don't understand how Tameka got that burned, especially with the brain trauma. One doctor even recognized that the major burns were in the chakra areas."

"What'd you say?"

"What could I say? My original explanation was that she touched a downed wire. You should've seen the looks on their faces—they knew it was bullshit. Grandpa will have to take care of it if they keep questioning."

"Where is Grandpa?" Trevor asked.

"He's gone home."

"That's Grandpa in a crisis. Never there."

She continued, "Tameka's burned over seventy percent of her body, and now there are *two* doctors who can't get over the chakra locations. She has second and third-degree burns. She'll be in recovery for a long time, and with a lot of skin grafts."

"And her brain?"

"She's not in a vegetative state, but she's not talking either. She can lightly squeeze the doctor's finger and move her eyes. She blinks yes and no. They said considering the trauma she's endured, it's a miracle. They also said it's normal for someone who has undergone this much trauma to be in shock for a while."

Poor Tameka.

I asked, "No one's heard from Jayden?"

She shook her head.

"What about Tameka's parents?"

"How can we explain this?" Serenity said. "The burns are inexplicable, her own husband's not here, and we're pretending to be her family!"

"How are we 'pretending to be her family'?" Trevor asked.

"They wanted to kick me out because 'family only.' I said I was her sister-in-law. I guess you're Tameka's husband, Trev."

Why did I feel a churning of jealousy?

Even for me, it was a little insecure.

She said, "The only thing we can do is call Grandpa. He can call his fixer, and then we can contact her family."

As much as I hated to admit it, Serenity was right. How *could* we explain what had happened? Tameka's family would throw a fit and demand answers, as any good family would.

I glanced at Trevor. "What about Tameka's in-laws, Jayden's parents?"

"I've never met them."

"What?! How? You were like brothers to Jayden for *fifteen* years. How is that possible?"

"His grandmother raised him."

I then remembered the BYF speech of him saying he was raised by his grandmother in a low-income family.

"Are his parents dead?"

"Not that I know of. He never said they died. I asked about his parents a few times, and he would change the subject. If a guy doesn't answer, you stop asking."

Men.

"Once in a while he would say he was going to visit his grandma in assisted living, but that's it. Again, I would ask how she was doing and he'd change the subject. I thought he was a private guy."

Serenity pondered aloud, "I've never met his parents either. Not even at Jayden and Tameka's wedding."

I said, "Serenity, you like to dig with people. You never asked?"

She shrugged. "Honestly, I didn't care. Jayden was never my favorite. The times I hung out with Tameka, we talked about her mom and sisters." She paused. "Come to think of it, Jayden's grandmother was at their wedding, right?"

"Yeah. She's an older woman from Jamaica. She seemed nice. For all we know, Jay could've hired her."

"True," I said. "If she's real, I'm wondering if she's a traveler? If one of his parents is a traveler?"

"One of them has to be," Trevor said.

"I can't believe with all your history with him that we aren't able to contact Jayden's immediate family. Everyone comes from *somewhere*."

"Who knows if he's been lying this whole time?" Trevor said. "We don't know what's real or what's not anymore."

Serenity hissed, "Enough about Jayden's family. Tell me what happened when you traveled."

Oh boy.

She looked at Trevor and then at me.

This was the time, but not the place.

"Is there a chapel here?" I asked.

"A *what*?" Serenity said.

"A chapel."

"Why? Are you going to pray?"

"We need privacy."

Trevor got up and talked with the nurse at the desk. He motioned for us to come over. He led us out of the burn unit and down hallways until we pushed open the maple doors of a chapel. No one was there.

"We have privacy. What's up?"

Serenity's compassionate mood had shifted to no nonsense. *This* was going to be brutal.

"I don't know how to tell you this, Ser," Trevor said.

"What?"

He hesitated.

"Just say it, Trevor."

Everything I had learned being a flight attendant was don't bullshit the rich pax. They didn't like FAs who cowered in front of them and apologized too much. If you had bad news, you had to rip it off like a Band-Aid on a really hairy arm.

I closed my eyes and said, "Your father is helping Jayden."

I let that land and sit for a moment.

She remained silent—a rarity for her.

Trevor said, "Dad's involved in the construction of the Machine and the funding of it."

"What the fuck are you talking about?"

He told her everything we saw.

She slumped onto a pew. "Fucker."

"Yeah."

"God, he's been a shitty father. The sad part is I can understand why he did this. He's a joke in the business world and has a massive chip on his shoulder. This is his one shot at a legacy."

I'd witnessed other children of billionaires who didn't inherit the genius. They desperately tried to outshine their parents and it never happened. This was SJ's life story.

We fell silent. I couldn't help but think of Tameka. All alone without anyone she could trust. She had discovered the reality of her husband—which she partially knew all along—but not to this psychotic level. I doubted that she would ever recover from any of this emotionally, mentally, or physically.

We were losing time. It was already afternoon.

My instinct was to visit Tameka. She needed someone. Obviously, I wasn't the best choice because she thought I was a stalker.

Yet I was the only option while Trevor and Serenity remained preoccupied. They continued murmuring about SJ. Once they were done, we had to return to the old psych hospital to hunt for the Time Machine.

I said to them, "I'll give you space and come back soon."

#

Tameka was propped up in a hospital bed. Her face was vacant, a barren landscape of expression. Bandages covered her forehead and cheeks and most of her exposed skin. She stared out the picture window and blinked every so often. Amidst the burns was that seamless face.

I didn't know what to do. Should I reach for her hand and hold it? She hadn't liked me the one time we conversed. I decided the best thing was to sit on the chair next to her bed. She could hopefully sense that I was supporting her.

A machine beeped while the footsteps of nurses and doctors echoed off the hallway floors. Tameka stirred.

I had an idea.

I took out my phone and searched for poems from the Harlem Renaissance fitting for this occasion. In school, I had read about this era. Instead, I found jazz music from the time and raised the volume.

She responded by releasing a sigh.

That was a good sign. I pressed the volume button to turn it up.

She began to slowly tap a finger along with the music. Then she softly broke into song. Her voice matched her exterior: it was haunting and enchanting at the same time.

The words…were not English or any language that I recognized. She annunciated each syllable, rolled certain r's, and clicked.

Was that light language?

My phone rang with FaceTime.

Mom.

I swiped to answer.

"Hi, doodoo."

Her face studied mine.

"Doodoo, have you been time-traveling?"

"Yes, why?"

"Where are you? All I see is a blank wall. I hear a woman singing, loud music, and a machine beeping."

"I'm at the hospital."

"What happened? Are you hurt?"

"No, Mom. I'm fine. I'm visiting a friend."

She said, "That song is…powerful."

Our internet connection weakened. She froze on the screen.

"Mom, can you hear me?"

She began moving. "Sorry, bad connection here. India, have you tried to change anything in your past?"

"Meaning what?"

"Have you tried to change your past in order to change your present?"

"No. Why?"

"Don't do it. That's how I think I almost died in that grocery store. The trip before that one, I'd changed the past where your grandfather never received the job offer in Boston. That way, we wouldn't have to move to the U.S. and I wouldn't have to leave all my friends and family."

"You didn't change anything, though? You still lived in Boston, married, and had me."

"Kind of."

"What do you mean 'kind of'? What are you talking about?"

Tameka sung louder.

"Can you quiet her?"

Jesus, Tameka.

"No, I can't and I'm afraid to move locations. I have a decent signal here. Spit it out. Fast."

"After that trip, multiple timelines of my life were created. In one, I am your mother. In another, I never left Trinidad, and in another, I died in that grocery store."

Tameka's voice resounded off the walls. Blood pumped through my eardrums.

"What did Kai say?"

Her face dimmed. "When she visited me yesterday, she wasn't the normal Kai."

She froze and the screen went blank. I lost connection.

I tried to get up, but I couldn't. Shock had cemented my butt to the chair.

Tameka's voice boomed.

"This is where you went," Serenity said and entered the room. "Whoa, she is *loud*."

Thoughts whizzed through my head.

The last time I saw Kai was on the Stone private jet *after* my mom saw her. She seemed fine to me.

Had Jayden begun to alter timelines years ago?

"Indy! Earth to Indy Kash!" Serenity interrupted. "What's wrong with you? You look like you saw a ghost. Did you see a ghost? That would be cool! Fuck, Tameka, you are LOUD…wait." She listened. "That's light language."

She confirmed my guess.

"How would Tameka know light language?" Trevor asked and entered the room.

I blinked a few times to snap out of my confoundment. In a monotone voice, I said, "Can you understand what she's saying?"

Tameka stopped.

"I understand some of the dialect. She was singing about a dark place, a tunnel? And then about things being turned upside down and inside out. I got the image of the Earth exploding from within."

The nurse came in. "The music's too loud and she needs her rest. You can come back later."

I said, "She sighed and was tapping her finger to the music *and* she was singing."

"I heard, but that don't mean anything. It takes a while for these patients to pull out of shock. It's good that she's movin' and singin' some, but we got a long way to go. All of you, out."

Serenity blew Tameka a kiss. We exited and stood in the waiting room.

She said, "We have to go back to *that place*—" She glanced at the nurses who were in distant earshot and lowered her voice. "—to find *the thing*."

Trevor ignored her and said, "Indy, are you okay? Seriously? You look…not good."

I heard their voices and registered what they'd said. This was not the time to numb out. "The last time we saw Kai, did she seem off to you?"

"No," they replied.

"Me neither."

"Why are you asking?"

"My mom called and said Kai seemed off the last time she saw her."

"Really? She's always odd."

"Yeah, but stranger than usual. I can't figure out what's going on anymore."

Serenity said, "Join the club. After hearing about our father, we can't either. It's getting harder to know who to trust."

No one responded.

Tameka's napkin from the diner popped in my head. "When I visited Tameka, she was writing on a napkin that had words and doodles. I didn't get a close enough look. The doodles could've been light language."

"So she's meta, like us?"

"She may've been sending a message with her singing. It aligns with what my mom told me. Mom changed something major in her past and it affected her present. Two new timelines were created somehow, and now three of them exist."

No one spoke.

Finally, Serenity said, "We're at critical mass."

"How do we fix any of this?" Trevor said in a louder-than-intended voice.

A couple in the waiting room glared at us.

He said quietly, "Are we in an altered timeline?"

"We could be," I replied.

That thought lingered among the three of us.

"We have to treat this timeline like it's the original one or we'll lose our minds," I said. "Let's think. How do we get to Jayden?"

"Tameka is the closest person to him," Trevor said.

"The second closest person has to be his grandmother," I said. "Do you know where Jayden's grandmother lives?"

"Last time I heard she was in an assisted living in JP."

All the way up in Boston.

"Do you have a phone number? Anything?"

"No."

My eye caught the clock at the nurses' station: it read 2:22.

We were down to less than seventeen hours if Jayden was to release the Time Machine at 9:00 a.m. tomorrow. The exact time was a guess, but for regular business hours it seemed right. Thirty minutes before the opening bell of the New York Stock Exchange.

Our only choice was to split up.

I said, "You have to find SJ. He needs to give you answers. I'm going to find where Jayden's grandma is, talk to her, and then head back to the old psych hospital. I hope she's been in contact with her grandson, if she really does exist. This is our only shot."

"Should we synchronize our watches?" Serenity asked.

"Huh?"

"I've always wanted to say that."

"You did. Congratulations. Let's go!"

CHAPTER TWENTY-TWO

My best resource was to call my former supervisor, Mrs. Moore, at the volunteer organization from when I had worked in JP. I texted her, saying it was an emergency for a friend, which *technically* it was.

She immediately called and I explained the situation in a roundabout way. I said I was looking for a JP nursing-home resident with the last name Mokashu hoping that was Jayden's grandmother's last name. I described her as a Jamaican lady who may have a grandson around thirty years old who came to visit and that his name was Jayden.

"You mean *the* Jayden Mokashu?"

"Yes, Mrs. Moore. The very one."

"You're playing with fire, Indy."

"You have no idea. Unfortunately, it's what I need to do."

She sighed. "Okay, Miss India. I'll send a group text and let you know if I hear anything. Promise me one thing?"

"Yes, ma'am?"

"You've come so far in the last decade. Be smart. Be safe."

I promised her that I'd try and hung up.

In the meantime, I tried to get ahold of Trevor and Serenity to no avail.

My phone chimed with a text.

Mrs. Moore wrote: "There was a woman by that description who lived in a JP nursing home. She recently transferred to your neck of the woods: Our Lady of Perpetua assisted living in Harlem. Her name is Vea Douglas. She goes by 'V.' My best to your friend. Talk soon."

Thank you Baby Jesus that she was here in Harlem. V was merely a taxi ride away.

I found the address to the nursing home online and ordered a car. During the ride, I thought about the fact that I didn't know what state V would be in. Would she be lucid or at an advanced stage of brain deterioration? Would she be a nasty old lady who loved her grandson and call the cops? Or would she help? Wrapping my mind around any scenario made me nervous. I was walking into yet another unknown situation without a safety net…and on top of all that, I had to deal with Jayden's *family*.

Yuck.

However, I was a little curious to see what type of crazy runs in that family tree.

We pulled up to Our Lady of Perpetua. She was a popular saint in the African-American community. Perpetua represented the divine feminine and was the saint of authenticity. Hopefully the latter would be the case with V.

The building was Harlem-historic with red brick and an embellished white façade. It seemed more like an elegant residence than an assisted living. It had to be costing Jayden a small fortune for V to live here.

I shut the car door and walked to the front entrance.

As I suspected, the building was locked. I buzzed. A person said, "Good afternoon, who are you visiting?"

"V Douglas. I'm a friend of Tameka's. Tell her it's India."

That was the truth, sort of. I had to say a name, so I used my real one. As bad as this sounded, I was hoping for a little bit of forgetfulness on V's part.

"Thank you. Wait one moment."

I prayed this would work and tapped my foot on the sidewalk. For sure, I thought my intestines would do their usual churn with anxiety, but today, I had noticed that my stomach wasn't bothering me as much. Was it all the metaphysical energy lately or from the crystals when they worked or both? Either way, I was grateful.

The woman's voice blasted through the speaker. "What's your last name, please?"

I squeezed my eyes and said, "Kash."

The door buzzed. A long sigh escaped from my lips, dragging my shoulders down with it.

As I entered the assisted living, I couldn't believe how nice it was. The inside was spacious and luxurious, similar to the lobby of a really nice hotel. The woman at the front desk waved me over and said, "You have to sign in."

I registered my information on the iPad.

"V is expecting you on the roof deck."

Yet another cold place.

She pointed to the elevator. "Take it to floor R."

When Time Flies by Jennifer Moreno (Ciotta)

I rode the elevator until it dinged. When the door slid open, I stepped onto the roof deck. A cold wind sliced and whipped. Flowerbeds lined the perimeter and colorful iron tables and chairs were arranged in the middle. The cityscape soared in the background. This was way nicer than any place I'd ever lived. I could only hope to die in a place like this.

A young man in scrubs and a coat smiled and waved. I did the same. A few residents huddled over a table, playing dominoes while a heat lamp warmed them. At the very edge of the roof deck was an older black woman in a wheelchair who had her back turned to me. She was gazing out to the skyline.

I wrapped my coat tighter around my body and carefully approached her. I touched her shoulder and said, "V?"

She backed up her wheelchair and spun around.

She was a stout woman with a bald scalp and dancing, purplish eyes. She was dressed head to toe in a purple outfit and a black designer wool coat.

We stared at each other.

Her face had barely wrinkled—just like my mom and grandmother, and hopefully me too. She wore makeup on her round, plump features. In each lobe was a diamond earring in the shape of a star.

"I'm India."

"Tameka doesn't have a friend named India that she's ever mentioned—not close enough to visit her grandmother-in-law unannounced. Would you like to start by telling me who you really are?" she said in a strong Jamaican accent.

I dragged over a chair and sat next to her. The attendant followed with a heat lamp—thank God—and switched it on. He shuffled to his faraway corner and cracked a thick book.

"Tameka is in the hospital."

Her eyes clouded over. I really had to work on my delivery.

I semi-explained what happened, using the "Tameka-touched-a-live-wire" excuse.

The orange horizon blazed.

"I'd appreciate you telling me the truth. What did my grandson do now? That's why you're really here, sweets."

"Are you close to Jayden?" I asked.

"Are you?"

I obviously couldn't lie to this woman. "No. He destroyed my life years ago, and I'm hoping to stop him from destroying others."

"Are you a traveler?"

"Yes."

"I had a feeling. I can travel, too. So could Jayden's grandfather, so he doubly inherited the gift."

Which *could* have made him doubly powerful and doubly prepared.

"How does Jayden travel?"

"Like me, I find a liminal space and go through it."

"Such as?"

"A bridge, stairway, hallway, tunnel, doorway."

Like Trevor.

"I have to be on an airplane."

"Air travel is a liminal space too. As long as you're in transition from one place to another."

My entire life was transitional lately.

"How did you end up here, in Harlem?"

"Tameka. We always got along. When she got in over her head with Jayden, she promised to move me to wherever she went." She paused. "Years ago, my legs worsened and he moved me into assisted living in JP, visited me once in a while, and kept me hidden—except when I was rolled out for the wedding with instructions to keep my mouth shut. It's a good thing Americans like small talk."

My heart ached for her. Jayden really did destroy every relationship.

"Oh sweets, don't worry about me. I've got plenty of friends and nice people here. I could be doing a lot worse."

Among all the dark and dank lately, her positivity was refreshing. I commiserated with her situation, enough to tell her everything. The words tumbled out of my mouth. When I finished, I didn't know if I had done something utterly terrible or inherently good. Either way, it was nice unloading the entire story on someone else.

"I remember seeing that Little Black Book. That was from a long time ago. He must've kept it throughout the years and added to it." She whistled. "Boy, was he prepared! Too well. That's the fault of my late husband and me."

"How?"

"We told Jayden when he turned thirteen. Now you tell that to anyone, especially a child, and they would laugh in your face. Not Jayden. He took it seriously and devoured everything he could on the subject. By the time Jayden turned thirty, I would say he was the world's most prepared time traveler."

I bet he was.

"We think the Time Machine is up at the old psych ward. Do you know exactly where he's hiding it?"

"He didn't tell me, sweets. It could be there or in any number of timelines."

That was the brutal reality.

"Do you know his real motivation for building a machine like this?"

She scrunched her ageless features. "Last time Jayden visited me in JP, he did say something odd."

My ears perked. "What did he say?"

"He asked about his parents, which he hadn't done since he was a child. We were honest with him. We'd always told him the truth: they had a disease called addiction and were unable to take care of him. My husband and I had cut all ties with them."

As heartless as he was, that was a flat-out rejection from the people who should've been his protectors, his everything, and I was sure he felt that grief and loss. Who wouldn't?

"When you last had contact with them, where were they living?"

"Oh let me see." She rummaged through her memory. "In a halfway house out in Framingham. A few months ago, a friend from the old neighborhood—she's a real gossip—told me they were back in JP and bragging on Jayden. Saying they were living with him in upstate New York. I asked Tameka, and she said nothing. Couldn't get anything out of her. That's all I know."

My phone chimed with a text. It was Trevor. All it said was "call me."

My phone then beeped with an email. It was my plane ticket information for tomorrow. Dammit. I had to fly to London to retrieve Blond Satan and her supposedly Keto-loving friends. I didn't know what to do, so I replied, "Received. Thanks." I'd deal with work later.

"V, it was lovely meeting you. I'm sorry, but I have to go."

"Yes, you do. You're on a tight deadline. Come see me again, sweets."

"I will. I promise."

I meant that. I couldn't believe this woman with a gentle soul could be related to Jayden.

I bent down and gave her a side hug.

She tapped my arm and whispered, "I'll take care of Tameka. Stop my grandson."

CHAPTER TWENTY-THREE

Outside on the quiet Sunday evening street, I called Trevor. "Hey."

"Hey," he said. "We grilled the hell out of SJ and broke him. What we saw was correct. He's helping Jayden with the Time Machine."

"Trevor, I'm so sorry."

"We don't have time for that. I'll deal with my piece-of-shit father later. His story is Jayden brought him in on a secret project and promised him the world in business"—as I thought—"but then he found out it was a Time Machine and wanted out. That was the first time he actually talked to me about being a traveler, and like Grandpa said, it freaks him out."

"Do you believe him?"

"He looked sincere."

"He did," Serenity hollered from the background.

They knew their father best.

"He said he funded the project. He bought two planes quietly, a Citation X and a Learjet, and helped break them down. When he found out what they were for, he told Jayden he was done, to which Jayden didn't take kindly"—no shit— "and said he would destroy Dad with all the info he had on him."

Jayden found dirt on SJ. No surprise there.

"Why did SJ *think* he was deconstructing planes? I mean, we saw him in the hangar. He seemed to be in on Jayden's plan?" I asked.

"Jay told him it was for a green jet company, to compete with Steven's."

That was a good cover. The way he held those wires, though, and directed people…I wasn't so sure that Trevor and Serenity were getting the whole truth. Their dad fudged some of the details to lessen the blow.

I continued, "So when we saw SJ in the past—"

"He said that was before Aire Aviation had opened, a couple months ago."

Like I had thought.

"He thinks Jayden is hiding the Time Machine in the old psychiatric ward, too."

I said, "He has SJ's funding plus the half billion from Stone Corp. Why wouldn't Jayden have his own private facility with lockdown security?"

"Dad said he's building a new facility but it's not done yet."

"It's a time issue." Just like ours at the moment.

"Here's the most chilling part: he's been experimenting on people besides Tameka."

That hit me like a ton of old red bricks. "Fuck. He's experimenting on his parents."

"What? How do you know that?"

"We don't have time. Where are you?"

"Serenity insisted we pick up some of Tameka's things and drop them off at the hospital. I don't know what Grandpa did but the staff is being *a lot* nicer."

"Good. I'll meet you there and we'll head upstate."

#

No one was in Tameka's hospital room.

Where did she go?

A nursed entered and curtly asked, "Who are you looking for?"

Serenity had registered Tameka under her maiden name. She didn't use Mokashu to avoid immediate recognition and leaking anything to the press.

"Tameka Harris."

She broke into a friendly smile. "Oh yes. She was moved to the nicest room on the floor. Please follow me."

Steven must've given a huge donation.

I followed the sound of her cushy sneakers.

"Here we go."

The door was closed.

"Just knock and the family will let you in."

The *family*? Why hadn't Trevor and Serenity informed me of this room change.

I rapped on the door.

A black woman cracked it open and looked surprised. "Yes?"

"I'm here to see Tameka. I'm with Trevor and Serenity."

"Who's that?" I heard someone murmur.

The door opened wider. Trevor and Serenity stood behind the woman.

"Hey!" I said. "We have to get going."

"We have to what?" Serenity said.

"Who are you?" Trevor asked.

The woman stepped aside. The expressions on both their faces said everything.

They had no idea who I was.

Two pairs of eyes studied me. I searched for recognition—for that little lift of familiarity, the half-smile that used to come so easily. What I found was absence. The kind of reserved vacancy you would give a stranger.

My stomach dropped. *No, no, no*! This wasn't right!

"It's me, *Indy*," I said, the words trembling into the silence. "You have to know me."

They exchanged glances as discomfort and wariness became apparent. My heart sunk. I was a stranger among them. How could they not recognize who I was? After all we were going through? Maybe this was their warped idea of a joke.

"Are you guys screwing with me? We don't have time. C'mon, let's go!"

Their silence was louder than any words. Every shared memory, secret, and moment of loyalty was gone. To them, I was no one. Again.

My voice cracked, "It's me! Indy! Indy Kash! We have to go upstate to stop Jayden!"

Trevor said, "Didn't I know you in high school? You were the girl who got kicked out, right?"

"Pyro Girl!" Serenity sneered.

They really didn't know who I was.

How the fuck was this happening?

"Listen, I don't know if you're some type of weird fan of our family or whatever, but we have a serious situation here. You have to go before we call security. Leave."

He slammed the door. I jumped at the thud.

My heart was about to beat out of its cavity and shoot through my chest. All the meta energy that had soothed my gut and intestines was no longer there. Bile squished and boiled in my stomach—a too familiar feeling. Tears poured down my cheeks.

Someone tapped me on the shoulder. "Miss, you have to go. Now." That friendly voice from before had turned sharp.

I dashed through the hallways to the elevator and out the entrance. My body heaved from sobbing and running at once.

What the fuck was I going to do?!

I wanted to call for Kai, but my mom said she was acting strangely. And now Trevor and Serenity. Could I trust anyone?

I slumped to the curb. As I cradled my head, I wept like I never had before. People walked by and glanced. I didn't care, because nothing else mattered. When did this happen? How did this happen? I'd gone from Trevor and Serenity calling me "family" to this. Between our phone call and now, the timelines must've become skewed.

It was so unfair. Yes, life was unfair and I knew that better than anyone. Yet I had started to come to terms with the present…and I had made friends, *real* friends, even a possible boyfriend. In an instant and without warning, it was all gone.

When I had no more tears left, I wiped my cheeks.

Where was I to go?

Nothing made sense anymore.

A notification dinged on my phone.

Boston Celebs Podcast.

I laughed in a maniacal way.

Maybe the world had already ended. Had Jayden's Time Machine messed up everything so badly that I was in the aftermath?

I didn't know what else to do, so I hit play.

"Hey, it's me again, your fav poddie host with an update!" He cleared his throat and switched to a solemn tone. "I have dire news for Stone Corp watchers. Jayden Mokashu's wife, Tameka, was involved in a freak accident earlier today. Possible electrocution. She is in serious but stable condition at the best burn center in Manhattan. We wish her a speedy recovery. We also received word from company insiders that Mokashu has a secret project he's releasing tomorrow. We'll be back then with an update. Bye-eee!"

I sniffled. Jayden's plans were still in motion. The Stones didn't know me and they possessed no knowledge of his plans.

They gathered in that hospital room with Tameka's family because they believed it was a freak electrocution. How Jayden had spun it, I could only imagine.

Everything was one gigantic clusterfuck.

I grasped the crystal necklace and pulled with all my might to rip it off.

It wouldn't budge.

Was this all a joke?

All I could recognize was the shambles of my life, head in hands, slouched on this curb.

A warm light touched the crown of my head.

"You're okay, Indy."

I turned around to see Kai's glowing figure.

I gave her a wary look and said, "Kai."

"I'm aware of what your mom told you. She was right about how I came to her in a timeline. Jayden had altered that timeline, I'm sure of it, and made me appear abnormal to Tina. The more he's using the Time Machine, the more everything is changing at rapid speed."

She sat on the curb next to me.

"Are spirit guides susceptible to altered timelines?"

"Usually no. This is a new occurrence. Jayden hasn't perfected anything, but he's doing a good job of messing with the spirit world."

Everything seemed hopeless.

"Do I seem normal to you right now?"

"Yes."

"I am, but how can you trust that? Your entire world has been turned upside down. Things from now on will take an even darker turn than we've seen. You need to focus—more than you ever have before, Indy."

Focus. Exactly what Mom said to me in the courtroom. I was always being asked to focus in situations beyond my control, and by a spirit guide who seemed like her normal self. Trevor and Serenity also seemed normal…until they weren't.

"You can't give up. You're the only human who can stop Jayden."

"How come I'm not in LaLa Land like Trevor and Serenity?"

"Jayden must be playing a game of timeline gaslighting. He'll make you think you're crazy until you walk off a bridge. He's choosing to slowly torture you."

Like in high school, I was a fawn to his wolf.

"He sees you as dangerous to his goal."

"I don't know how to stop him. Going upstate, if he's onto me, he knows that's where I'm headed. It's bait. I'm dead on sight."

"There's always another option."

I used to believe that too. If Jayden had started preparing for all this at thirteen years of age, how could I erase nearly two decades of studying and perfecting—

"I have to return to the plane. The elders are expecting an update. Indy, find another way."

With that, she disappeared. I was left alone once again, the way I had begun this journey.

But I had gained knowledge.

This knowledge told me that if I were to stop Jayden, I'd have to travel to his original past and somehow halt his childhood ambitions. That was the only way.

My mom warned me not to screw with the past, though. Damn.

Well, sometimes you had to go in and fuck some shit up.

That was exactly what I planned to do.

CHAPTER TWENTY-FOUR

I returned to the only familiar place I could think of: my apartment. I unlocked the door and Snowball meowed when I entered. Her fishy cat food remained half-eaten in her bowl and she had plenty of water. Mrs. Albright had been here. The last time I saw Snowball was at Trevor's apartment with Frank. The timeline had definitely been altered.

The time on the oven read: 5:55 p.m. As Serenity had said, we were at critical mass. I had to think fast.

What confounded me was why my family used air travel solely as their liminal space to travel, while Trevor's family, V, and Jayden used ordinary spaces. Could I use a liminal space too, or a liminal state of mind to return to where I wanted in the past?

My ancestors technically could. They were able to astral travel.

Even if I could harness this ability, I would return to my own childhood. I hadn't met Jayden until I attended Brookline Prep.

V had access to Jayden's childhood. I could follow her through a liminal space!

I looked up the number to Our Lady of Perpetua and called.

"Our Lady of Perpetua assisted living."

"Hello, I met you a few hours ago. I was there visiting V Douglas. May I be connected with her?"

The person on the other end was quiet for a moment, then said, "You must be mistaken. I regret to inform you that V passed last week."

Adrenaline coursed through my body.

No.

I refused to believe it.

"Are you sure?"

"Yes," the woman said. "We know when a resident passes away. V died *last week.*"

"I just saw her a few hours ago—"

"Miss! Unless you are family, I do not have any more information for you. I am sorry for your loss, but there's nothing more I can do."

She slammed the receiver. Like Kai had warned, my world was becoming a lot more sinister fast.

V wasn't an option.

Who could get me into Jayden's past?

His parents.

My fingers clicked away on my phone. I winced the entire time I scoured social media. Even though I wasn't supposed to, I used the logins from a couple volunteer organizations for whom I had worked. Luckily, they hadn't changed their passwords.

An Instagram account popped up when I searched for the name "Mokashu."

It was of a woman named Barbara with frizzy, platinum hair and missing teeth. She was so thin and pale; sadly, you could tell she was an addict. Next to her stood a man with his arm around her waist. He was lanky with a fade haircut and large teeth. I expanded the photo. Together their features melded into Jayden's—they were definitely his parents. The tag for Jayden's father read: Zion Mokashu. Other than that photo, Barbara's account was void of information and Zion's was blank except for a zoomed-in profile pic.

I observed this time and time again at my community service jobs. I served food, folded clothes, and packed meals for those on meth, heroin, methadone, cocaine, alcohol, prescription drugs, and more. The sadness and loneliness that poured out of their souls was enough to frighten anyone.

Barbara and Zion were the perfect guinea pigs for the Time Machine. They were long-time addicts; no one would believe a word they said. I hated to be this critical, but the shape they both were in, after years of drug and alcohol abuse, it was hard to look at them. Society turned away from anything scary or grotesque—the darkest parts of the human psyche.

When I had listened to the stories of the food pantry clients, I saw myself in them. We were all people with life struggles, bullshit thrown our way, and that as humans, we knew the meaning of unfairness.

I had to find them.

Barbara and Zion had to be in the vicinity of the Time Machine. As much as I wanted to crawl into bed, pull the covers over my head, and pretend it was four days ago, I couldn't avoid the thing I had to do.

So, I fueled up on leftover beef stew in the fridge, a can of tuna I shared with Snowball, and potato chips made with avocado oil. I texted Mrs. Albright to take care of Snowball. She responded, "I know, honey. I've been doing it all week." Apparently, she wasn't at her sister's in Maine.

I snatched my spare set of car keys from their wall hook—was my car there or at Trevor's in the city? I pressed the key fob and heard a beep.

Phew.

Snowball pawed me. When I bent down to plant a kiss on her furry head, tears formed. This could be the last time I saw the most special and precious part of my life. We'd been through everything together. Her green eyes penetrated mine, as if saying, "It's okay, Mama. Go get 'em."

I nuzzled her, wiped my tears, and flew out the door.

#

Once again, I stood at the teal door. A soft lullaby filled the air. I looked around me. No one was there.

The song grew louder. I recognized it.

It was Tameka singing.

How could I hear it?

She had reached me despite the mess of this altered timeline. Though I couldn't understand light language, I felt the power in her words. She must be an incredible poet.

Serenity said Tameka was singing about a dark place, a—

The underground tunnels!

They were hidden and dank—the environment Jayden preferred like the swamp creature he was. V mentioned a tunnel as a liminal space—Jayden could be using it to heighten the powers of the Time Machine.

Where was a tunnel entrance?

I raced around the building and then the next. In the very back corner, where concrete met grass, steam rose from a vent.

This had to be it.

I rushed over to it, heaved the grate, and let myself down through the hole. As I held onto the opening, my feet dangled.

The vapor of steam had dissipated for the moment. I would have to trust and let go.

I could do this. It was time to have faith in myself and set myself free. I squeezed my eyes shut and took a second to muster the courage. My hands released.

I landed with a thud on the ground.

The lullaby ended and I knew I was alone. I thanked Tameka for helping me.

Water trickled. I stood up, turned on my phone flashlight, and ambled on the uneven stone of the earth. The frigid air and dampness swept into my lungs and made me cough.

As I rounded a corner, I smelled burning—that reek of Tameka's smoldering flesh. My body filled with dread. I bent over and vomited. Chunks of beef and carrots spewed on the ground. My body heaved from the exertion and I stood up. The stew might have been exorcised from me, but the terror lingered in my buckling knees.

I had to move forward, even with wobbly steps.

The tunnel seemed to contract and the air flow lessened. I reminded myself that not every experience was a pleasant one. As humans, we all wanted our lives to be easy and pleasant. That wasn't life; that was a perfection no one could attain—not even the Spirit Council. Though it pained us and went against every happy ending we ever watched, this was the truth…

Sometimes we had to fight.

At the far end of the tunnel, there was light. I doubted it was a healing light, yet I was compelled to walk toward it. My brain nudged my right foot and then my left. Slowly, I traversed the long, dark path that would get me to somewhere I didn't want to be.

The light glowed and flickered like an old incandescent lamp. The burning smell was so horrendous that I covered my mouth. The dormant crystals around my neck gently bounced against my skin. Water kept dripping on my hair. I absolutely hated frizz, but this really wasn't the time to be vain.

A roar echoed throughout the tunnel. Lasers beamed and swished…until the tunnel went black.

The Time Machine was here.

I found it. Finally.

My heart lurched with relief that I had accomplished something deemed insurmountable. If I could do this, I could do more.

I navigated through the dark, listening for any sound that would guide me. I crept along and splashed in puddles for what seemed like an eternity, or like waiting in a *really* long line for coffee.

My foot kicked an object that was hard but not heavy. I bent down to pick it up. The blood drained from my face.

It was a bone.

I dropped it.

I didn't know anatomy well; it looked like a femur. It could be from an animal—I was sure they existed in this sewer-like environment. I examined it closely; it was human. This thigh bone did not have sinewy flesh attached—thank goodness. But it did have a marking. A black line from the middle of the femur extended upward, as if it were leading to the sacral chakra.

Was the Time Machine eviscerating its human subjects and leaving them as skeletons?

"Who's there?"

FUCK.

That was Jayden's voice.

It sounded distant, like it was way down the tunnel.

"You imaginin' things, man. Ya ears are goin' bad. Ya said we'd be in and outta here quick. We hungry, boy."

The voice resembled a much older Jayden. Zion?

I recognized the tone of a man who'd been around the block too many times. I waited for Jayden's response. Minutes passed and nothing. I continued my walk into the black abyss until I rounded another corner.

Where were they?

My eyelids fluttered. I let out a gigantic yawn. My legs grew heavy and dense. The air morphed into the sickening burning combined with an undertone of chemical. My head grew woozy. I had to stop.

I knelt on the ground, then sat and leaned against a wall.

Was I being drugged?

I forced myself to stay alert, but my eyelids pulled. The next thing I knew, I wasn't in the tunnel anymore. Where was

I? I blinked to try to regain focus. It proved impossible as panic ripped through me. My heartbeat hammered. My skin prickled to where I wished I could've jumped out of it. Every nerve sparked in wild disbelief.

#

This was not the normal non-dizzying spinning or the black space. Instead, I felt so nauseous that I puked again. The vomit separated into particles, formed a line, and zagged away.

Oh my god! What's happening! I thought in my frenzied haze.

The gentleness of when I traveled with Kai, when Trevor had a soft landing, or traveling on my best solo trips was absent. Without warning, a force shoved me around in the dense air.

Jayden appeared.

He was covering his ears and crouched against a tunnel wall.

My head swung left then right. Feared coursed through every part of me as the trauma awakened of the relived arson event. My intestines began their inevitable coiling. I needed to find a way out and couldn't—a reminder of exactly what happened before. The door that wasn't there, feeling trapped and alone. I should've been used to those emotions by now. This was different. It was a feral, primal need to save myself in a way I hadn't ever known.

The colors of the rainbow withered, and discordant traffic horns blared.

I covered my ears.

It smelled like a dead animal. The sweetness in my glands overtook everything and I heaved yet again. Nothing came out. My mind slipped in and out of consciousness.

What was happening?

Had Jayden created a black hole and I was stuck? That couldn't be possible, because if I were truly in a black hole, gravity would've stretched me like spaghetti.

I mustered all my vocal strength and screamed at the top of my lungs:

"JAYDEN, TURN OFF THE MACHINE!!!"

He wheezed and clutched his chest. His five senses were completely bombarding him, as mine were too.

I kept focused. Though my consciousness wavered, I fought through it. One thing was for sure:

Jayden Mokashu was NOT taking me out.

From my battle with UC, I understood that a knight in shining armor wasn't going to ride in on a horse to save me. I learned the hard way: there was no cure. I had to save myself.

I couldn't allow the noises, smells, and sights to override me.

The protection crystals heated against my throat.

"Stay awake, stay alert, I will get you out of this," Kai said.

I had no idea how I heard her voice. It sounded like the Kai I knew, but I couldn't be sure. It was best to rely on myself.

My intuition said, *shut down your senses one by one*. I concentrated as best I could on eliminating smell, sound, taste, touch, and finally, I inhaled and closed the door on sight. I was a blind-deaf-tasteless mute who couldn't feel the crystals anymore. I had morphed myself into an object that rested on the ground and simply took a break.

How I had figured out how to do this…I wasn't sure. It was shocking, yet Kai's advice proved true. If I focused like my life depended on it—by the way, it did—I could do things I never thought possible.

I was suspended in animation, a limp, boring human body without anything to do except think and lay there.

A scene poured into my consciousness of a little boy—*of Jayden*—was he eight? He played with a miniature car, a toy DeLorean—of course, he knew what a DeLorean was. I heard him say "zoom-zoom" while the younger version of V smiled at him with fondness. The scene changed to him as—perhaps if I evoked incredible compassion—a thirteen-year-old boy who felt deep sadness and anger toward his parents and the world. The sociopath was in there, but looking at him, it was hard to see anything but a child.

In this moment, I felt exactly what it was like to be Jayden. His fury ignited into a teenaged lust for power without an understanding of how to achieve it. Chemicals swirled and restructured themselves, as if I was slowly morphing into a monster. I was him, thinking ahead at all times, plotting and strategizing. I flashed through Jayden's sick, twisted mind, and it exhausted me until the scenes slowed down to…

Him as an adult, and his plan for selling Timeline Tourism.

He knew it was an idea that could end the world…yet he saw the reward over the risk. His ego and impatience clouded his judgment. After he was able to block Kai and the Spirit Council, he thought, *I can do this*. I experienced him watching—of all things—Home Shopping Network over and over late at night. He thought, *I could dole these babies out and make a fortune—and finally get the recognition I deserve*. His plan was to perfect the Time Machine—which he hadn't done—and mass produce with the backing of Stone Corp.

My intuition said, *this is the surface reason. Dig deeper*.

He would convince the public that he could—my consciousness wavered here. I couldn't quite understand his intention—wait.

My focus resharpened.

Adult Jayden, who looked the same age as he did in present time, hacked and coughed blood into a tissue.

He was sick.

Only he knew.

His ultimate goal was to play God for himself.

A new sensation washed over me. What felt like a gentle broom swept out my consciousness. A bright light surrounded me. I was able to see again; the light restructured into the soul star chakra. It showered me in its highest vibration and most primal forms of joy and love. I yearned to bask in its rays and stay here forever, but alas, I had a job to do.

I asked my consciousness to restore my five senses and human body.

It obeyed.

Swiftly, I returned to the tunnel, and in that instant, I stood face to face with what I dreaded most.

CHAPTER TWENTY-FIVE

Like the disappearing photo had foretold, Jayden had me hooked up to the Time Machine.

Here I was, standing like the Vitruvian Man against my will. My body had involuntarily shifted into that position.

Jayden had removed my coat and the top half of my clothing—my teeth chattered—and connected me with the chakra wires. I only had on a bra and the necklace; this wasn't the time to give a shit about modesty. My head could not move. The magnets touched my chakras, one through seven. I shook with coldness and fear—the latter I tried not to acknowledge.

Even though the Time Machine wasn't on, the wires still paralyzed me. I desperately tried to move an arm, then a leg. I couldn't. The magnets felt warm; I could only assume that they and the wires had enough energy from its last run to stifle my chakras and freeze me in this position.

Next to the Machine, a battery-operated light shone. Slumped against the tunnel wall near the Time Machine was a man and woman.

Zion and Barbara.

They looked so thin and gaunt—much worse than they looked on Instagram—shells of the humans they once were. They resembled corpses, though they weren't, because I saw their bodies rise and fall with breath.

I scanned the area as best I could. No sign of Jayden. It was me, his parents, and the Time Machine. The tunnel was absent of the burning smell. It was just cold and damp, like any underground place.

"Barbara, Zion!" I whisper-yelled.

Zion opened one eye. "Jay got you hooked up too. Ya like the others. Enjoy the ride."

"What others?"

"The people he experiments on. You, me, and the others, the homeless people."

"Where's Jayden?"

"I don't fuckin' know. Stop botherin' me, bitch."

With that, he fell into silence and began to snore. I studied both Barbara and him. Were they burned?

"Lady, my son will kill you. You gotta get outta here."

"Barbara, did he connect you and Zion to the Machine?"

"Yeah."

She pointed to her pale face, which had small burns, and then to her blond hair. In the center was a bald spot from the crown chakra connection.

"He said he wanted to heal us. He finds sick people and tries to make 'em better."

How was healing the human body possible with a Time Machine?

What I saw and felt about Jayden in my altered state of consciousness was true. I understood why he kept his illness to himself. It must be newly acquired and aggressive, because I'd seen him as his recent, adult self. The Spirit Council and Kai didn't know. He was on a solo mission: cure himself, play with humans like ants on an ant farm, and rule the world.

"You gotta get outta here, lady."

"Where's Jayden?"

"I dunno. He said that was round one. He comin' back for round two."

I was round two.

"Lady, promise me somethin'? If that machine don't kill us, you've got to. We'll do the same for you, if we survive."

All I could do was nod.

"My teeth hurt. I'm goin' to sleep now," Barbara said and turned her body away from me.

The silence was crushing. I was alone with two nearly dead humans and my own thoughts.

"My parents are cool, right?"

I did not see or hear Jayden approach. Only an evil creature could move that quietly. His shirt was untucked, and red spots—presumably burns—dotted his exposed hands and forearms. He crouched next to the Time Machine and fiddled with a wire.

This was real life. He wasn't a TV villain where he'd launch into a long speech and confess every detail of his plan.

He was gonna rev that baby up like a lawn mower and fucking go.

He kept adjusting the solar plexus wire. The magnet stirred on my stomach.

"Thanks for breaking my Machine."

I willed myself to squirm and stretch to get out of this position and break the Machine for good. But as hard as I tried, I was frozen.

I heard a click, then a whir. The transporter came to life.

"Let's hit it!" Jayden croaked.

He still had to turn on the cyclotrons and power the eighth chakra by making the wire dance. So far, it sat motionless on the ground. If my heart exploded out of my chest, I wouldn't have been surprised. My intestines were so scared they froze into a pipeline.

The magnets heated and my chakras whizzed one by one: first my tailbone spun, then the sacrum, then the solar plexus, the heart, the throat, the third eye, and finally the crown. The lasers flashed and swished, while the transporter let out a deafening roar.

All of these chakras spinning and vibrating at such a fast speed, it was like doing the energy cords in acupuncture times a million. The energy zigging and zagging around my body was so intense that I was close to passing out.

If he connected the eighth chakra wire, I was toast. My petite self could not handle one more iota of energy. No human could.

Jayden hollered, "My Machine isn't solely for traveling. It'll pull your physiology from another timeline where you aren't sick. Imagine a world without Alzheimer's, Parkinson's…lung cancer." He paused. "And what do you have? Inflammatory Bowel Disease. Everyone would be healed"—or dead—"that's why you're the perfect candidate—"

A coughing fit overtook him.

From what I knew about medical intuition, lung cancer made sense for Jayden. Grief and sorrow that hadn't been addressed usually culminated as disease in the lungs. Considering that both of his parents rejected him, he was—like me—on par with holding onto old emotions.

That was my last clear thought. My brain was fogging over. The energy consumed me to a level I could not withstand.

My body jolted and zapped. Tears flowed. I understood what Barbara had told me; I'd rather be dead than feel like this. I lost control of my bodily functions and openly wept. I didn't care what Jayden thought of me. I was dying, and these were my last moments. Memories swirled through my mind of Trevor and I having sex, him calling me family, petting Snowball's plush fur, Mom admitting she was a time traveler, Serenity as a child in her room with kitten Frank, and Kai's glowing tears.

The eighth chakra wire gradually snaked into the air. With each turn, I sobbed harder. Somehow, I managed to cry out for everyone to help me, including my ancestors. I could not hear myself over the Time Machine.

The wire danced higher.

My tears, piss, shit, and the natural moisture of my body floated and gathered in the air. They morphed into particles and disappeared.

I spasmed and contorted. The eighth chakra wire was about to connect. My muscles and tissues heated; any second now they would begin to cook.

I gasped for breath.

My heart stopped.

In a millisecond, I was out of my body, floating above the entire scene. I peered down on my lifeless corpse, the grin on Jayden's face, and his fist pumping in the air with celebration.

Barbara and Zion lay in a corner, motionless.

The incredible part was I felt no pain; I was the pure version of myself. No UC or excruciating electrocution. In the distance, a light shimmered and expanded. It coaxed me toward it; it was the most profound feeling.

It stretched beyond words—ancient, steady, and all consuming. It settled into my heart chakra like something sacred…and endless. I was rooted in this unfiltered and blinding truth of a depth that I never knew was possible.

I was connected to the entire Universe.

I floated down a tunnel toward it.

Soft, ethereal music played and heavenly chimes tinkled. I witnessed my life in review from birth to the moment I had died. It was objective and without judgment…and displayed the most beautiful thing I had overlooked: the impact of my years of service.

I observed the smile that I'd brought to someone's face while dishing out soup. A little girl with leukemia jumped up and down as she boarded a private jet. A homeless man with sparkling blue eyes felt seen by me.

The most exquisite non-binary spirit guided me to a verdant garden that possessed otherworldly colors and plants, like something out of Avatar. I sat on a bench. The being sat next to me, leaned in my ear, and whispered, "I don't have to show you your mission. You already know it. Now get back there."

The gloom of returning to my human body was like diving into an ice-cold pool. It felt heavy, cumbersome, and unkind— by far, the worst human experience.

The eighth chakra wire had connected. My body jolted to a Grand Mal seizure times a hundred. I braced myself for a final zap, but suddenly, the Time Machine died.

I let out an enormous moan, fell to the ground, and gasped for air.

That fact that I was still alive was impossible. That fact that I could still formulate thoughts and breathe was even more impossible. Though my heart thumped too fast, it was beating again.

I smelled burning human flesh—probably mine.

I could barely move and avoided checking to see which body part would need amputation or what chunk of skin or organ was missing.

My mouth was shut. Was I still moaning?

No.

It came from near the tunnel wall.

I blinked and did my best to focus. My head and chakras were spinning.

The moaning was Barbara and Zion.

Where was Jayden?

In the distance, a light flickered in the tunnel. It dimmed to gray and then to black. I smelled dead animal again and heard an eerie creaking sound, like a basement door opening in a horror movie. The spinning in my head and chakras lessened and my vision sharpened.

Maybe the energy was too powerful for the Machine and that was why it'd stopped? Had Jayden imitated the Philadelphia Experiment and cranked it to full blast?

Parts must've come off and flown down the tunnel. Jayden was bent over, picking up a shiny metal object. I could hear him hacking and swearing.

My instinct was to rush over to Barbara and Zion. Obviously, I couldn't. I had to lay here, completely and utterly helpless.

I looked at them.

They had ceased moving; their chests did not rise and fall.

Despite the freezing temperature, I wasn't cold. This signaled my body was in shock. My job was to snap out of it.

Jayden lugged the piece of metal to the Time Machine. He stood it upright and tapped it into place. He unzipped a bag and removed a screwdriver and screws and refastened the metal box.

It was all so…primitive. This was a human who could time-travel, possibly heal disease, and exceeded all scientific expectations…yet here he was, attaching nut to a bolt.

In my brain fog, I saw Jayden for what he actually was: fallible.

The crystals had remained pleasantly warm.

I strained to lift my hand to touch them.

My fingers outstretched and hovered above the ground.

Jayden had refit the Machine and the transporter whirred in slow motion. His next step would be connecting the wires to my body. My hand lifted an inch higher.

He coughed and mumbled to himself as he picked up each wire off the ground.

He was a fumbling, muttering mess who was no longer the cool, collected guy that everyone knew. I understood what Trevor meant when he said Jayden had become moody. That must've been a tough act for all these years pretending to be the nicest guy in the room—*then* pretending not to have cancer. The man I saw in front of me was splitting at the seams.

"Fuck!" he yelled and dropped a sparking wire.

The transporter whizzed at a higher speed. My close proximity to it caused my cells to dance. It wasn't like before, when they were breaking down. It was like an opera singer belting out her peak note. The feeling was stimulating and irritating at the same time.

Jayden had separated the wires, and with gloves, was reattaching the magnets.

My hand reached higher.

Behind him, Zion had woken. He got on all fours and crawled over to his son. He yelped, "Boo!"

Shocked, Jayden's body sprung up and he whipped around, already in fight mode.

This was my chance.

Zion was cackling as Jayden lunged at him. With all the physical and mental strength I could muster, I reached out and seized hold of Jayden's ankle.

A jolt pierced through me. I wouldn't let go. My hand wanted to release his ankle. My innate stubbornness refused.

He kicked and I grasper harder.

The transporter roared softly this time, more like a teenage cub than a full-grown lion.

I dug my fingers into his ankle bone and tissue. An evaporating sensation overtook my body and I was whisked into the dark unknown. I was still attached to Jayden, so together we zoomed in harsh time-lapse fashion through time and space. It moved too fast. I squeezed my eyes shut, praying that it would end.

Then it did.

Of all the places I thought I could go, it never occurred to me that this—*this* place was even an option.

Yet here I was.

CHAPTER TWENTY-SIX

My mind raced. How am I here?! Where is he?

I was on Blond Satan's G4. My eyes darted to her large phone screen and read the day and date. It was Tuesday afternoon. I then glimpsed the flight map. The trip originated in Luton, England, and our destination was Teterboro. It was two days after I'd been struggling with Jayden in the tunnel.

Goosebumps rose on my arms. Usually in my time travels and while working on jets, I felt cold. This time, I was sweating and trembling.

I had to get ahold of myself. I was clearly not in reality and needed to figure out how to leave this timeline.

Nothing came to mind for an immediate escape. For right now, I would act as a flight attendant and observe this timeline.

There was Blond Satan herself and her usual gaggle of friends and a handsome young man with black hair…and Serenity? There she was, howling with laughter and gesturing wildly—her usual life-of-the-party self.

Would she recognize me? Had the timeline snapped back to its original state, or was this a new one entirely?

The buffet of all kinds of food—not all Keto—was spread throughout the plane, on the tray tables, side boards, and credenza. Little Miss Satan munched on a handful of pretzels and was that a—pina colada?!

Why would that bitch insist on a Keto menu—okay, Indy, so not the point right now.

Serenity sipped on champagne and her glass was almost empty. I grabbed the bottle out of the ice bucket and sauntered over to her.

"More champagne, miss?"

She looked me dead in the face and said, "duh!"

The group broke into a fit of laughter.

My cheeks burned. I poured and blinked away tears. We didn't know each other. The real Serenity—even if she was pretending in front of Blond Satan—would've given me a wink or another type of signal. This was a version of her I instantly loathed: cruel and entitled.

"My husband's glass is empty too. You might wanna fill him up while you're here," she said and pointed to the man's outstretched hand.

Her husband?

Could altered timelines make someone switch their sexuality?

I poured again and studied him. He was a twenty-something man with olive skin and timeless features—the Latin version of her.

With my tail between my legs, I moped to the galley. I heard Serenity say, "Jesus, it's so hard to find good help these days! You have to tell them exactly what to do!"

"Don't be mean, Seri. Indy's a great flight attendant. Be nice."

Was that Blond Satan?

Whoa.

Blond Satan being nice was way creepier than Serenity being mean. This wasn't a future I could stomach.

I set the champagne bottle on the counter and began to wash the dirty silverware.

Kai, Trevor, Mom, or hell even the Spirit Council never talked about traveling to the future. I was sure as I kept traveling normally—whatever that meant—the question of jumping into the future would've been raised naturally. It must've been a quirk of the Time Machine energy or Jayden's ability to travel into the future that no one had yet discovered.

Had he sent me to another timeline while he was back in the original one?

The lav door cracked open. I heard a woman's giggle and a man's voice.

She stepped out first.

Anna.

The supermodel Trevor had been "dating."

Behind her was…

Trevor.

His arms encircled her waist and he was nibbling on her ear. She squealed with pleasure.

I stopped washing a fork midair. My heart plummeted to a depth that I didn't know was possible.

"Oh wait!" he said and zipped up his pants.

Serenity hollered from the front, "That's my brother! You whore!"

I couldn't look at him. At either of them.

I felt a tap on my shoulder.

"Hey, make me another vodka soda with lime. Thanks," he said.

With tears about to spill down my cheeks, I nodded and turned away. He and Anna gyrated back to their seats, though music wasn't playing. The dam broke and I sobbed my way into the lav and shut the door. I sat on the bench with the toilet hidden underneath.

Was I trapped in my version of hell?

When I was at my lowest point in the midst of Pyro Girl, I'd spent a lot of time in my room on YouTube. I stumbled upon a video that discussed "Appreciating the Basic Concerns" or the ABCs. I sniffled and went through the ABCs.

I had food, clothing, and this plane and my apartment counted as shelter, and enough money to get me home, wherever that was. I could breathe air, had all my five senses, and could walk and run if need be. According to the ABCs, I had much to appreciate—yet I wasn't feeling grateful.

The last thing I wanted to do was serve these assholes, especially my former friends who once called me "family."

As much as I wanted to, I couldn't keep hiding in this lav.

My experiences with Trevor and Serenity…I still had those memories. Even if this timeline had changed, or like Mom had experienced when other timelines were created, I was still me—and that was the most important thing.

I stood up, wiped my face, and caught a glimpse of myself in the mirror.

Black speckles dotted my face—like Kai's aura. I touched one. Cold air ran through it.

I gasped.

It was a hole in my skin.

I examined closer. Another one popped up under my right eyelid. As a kneejerk reaction, my hand jumped to the crystals and smacked them. They were limp against my neck. I gulped. At least, my hands didn't have the holes…yet. If they started popping up everywhere on my body—my breath caught in my throat.

Had Jayden messed with this timeline that fast? Not even twenty-four hours after his release of the Machine?

I took a deep breath. I was the only person who could figure out what was going on in the future and hopefully fix it. I couldn't save the world in a private jet lav. Despite the holes poking through my face, I pulled open the lav door and stepped into the galley.

"Indy!"

Blond Satan.

She touched my shoulder. "Are you okay? I saw you crying." She nodded to her friends. "Trevor was annoying and kept demanding his drink. Don't worry, I made it for him. And I told them to lay off you. You take your time and serve us when you're ready, okay?"

This was too much. I could not handle an empathetic Blond Satan.

"Thanks."

She gave me a wide-tooth grin, and as she did, I saw a few black speckles dotting her face too. As she walked to her guests, she carried a tray of drinks. Her hands had the speckles.

Were we disappearing?

I couldn't stand by and wash another fork. They obviously didn't realize they had holes because they gesticulated, chortled, feasted, and drank with glee. Perhaps I only saw them because I had been involved with the Time Machine. At the moment, it was fun and games…until they discovered there were gaping holes in their bodies.

I dropped the fork into the sink, put on my bravest expression, and marched over to the pax.

About to open my mouth, Serenity blurted, "Isn't Jay a fucking legend?! He's a genius! Now we're all going to be rich!"

"We're already rich. Plus, all this stuff is way dangerous," Trevor slurred while downing the vodka soda.

"You know what I mean! This invention will bring in trillions and we can fix our dumbass past mistakes. Trev, where would you start?"

Everyone laughed.

"It's so exciting—" Blond Satan paused for dramatic effect. "I could start a foundation for those less fortunate to have financial access to the Machine."

Oh God, I might puke.

This was straight-up Jonestown. They had chugged Jayden's Kool-Aid.

Trevor yelled, "That's my bro! I wish he were here. Let's toast to him anyway." He held up his empty glass. "To Jay-man!"

Really, Jay-man? Could this get more foul?

"To Jay-man!" the others repeated.

Well, there was no convincing them that Jayden was an evil mastermind who was destroying the world.

"More drinks?" Blond Satan asked her guests.

"Fuck yes," Trevor replied and then nuzzled Anna's neck.

"I have to pee first, then I'll get them."

She traversed to the lav and closed the door.

I'd seen my holes in the mirror—would she?

Suddenly, Amanda shrieked and threw it back open.

She rushed past me to her friends. "Guys, I had the best idea! We should all time-travel back to my twenty-first birthday party. Remember how fire it was?!"

"Iconic!" Serenity yelled. "We could also preserve our youth. We'll get beauty treatments, lasers, even surgery early, so we can look twenty at age forty." The women squealed in delight. "Cheers to my brilliant idea, motherfuckers!"

The last thing I saw was Serenity toasting with her champagne glass—oh wait—and I caught a glimpse of Trevor feeling up Anna under her shirt.

Then I was whisked into a harsh time-lapse. I sped through a mucky tar that stuck to my body and smelled like decaying flowers. The tar formed into particles and disappeared into a vast, dark space. Next, an out-of-tune violin screeched. I covered my ears. My body twisted and spiraled. The taste in my mouth was a combination of rotten teeth and bad breath.

My intestines became inflamed and hot. Like Alice falling into the rabbit hole, my body shot into my colon. I touched spots of festering black, and the smell was metallic and acidic. My intestines groaned and contracted at the mere idea of food and water.

This was hell.

"I will get you out of here!" Kai said. "Hold on."

Something pulled me up. The ghastly sensations halted and I traveled across time and space onto…

Another private jet.

Rap music blared. All the heads in the cabin bobbed to the rhythm. A young woman pumped breast milk while she vaped. The smell of mimosas, Johnny Walker Blue, and Casamigos wafted into my nostrils, lingered, and nearly inebriated me. A man and woman simulated a blow job while the others cheered them on.

Orange-juice residue stuck to empty glasses, and lipstick stained the cocktail napkins.

I quickly counted: 13 pax.

They sung, laughed, and shrieked. I checked the flight map which read: 9:00 a.m. We were headed from LAS, Las Vegas, to LAX, Los Angeles. The pax were celebrating with as many drinks possible in a forty-six-minute window. I had always hated these trips.

Fuck this.

I had to get out of here.

"Kai, can you help me?!"

I waited

No answer.

As a last resort, I marched up to the cockpit. Maybe the pilots could give me a clue into what was going on. I tapped the captain's shoulder. "Hey! We have to talk."

He didn't respond.

I then tapped the co-pilot's shoulder and repeated myself. Nothing.

Were they asleep?

I slapped the captain's shoulder as hard as I could.

It was like smacking a lifeless piece of meat. I wedged myself between the pilots and turned toward the captain. He didn't have black speckles; he had gaping holes.

I gasped.

I could see right through him. I froze.

The co-pilot was the same. Both their eyes had morphed into black coal and there was no movement. It was as if two test dummies were flying the plane.

Shock hindered me from taking any action. But what action could I take? We were on autopilot, and time was running out.

How could I communicate with ATC?

The headphones!

I ripped them off the captain's head.

Once I jammed them on my head, I screamed into the speaker, "Mayday. Both pilots are under duress! They cannot land the plane. This is the flight attendant."

ATC wasn't responding. I didn't even hear static.

Shit! I had to push a button or something to connect with ATC.

I patted myself down to find a cell phone.

Nope.

I'd tell the pax we were emergency landing and to give me one of their cells to call 911. I tore off the headphones and pivoted to race into the cabin. Unforeseen turbulence caused me to lose my footing. I stumbled and fell onto the carpeted floor.

I managed to crumple into a fetal position and lay there. Oh God, bile was shooting up my throat. My eyes squeezed until I thought I had passed out.

Then I heard the sound of bees buzzing.

"I'm going to get you out of this, Indy. I promise."

Kai again.

The bees buzzed louder.

"I'm trying to get you to the etheric plane for psychic surgery. But I can't."

For psychic what? The idea of surgery in this extreme situation was probably a really bad idea. I was still in the fetal position. The bees grew distant, and there I was again being whisked against my will into the black tar and decaying plant odor.

Then I landed in a pleasant scene. One that I actually recognized.

Manhattan Beach Pier.

All the tightness and franticness in my body was gone. For once in my thirty years, I didn't have a care in the world.

It was a new, strange way to feel. The over-thinking, worrying, disappointed-in-herself Indy had gone away. Now, I was perpetually vibing, operating at a steady 4:20 frequency.

When Time Flies by Jennifer Moreno (Ciotta)

I basked in the glorious rays of the Los Angeles sun and peered at the mansions and smaller luxury homes along The Strand.

Saltwater seeped into the pores of my exposed skin. I plodded through the wet sand and stopped to kick off my shoes. The waves lapped over my feet. It felt so nice.

At the pier, I brushed the sand off my toes and slipped on my chucks. Like a tourist, my white jeans were rolled to mid-calf. It was a dry, seventy-degree day. The breeze tumbled through my messy hair.

I stepped onto the concrete pier. It extended into the sea quite a ways with a red-roofed aquarium and cafe at the farthest point. Tourists strolled or rested their forearms on the turquoise railings to gaze into the azure abyss.

Even though the world was collapsing, I didn't care.

It felt like I was on extra strength Xanax. My lips formed a gigantic, ridiculous grin.

I reached into my pocket for my cell and it was there. In the phone camera, I saw myself with a lion's mane for hair and a broad smile that flaunted my white teeth. In the background, ocean waves stroked the blue sky.

My thumb pressed the circular button to snap a photo.

"I can take the next one."

I lowered the phone to see…Jayden. He was dressed in a gauzy shirt and pants. Between the clothing and his black, brow-line glasses, he resembled a Buddhist and Malcolm X.

Upon staring at him, I should've been wanting to rip his face off.

But I was unable to conjure any ill will toward him.

My eyelids were half-lowered and my lips parted as if I were hovering on the edge of sleep. My breaths barely disturbed the air. There was no tension, just the knowledge and memories of what he had done. I had to snap out of it. I wanted to stay here, though. Just a day at the beach in my favorite weather. Next, I'd go shopping at one of my favorite boutiques on The Strand.

"Indy, snap out of it!" Kai bellowed from a distance.

Maybe Jayden is nice in this timeline?

Perhaps he is curing cancer and UC, and helping us become better versions of ourselves?

When I saw myself in the phone camera, the black speckles were absent. This was my true, loving self who embraced the moment.

"Indy, this is an illusion!" Kai barked.

Anything she said didn't matter.

The Earth welcomed me into her tranquility and surrounded me with the love of a newly planted seed that was waiting to form. I imagined it sprouting and blossoming into a bud that poked out of the sandy beach and stretched into the new world. It grew, fought against the harsh winds of a tsunami, and soaked in the droplets of the ocean. Then it stood, tall and humble, against the bright blue sky as it shined in all its glory.

I smiled at Jayden.

He grinned.

That snapped me out of it. It was like being dunked in ice water—the trance shattered in an instant.

What was that nonsensical babbling about a sprouting flower?

I had to keep the illusion going.

"Hi Jadyen," I cooed. "Nice to see you here."

"India—"

My skin crawled when he said my name.

"It's time to walk off that bridge." He pointed to the end of the pier. "Then you can finally move on to the afterlife. There's no space for you here. There are no timelines to run back to. This is it."

He and Kai had alluded to or told me to walk off that bridge, when they knew I wouldn't do it. Maybe it was exactly what I needed to do? It could be a remnant of the trance talking, yet my mind was clearer than it had ever been. The crystals tingled on my neck.

"You can't run anymore."

His eyes shifted toward The Strand. A humongous, electronic billboard played Pyro Girl on repeat. Tourists gawked, pointed, and hooted with laughter. I stared at it, knowing the old me would've been mortified. The new me wasn't. I was realizing there was a lot more to Indy Kash. On this incredibly bizarre journey of merely a few days, I had learned strength, resilience, and the power of not letting someone like Jayden get under my skin. I was sure I'd encounter more assholes like him—okay, maybe not with all the superpowers and genius-level smarts.

Still, I had to keep up the façade and pretend that I cared.

My mouth twisted into a scowl and yelled over the waves, "Take that down! Now!"

"This is your reality. Welcome to Timeline Tourism. You can't change a damn thing, just like the fire."

It all clicked. "Me taking the fall was an altered timeline."

"You say 'altered.' I say new."

That explained why the door wasn't there when I traveled back to the arson event or the large mirror-window in the courtroom I'd never noticed the first time around. Or Serenity knowing me in her past or me traveling with Trevor to his past, though I was never originally there. The one thing I was right about: the timelines had collapsed into full chaos.

I truly felt small and insignificant, like a tiny grain of sand on this beach.

"Go Indy, walk. You'll feel better."

In this timeline, Jayden had returned to his collected, self-assured demeanor. Under the guise of fear, I studied his face. A tiny black speckle had formed on his forehead and pulsated. His mouth twitched. I knew he could feel it.

Kai was right. This was an illusion…for him too. He was losing control of the timelines. My crystals surged with a pleasant warmth.

I felt different. My chakras spun clockwise. For the first time in my life, from within myself, nothing seemed unbalanced.

If Jayden had total control over the timelines, I would've been gone a long time ago.

He grimaced. I could tell he wanted to touch his forehead so badly, but he couldn't risk me noticing. It was an itch he desperately yearned to scratch, like a big, honking chicken pock.

I'd been to this beach so many times. The fall wouldn't kill me because it was too shallow. The waves crashed at a normal pace, and I could swim to a pillar and hold tight. He wanted me to walk off that bridge and swim to where I couldn't paddle my arms and legs and simply drown.

I put one foot in front of the other and slowly walked down the pier. I turned around. Jayden waved and then stuck out his middle finger.

I continued on, knowing for certain that he'd been distracted. A bridge was a liminal space. If I could focus like I did in the old psych ward, I could cut through space and perhaps time.

I turned my mental state into a walking meditation and focused on what I knew as the original timeline and traveling back to Trevor, Serenity, and Snowball. The love that had emanated from them in that timeline enveloped me and carried me down this pier.

I stopped and turned around. Jayden was swatting his forehead.

When I reached the end of the pier, I looked out to sea. The blue sky met the blue water. The waves pummeled against the pillars—I, uh, think I was wrong about the current. Standing directly above the pier, I realized the undertow could be my demise. My heart beat like a distant drum. I recognized the danger and felt the need to do whatever was necessary. I was more than me. I was the person who had to get shit done for everyone else. The world was counting on it.

Tourists had gathered and were enjoying the view and cool mist. There was a railing surrounding the plank. I would have to jump and startle everyone around me.

I hoisted my body over the railing and sat there for a moment. Out of the corner of my eye, onlookers pointed and spoke indistinctly. I thought back to the idea of the emotional liminal space. I was in one. My undecided thoughts wavered in a transitory state of moving from this timeline to another one.

I lunged forward and let go.

CHAPTER TWENTY-SEVEN

Oh, the beauty and magnificence of the sea. At first, it wrapped me with its salty essence and coaxed me into its depths. I held my breath and swam like a fish. My body flexed to and fro until I reached a pillar and held on tight.

The current strengthened to where I was no longer a sun-bathing creature bobbing in the ocean. I clenched the wood and gasped for breath. Water pressed into my lungs.

When I had jumped, I heard the unmistakable screams of tourists. Surely, they'd called 911 and help was coming at any moment.

I gripped the soft driftwood pillar as the waves splashed over me. My main goal was to suck in enough air before the next onslaught of sea. Physically, I was in my most vulnerable state, hanging on and letting the water lacerate me. The exhaustion consumed my muscles and bones. I wouldn't allow it to deplete my spirit. I remained here for a while, yet no one came.

Several minutes later, the tide had retreated enough to where I could get down and walk on the sand.

My feet collided with the mushy earth. A massive bruise had formed on my back where the water had pummeled. Thank God the pain and injuries from the electrocutions had not followed me through the various timelines, because with this back pain, I didn't know if I could withstand much more.

Here I was, next to Manhattan Beach Pier. I had failed to travel to my original timeline.

Instead, I was a sopping wet mess of a human who was staring at the worst moment of her adolescent life flashing across a billboard.

Jayden could be right: this could be it for me.

I fell to my knees on the beach as the tide washed over me.

"Don't give up," I heard Kai say. "There's always another option."

The crystals danced on my neck.

In the distance, a ship's foghorn blared.

I squinted to find the vessel. It was a dark speck chugging along the horizon.

It reminded me of…

The Philadelphia Experiment.

I moved to the dry sand and sat down with my legs folded close. My arms encircled them and my chin rested on my knees.

I touched the heated crystals, "Kai, are you there?"

The ocean breeze tumbled past me.

She didn't respond.

Thoughts began to flood into my consciousness.

Teleportation.

Long-distance reiki.

Wait.

Could this be the solution?

The electromagnetic field surrounding this timeline and all the other false ones had to be "healed" somehow.

Jayden had released the chaotic energy that created these timelines, and he was energy too. He couldn't be destroyed. I couldn't kill him if he'd embedded himself into an infinite number of timelines.

Everything in my body was screaming *no*, but I had to return to the Time Machine. Healing the timelines by healing the energy of the electromagnetic was now priority. Like or not, it was up to me to figure it out.

This wasn't the *Wizard of Oz*. I couldn't just click my heels and go home.

As much as I wanted to label the past as "traumatic" or painful, it was the thing that brought me answers in the present…and the future. Returning to my past and delving into memories, instead of ignoring them, had begun to heal me. I was always so afraid of it and blamed it for shaping my terrible life. I realized that to move forward, I had to know where I came from. I had been an ordinary girl living an ordinary life until trauma had changed my path. Was it for the better?

No.

It was a path, much like a timeline. I could have fought harder and taken my fate into my own hands. I was doing that now—a little late, I admit, but no time like the present—or a version of the present. It might have been time travel that woke me up, but it was my inner strength and resilience that carried me to the finish line.

Anyway, my original life wasn't so terrible after all.

In fact, I had begun to embrace it.

With all these shifts in consciousness lately, I finally understood what all the gurus and thought leaders were saying: my thoughts formed my reality. With time travel, I had escaped "reality" and it provided me with an outsider's view of my own life.

What a gift.

All I could do was find a liminal space and pray.

In front of me was the shoreline.

I lifted my chin off my knees and rose.

The wind grew stronger, pushed me closer to the water, and whooshed through the gaping holes in my body.

My feet converged with the lapping waves of the shoreline and I thought about my original life in review—all the good and bad. I thought about wanting to return to the Time Machine and how I could end the chaos. I felt it all in the sinew of my bones and took another step forward.

Immediately, I smelled lavender, rose, and honey. An angelic white surrounded me and I was traveling through cotton-candy space. The bees buzzed again and I was transported to a plane of electric purple, pink, and white. The frequency of healing and DNA repair, 528 Hz, filled the air. I recognized it from all those meditation mp3s. Every muscle loosened and unshackled at once. White light enshrouded me. Like my ancestors, I had astral-traveled. Somehow, I ended up on the plane of love and healing. I, Indy Kash, broke the generational patterns of air travel and did what my grandmother and mother couldn't do.

For once, I was in awe of…

Me.

As quickly as I had entered this astral plane, I was off again.

Then I landed…

In the exact place I needed to be,

In the tunnel at the Time Machine.

CHAPTER TWENTY-EIGHT

The Time Machine was pulsating.

Barbara and Zion weren't there. Jayden had to be close if his precious baby was here.

The wires sparked.

I had to somehow reverse-engineer this thing and create an electromagnetic field that was *healing*, not damaging.

Any self-doubt was absent. I was laser-focused on what had to be done, and I knew I could do it.

My body had returned to a perfect specimen of its original self. The dampness and chilliness of the tunnel seeped through my bones. The important thing was I could rotate, bend down, and jostle the metal box and the wires. The energy that Jayden had released from the Machine wasn't affecting me.

Voices resounded in the distance.

Jayden would be back soon.

I knelt down to examine the box. As I exhaled, my breath formed a misty cloud. My mind quickly intuited. Healing energy imbued the chakras, and Jayden had manipulated that energy. To conjure their healing properties, they would have to return to their original state. The eighth chakra was the most powerful one. If I could connect to it in a positive way, it could end all this horror.

I needed energy to do that—not the transporter.

The cyclotrons were natural magnetic fields that revved up to high speeds. If I could ramp up the electromagnetic field— like a healer performing reiki—I could turn it into a restorative one.

Lucky for me, I knew how to do that.

It was time to bust some motherfucking ghosts.

The voices boomed in the foreground. I heard Barbara crying and Zion swearing. In between hacking, Jayden was barking at them.

I crouched in waiting.

As soon as I saw Jayden's figure, I heaved the battery-operated light and banged it against his head.

His body thudded to the ground.

"Nice hit," Zion said.

I thought, *please let this fucker be alive.*

His arms and legs twitched.

Good.

Barbara and Zion fell to the ground and crawled away from the Machine to the far end of the tunnel.

I maneuvered Jayden's body into the Vitruvian Man position and rolled him so I had access to his root chakra. He was wearing protective gloves. I tugged them off and put them on me. Then I yanked each wire from the metal box. I attached each one to Jayden. They had so much energy they stuck to his skin.

He moaned.

A goose-egg shape emerged on his forehead, right where the black speckle had been.

How ironic.

On the opposite end of every wire, there was no magnet. Energy coursed through them like water through a hose. I gathered them in a bunch and stood next to Jayden's body. I exhaled. It was now or never.

I placed the opposite ends of the wires directly on my solar plexus.

They gyrated and sparked, and hummed like an old TV gone static.

I felt like I was falling down an elevator shaft with no bottom. Absolute bliss consumed me. I thought of the non-binary being and the verdant garden of my Near-Death Experience, Trevor and Serenity, playing in the sandbox, solving equations in physics class, Snowball purring, and Kai's support.

#

The eighth chakra wire tugged itself out of the bunch. The soul star formed on the tunnel ceiling and the wire plugged into that.

The electromagnetic field around me was one of pure healing and light.

I saw millions of timelines collapsing without a sound. A starry dust signaled their welcome end. A gray mist lifted and exposed the astral plane where Spirit Council beings floated and scurried. I watched in awe as the Universe was being restored to its natural order.

Underneath my feet was the glorious rumble of the timeline piecing itself together like a jigsaw puzzle. The chakras let out a collective orgasmic sigh as sunbeams radiated to every corner of the Earth.

This time, I cried out of joy.

My arms and legs flailed. I jarred back into my body, as if awakening from a deep slumber where my soul reentered its human owner.

Water dripped and I opened my eyes. The feeling that surrounded me was…

Normal.

A perfectly imperfect human. No electromagnetic fields on either side of the spectrum. Humanity had landed somewhere in the middle where we were supposed to be.

Jayden stirred and rubbed his forehead. "What happened? I feel…different."

Energy *could* be teleported.

He seethed. "What the fuck did you do?! My Machine!"

The next thing I knew, Kai was standing next to me.

"Nice job, Indy. You took away his meta abilities. He can't time travel anymore."

"I did that?"

"Yes, you did."

"Who are you talking to?" Jayden asked, trying to get up.

"He can't see me and I'm not blocked from his energy field."

I asked, "What do we do with him?"

"His ability was one in a gazillion, and now it's gone. His career and life as he knew it is over. From now on, the Spirit Council will be watching his every move."

"Can't you create a wormhole or something and throw him in there?"

"A what?!" Jayden yelled then coughed.

"Nah. The Spirit Council has a subsidiary that handles these types of situations, though he is unique. In other words, he qualifies as: not my problem. I have to get back to the plane. There's a lot of debriefs and meetings. Peace!"

She left.

The bubble of white light popped and I fell on the ground.

Though the chakras were healing, they still expended too much energy for my human body.

I lay there for a while, wincing in pain.

Footsteps pealed through the tunnel.

"There she is!"

In a flash, Trevor and Serenity were by my side.

I had never felt such a massive tsunami of relief.

"Don't touch me," I whispered.

"Fuck that," Trevor said and bent down to pick me up.

When he touched my arm, a static shocked buzzed. He jumped.

"I told you. Where did Jayden go? He was right here."

"I'll find him!" Serenity took off.

Trevor knelt beside me. "How are you alive, Indy? Let alone talking."

The crystals rested on my neck. "I learned to fight, to really fight."

"I guess you did. When you didn't come to the hospital, we assumed you came here by yourself. When we arrived, we noticed smoke rising from the vent. The grate was lying on the ground. We heard the Time Machine roar, went into the tunnels, and eventually found you. We need to call an ambulance."

He whipped out his phone and then halted. "Wait, no. We can't. We'll have to explain *twice* to the EMTs and the hospital that *two* people were mysteriously electrocuted on this property."

I grimaced. "You're right."

"Let's get you to my apartment and call Dr. Munk."

CHAPTER TWENTY-NINE

Yet another phone was a goner.

Though it was in my coat which Jayden had thrown on the tunnel floor, the energetic impact had incinerated it. Serenity called her 24-7 concierge to deliver another one.

Dr. Munk could not believe that my brain was functioning properly. I would have to go to the hospital this week and get an MRI.

I had many first-degree burns, as well as eight small second-degree burns. They hadn't opened or blistered, so I didn't need to bandage them.

She handed me a natural salve and told me to rub it all over. Luckily, I only sustained a few burns on my face, the most noticeable one on my third eye. The deepest burn was located on my solar plexus. It resembled a giant purple blob, as if I did a hardcore cupping session. Upon seeing it, Dr. Munk shook her head.

She explained that as electricity flashed over my body, it would normally come into contact with sweat. When water turned into steam, it created a vapor explosion, which could have resulted in severe burns. I had described to her in a roundabout way how dry my body was at the time of electrocution. I purposely omitted how all the moisture, tears, piss, and shit were sucked out and turned into particles that vanished.

She said, "Your explanation is humanly *im*possible, but I'll let it go."

Dr. Munk then warned me of confusion, cardiac arrest—been there, done that—memory loss, debilitating headaches, seizures, vertigo, periods of deafness, personality changes and mood swings—lucky Trevor—nightmares, and more PTSD and chronic pain.

Awesome.

From the look on her face, she knew we were all bullshitting her.

"Indy, you need weeks of rest. I'll write a letter to your employer."

That's right! Tomorrow was the commercial flight to meet Blond Satan's jet in London. I had completely forgotten and would have to contact Ron.

The next time I'd fly Blond Satan, I actually looked forward to her bitchiness. Who would've thunk it?

"Umm," I said to Dr. Munk. "I can't say I was electrocuted twice. There will be too many questions."

"I'll say you were in a car accident."

I thanked her and gave her Ron's email address. Her fingers clicked away then pressed Send.

I reached for my new phone on Trevor's nightstand. It read: 12:12 a.m. It was Monday.

My head pounded, and every time I tried to get up there was vertigo…and the burns seared. But I was okay. I would survive.

Dr. Munk first prescribed me high-dose NSAIDs, which I couldn't take because of the UC, so she recommended Boswellia and arnica instead. There was Serenity, my nursemaid, conversing with the concierge to find an all-night pharmacy that carried Boswellia and arnica.

Meanwhile, Trevor sat next to me and held my hand.

Frank and Snowball cuddled on either side of me.

My family was here. Tears swelled up out of happiness. I finally knew I would be okay. I wasn't isolated or alone. People cared about me, and I cared about them, too. This was a new feeling that I wholeheartedly embraced.

Dr. Munk left. As soon as she did, Kai appeared—minus the war paint and speckles. She glowed brighter than any of the other times I saw her.

"You're one lucky human," she said.

The cats stood at attention.

A thought popped in my head. "Am I still in the timeline where I was convicted of arson?"

"Yes," Kai said. "All the changes from your original past and the photos appearing on your phone, those were timelines in chaos created by the Time Machine. As far as the Spirit Council can see, all chaos ceased when Jayden lost his powers."

"Jayden! Where is he?!"

Serenity hung up with the concierge and said, "I couldn't find him in the tunnel. The slimy bastard must've found another way out. I called Grandpa and told him everything. He organized a witch hunt and found him."

"Was he arrested?"

"For what? How could we possibly explain anything that happened to the police?"

"Why couldn't I testify along with Tameka, Barbara and Zion?"

She gave me a sharp look. "Really? A woman who can't speak because of traumatic injury, and two serious addicts? Plus you. And how are you going to explain the two 'electrocutions' to Boston's finest? Unless you're topless in a Red Sox thong, they're not listening to a word you say."

"That's valid."

"Yeah. We'll keep a good eye on Jayden."

"How?"

"Grandpa can do anything…except time-travel well."

"Where is Jayden now?"

"Let's see." She tapped her phone and showed me a video. "He's fumbling around his penthouse in the city."

There was Jayden in black and white, pacing, coughing, and muttering to himself.

Kai said, "Don't worry, Indy. The Spirit Council is monitoring him closely too."

Serenity piped up. "Kai filled us in on the altered timelines you endured and what Jayden had done. You know that Trevor and I would never treat you that way, right? You're family."

My eyes glistened with tears. All I could do was nod.

I remembered Jayden's lung cancer and told them.

"That explains a lot," Trevor said slowly. "He told us he'd had a bad bout of COVID and then that he had Long COVID. Good cover."

Kai said, "Now that the Spirit Council isn't blocked, we—I'm on the Council now—were able to evaluate the Time Machine. We think he developed an algorithm where he tuned it to his frequency—combined with the negative energy density—to create a stable time-travel environment. Human scientists have always deemed that impossible, and Jayden did it."

Trevor whistled. "You've gotta give it to him."

I nodded. "Congrats on your promotion, Kai."

"It's all because of you and your brave, selfless act. You saved humanity."

I had certainly put on my big girl pants. Everything was so surreal to me; I didn't know how to revel in defeating Jayden. All I could feel was happiness to be alive and to return to normal human existence.

I squeezed Trevor's hand and smiled at him.

"No more war paint?" I said to Kai.

"Not for now. The battle is over, but there's always a war brewing in the human world."

Serenity asked, "What about the Time Machine—is it still in the tunnel?"

"That's been taken care of. Now that the Council's energy isn't blocked, we beat the shit out of it. *Office Space*-style."

Trevor, Serenity, and I broke into laughter.

"Where are the pieces?" I asked.

"We set them on fire. They disintegrated into particles that we've secured on the plane."

As I glanced around Trevor's bedroom, with these two humans, my spirit guide, and the animals showing me unconditional love, I couldn't help but be grateful. For the first time since childhood, my future looked bright.

Through this whole experience, I'd learned the best place to live was in the present.

So I would.

#

A couple of weeks later, I was lying on Trevor's couch. Snow fell outside and I curled up with a blanket and Snowball. Trevor had run out to get me my favorite beef soup because the restaurant wouldn't deliver through an app or concierge service. He actually had to walk. And he did, in the snow, for me. I smiled.

Of course, without warning, Kai appeared. She glowed even more. Snowball perked up to her perkiest degree.

"Indy?" Kai said.

"Yes?"

"Where's my PSL?"

I giggled and reached for the milk frother that had materialized.

Today, I would take my time making Kai's drink. I was learning that time was not something to be rushed, manipulated, or taken for granted.

Time was always a gift.

Who doesn't love a good gift?